PYRAMID

Tom Martin lives in Oxford.

For J

Acknowledgements

For their skill and intelligence, I would like to thar
Straus, literary agent, Maria Rejt, editor at Pan Ma
and Anna Valdinger, assistant editor.

Inspiration for this book came from many sour   _ost
notably the following: Charles H. Hapgood, *M   _f the
Ancient Sea Kings: Evidence of Advanced Civili   _on in
the Ice Age*; Giorgio de Santilla and Hertha Von   _chend,
*Hamlet's Mill: An Essay Investigating the Origins   _Human
Knowledge and Its Transmission through My   _Manly
Palmer Hall, *The Secret Teachings of All Ag   _ Edward
Goldsmith, *The Way: An Ecological World-View*; the works
of Lee Child and James Twining; and the works of Joseph
Campbell.

PROLOGUE

High up in the thin mountain air of the Andes, Professor Kent looked out for one last time over the moonlit beauty of the ancient ruins of Machu Picchu, stretching away along the valley's edge three hundred feet down below. Only ten minutes earlier he had been lying sound asleep in his warm bed in the Hotel Ruinas, not far from the world-famous UNESCO heritage site, when suddenly, without warning, he had been shaken from the depths of sleep by two strangers.

Before he could cry out for help, they had gagged him and dragged him from his bed. Without uttering a single word, they had marched him barefoot down the corridor, through a fire escape door and out into the chill of the night.

So they have finally come for me after all these years.

It was a horrible affirmation. He had begun to doubt his own sanity these last few months but this night-time abduction proved the discoveries he had made were as important as he had thought . . .

For years he had suspected that if he continued with the breakthroughs he was making he would draw the forces of evil out of the shadows. Each of his discoveries must have tempted them a little further until, finally, they could sanction his presence on earth no longer.

Where are they taking me?

The freezing night air drew the heat from his shivering body. Professor Kent stumbled as he was frog-marched along a steep narrow track, up into the wild hinterland of the mountainside. He looked a pitiful sight next to the burly frame of the thug who was pushing him upwards through the darkness. His white beard and thinning hair were matted with perspiration and his pale face was almost ghostlike in its appearance. But even now he was consoled by what he saw around him. Lit up by nothing but moonlight, the landscape radiated an intensely sacred beauty.

They reached a small plateau and the shorter of the two kidnappers, who had been scrambling along the path ahead, turned around, pulled a small box out of his coat pocket and opened it. In the darkness Professor Kent couldn't see what was in it. The big thug who was holding him in an armlock suddenly forced the terrified old man to his knees.

In a blind panic Professor Kent began to struggle but the huge man simply pushed him harder until he was lying face down in the scrub, pinned to the ground. A moment later he felt a rough hand tear the gag from his mouth.

When he saw his other captor crouching down next to him with a syringe in his hand Professor Kent began to scream. Slowly – incredibly slowly it seemed – the man brought the syringe up to the professor's face. In the moonlight, a droplet of mercury-like fluid could be seen glistening at its tip. Then the small man spoke: an evil hissing in the professor's ear, 'Do you have anything more you would like to add to your tapestry of lies, old man?'

His accent was foreign, but of unknown provenance. Professor Kent twisted his head up as far as he could until, out of the corner of his eye, he could see the face of his interrogator. With a great effort he managed to rasp out a question.

'If they are lies then why have you come for me?'

The sinister man laughed scornfully, then leant forward and brushed the tip of the syringe across the professor's neck. Kent barely felt the scratch but he knew it was enough; immediately his lungs began to tighten.

As he sensed the poison coursing through his veins

he suddenly knew he had been freed of a tremendous burden. All he wanted now was to be left to die in peace, but his executioner continued his taunts.

'You are a demon, Professor Kent. And demons must be returned to hell – where they belong.'

'There are no demons in my philosophy and no hell either.'

'That's enough!' the small man shrieked. His accomplice forced the professor's face further into the scrub. He could feel himself slipping away.

'I do not want to listen to your lies. Did it never cross your mind that the past and the future are private property and they don't belong to you, Professor Kent? They belong to more important people.' There was anger in the executioner's voice. 'You thought you could outwit us? Did you really imagine you would ever be allowed to reveal what you have discovered?'

As he spoke, something flashed in his hand. It was a razor blade.

What is he doing? The professor turned a weary glance towards him. *He has already condemned me to death with his poison.*

The small man continued to talk, sarcasm dripping in his voice, 'We are generous. We feel that like the Greek philosopher, Socrates, who was offered the chance to take his own life, you, too, should be allowed to do the honourable thing . . . We don't propose a shocking death for you. It might spark enquiries, a sudden interest in the obscure workings of your so-called theories. Suicide is far less sensational than murder – don't you think?'

With that Professor Kent felt the giant release his grip. Instinctively he tried to move but his body would not respond: he was paralysed.

Almost casually, his persecutor rolled him onto his back. He reached for the professor's right hand and then slashed along the wrist with the razor. Blood spurted over the forest floor and then began to flow steadily from the wound. He dropped the limp right hand back onto the ground. Then, picking up the left hand, he placed the razor in its palm and closed the fingers around it. He then carefully laid the hand back on the ground.

'We will let God decide on the punishment for your blasphemies. Your time on earth is done, old man.'

The professor summoned all his will-power in an effort to open his hand and let the razor fall, but nothing happened. There he lay, paralysed – his own executioner.

'There is no biblical God who can punish me. My proof will be found . . .' The professor's voice trailed off as the muscles of his voice box succumbed to the poison.

The small man snarled to his companion, 'Is there

no end to this man's stubbornness? Where does he get this sickening belief? He is like a cockroach – impossible to exterminate.'

He bent down and dabbed the professor's neck with a piece of cotton wool.

'To think that a mere academic could cause us all this trouble. There – we don't want any misunderstandings. Let's get back to the hotel and search his room. We must destroy every scrap of evidence.'

They looked at the motionless body for a few seconds longer then melted silently into the night.

Professor Kent, his body totally incapacitated, stared upwards at the stars above. For years he had studied the mysterious heavens as part of his quest for the great truth and even now, despite his enfeebled state, his mind picked out all the familiar patterns of the constellations. As his strength ebbed away, he thought of his final discovery.

So, my intuition was correct. I have solved the final mystery. But this means the world is in grave danger. Are the maps safe? And with me gone, will anyone understand what they mean?

Then all was darkness.

PART ONE

PART ONE

1

It was five minutes to twelve on a sunny and unseasonably warm Tuesday morning in March. Catherine Donovan, at twenty-nine one of the youngest ever prize fellows at Oxford University, stepped through the small doorway set within the massive wooden gates of the lodge and into the calm of the pretty front quadrangle of All Souls College. Sunshine streamed across the lawn, bringing warmth to the Cotswold stonework while the bells of the university peeled brightly, announcing the imminent arrival of midday.

All Souls, where Catherine held her fellowship, was the most prestigious if secretive of all Oxford's thirty-five colleges. It had no undergraduate students at all, whereas most colleges had at least 200 and the largest accommodated as many as 400. Quite simply, All Souls was the exclusive abode of world-class scholars and its rarefied membership was dedicated to furthering human knowledge, in subjects as diverse as nuclear physics and Islamic art.

The only way an outsider could join this elite club was by the most rigorous recruitment process undertaken anywhere in the academic world. But for those who made it through, it was worth it. The fellows were treated like royalty. The college wine cellar was one of the finest in the university and those fellows who took up their apartments in college could still choose to be woken in the morning by a butler bringing tea, toast and the morning newspaper, all served on a silver tray. But most importantly, none of the fellows was obliged to do any teaching – each could devote their time to making groundbreaking discoveries in the specialism of their choice.

For Catherine, a beautiful young woman and an American, All Souls was a particularly strange environment. The other fellows – who were used to all sorts of eccentricity – simply regarded her as another misfit in a college of misfits, and so they welcomed her, content in the knowledge that she was already a world leader in her own chosen field: astronomy.

Catherine Donovan glanced at her watch. *Five minutes before I'm on.*

Quickly, she dashed into the lodge and, searching

her pigeonhole, grabbed her morning's mail: a couple of uninteresting communiqués from the astronomy department and a large brown envelope, clearly posted from abroad. Hurriedly she examined it and instantly recognized Professor Kent's handwriting. The last thing she wanted was to be late for her final lecture of the term, so she stuffed the envelope into her bag and set off at a brisk pace round the quad in the direction of the auditorium.

As was usual for all of Dr Donovan's lectures, the beautiful ancient stone room at the heart of the college was crowded with students drawn from across the university. Her lectures were by far and away the most popular in the department. She gave them out of choice because she appreciated some contact with the students. They responded by attending loyally, their numbers increasing as the lecture series went on. Only the day before over coffee in the senior common room, one of her friendlier colleagues had teased her about it mischievously – saying he had overheard two students describing her as the most attractive don in the university.

With shoulder-length brown hair, exquisite high cheek bones and the grace of an athlete, she would have commanded attention anywhere, and she knew it.

This morning, however, Catherine was nervous. Tradition had it that the final lecture of term was always used to inspire the students for the long vacation. Today she intended to surprise them by explaining one of the strangest and most inexplicable mysteries in the cosmos – a mystery that could have truly frightening implications for the whole of humanity. The students were a bright bunch, but they were very young and it was important that they were reminded of the frailty of human knowledge in the face of the unknown.

Looking up from the podium on which she stood, Catherine surveyed the sea of faces that confronted her. Clearing her throat, she began: 'Good afternoon everyone. Many thanks for coming. I want to begin today by seeing if any of you can solve one of the greatest mysteries of all time.'

An excited murmur filled the hall and the eager eyes of the students stared at her in anticipation.

'As we all know, the brightest star in the night sky is Sirius. There are one or two stars that are a little closer to our solar system, but none of them burns as brightly. Perhaps this is why Sirius occupies a central position in almost all the mythologies of the ancient world.' Catherine glanced at the sea of faces. *Good – they look keen.* With a conspiratorial tone to her voice she continued, 'But maybe – just maybe – there are other reasons too.'

Again she paused, this time to take a sip of water from the glass that rested on the table by her side. She looked down at her laptop and clicked. Immediately, a slide was projected onto the giant white screen attached to the wall behind her.

The slide contained two images arranged side by side. The first image was a photograph of a drawing that had been scratched into sand or fine loose earth.

The second image was clearly generated using the latest astronomical software. It was a graphical illustration of a distant object in the heavens as it moved majestically along its ancient course. There was also a second, smaller object. Its course seemed to spiral round and round its larger neighbour as if caught in an attraction from which it was struggling to escape.

Catherine glanced up to check that the images were clearly displayed on the screen,

'Now, as distances between stars go, Sirius is virtually our next-door neighbour. Does anyone know exactly how far away it is?'

She surveyed the audience once more. An arm went up from a shaggy-haired young man in the third row. Catherine smiled encouragingly, but as the soft gaze of her beautiful green eyes settled on him, he seemed struck dumb. Smiling sympathetically but with just the faintest hint of impatience entering her voice, she tried gently to coax him to speak.

'Yes?'

With a bright red blush flooding his face he began to stutter out his answer, 'It's . . . It's 2.67 parsecs away . . . which is 8.7 light years or fifty-two trillion miles.'

Catherine was impressed.

'Yes! Very good. Thank you. Now in 1844 Friedrich Bessel, the German astronomer, speculated that Sirius must have an invisible twin. Bessel had spent a lot of time taking extremely careful measurements of the slow movements of Sirius and he had noticed a small wiggle in its regular journey. Bessel thought this could only be caused by the gravitational pull of an invisible next-door neighbour but he couldn't prove it. At that time no one had managed to build a telescope that could see as far as the Sirius star system.'

Catherine walked closer to the projection on the board.

'It wasn't until 1862 that the American telescope maker Alvan Clark, using one of his own inventions, saw, for the first time in human history, the faint companion of Sirius – thereby proving that Bessel's theory was correct.

'But was it the first time?' she asked mysteriously. There was an excited murmur from the students and again Catherine paused dramatically.

'Today, we can of course see both objects very clearly using our massively powerful telescopes. We call the big star, the original Sirius – the Sirius visible to the naked eye – Sirius A and its companion star, the heavy, invisible Sirius – Sirius B.

'Now, the question I have for you today is a very simple one, but if you can answer it correctly, NASA will probably appoint you as their head of research.' Taking a deep breath and then speaking slowly Catherine posed her question. 'If Sirius B is entirely invisible to the naked eye, how come there exists an African tribe that has kept a complete and accurate astronomical record of it for the last two thousand years?'

There was a gasp of amazement from the crowded lecture hall.

'The tribe I am referring to are called the Dogon. They live in what is now called Mali in West Africa. In their ancient oral tradition the bright star Sirius is accompanied by an extraordinarily heavy, very dark object, called Po. It is worth noting at this point that Sirius B is in fact a white dwarf – it contains as much matter as our sun but is tiny by comparison: one teaspoonful weighs nearly a quarter of a ton. So it would seem that not only did the Dogon know that Sirius B existed – which is strange enough in itself – but they also knew that it was a particularly dense type of star ... And what is more, they also knew that it completes an orbit around its larger sibling every fifty years.' Catherine smiled at the looks of amazement on the faces of her audience. 'The Dogon beliefs – if that is the right noun for their astronomy – were first communicated to the outside world in the 1940s, to a French anthropologist, but we know for sure that their theories are at least 1,800 years old and almost certainly much, much older. The Dogon used sand diagrams to illustrate celestial movements. In my lecture I will tell you how these have been preserved. But here you can just see the Dogon diagram of the interlocking orbits of Sirius and its dark counterpart on the left-hand side of the slide. And here on the right-hand side is the modern astronomical record of the movements of Sirius A and B.'

The audience gasped again.

'As you can see – a perfect match. Nowadays we know that the orbital cycle of Sirius B, or Po, is exactly 49.1 years – so fifty years wasn't a bad guess for a Neolithic tribe. And the Dogons' knowledge of the cosmos didn't stop there. For example, they maintained that Jupiter has four moons and Saturn has rings. Now, just as with Sirius B, the rings of Saturn and the moons of Jupiter cannot be seen with the naked eye – you have to have a telescope and a good one at that. So can anyone explain how the Dogon knew all these things?'

A hush fell across the crowded room. Privately, Catherine was sure that one day a rational, scientific explanation for the mystery of the Dogons' knowledge of Sirius would surely be found. After all, it was quite inconceivable that in the depths of the primitive past, mankind could ever have had the highly advanced technology required to view the smaller star. Nevertheless, it remained one of her favourite cosmic mysteries and it never failed to have the desired effect. Mouths agape, the wide-eyed students in the front couple of rows craned their heads round to see if anyone further back had any idea. All were silent.

At that moment, as if on cue, the door at the far end of the lecture theatre clicked open. The entire audience rotated in their seats.

It was one of the porters from the lodge. He was looking a little anxious and coughed nervously before raising his hand in a confused gesture.

Catherine glanced back across the room.

'Please excuse me for one minute.'

Nervously straightening the fall of her skirt with her hand, she walked quickly from the podium and, feeling a little self-conscious, strode down the hall to meet the porter. He scuttled towards her and they met halfway.

'I'm very sorry to interrupt you, ma'am. The warden wants to see you urgently.'

'What! Can't it wait another half an hour?'

'He said not, ma'am. He said he has some very bad news.'

Catherine's heart started to race. Turning to the room at large she addressed the audience again: 'Excuse me, everyone. I am afraid something serious seems to have come up, and I am being summoned away urgently. I'm sorry about this. I do hope this mystery – and believe me it really is a mystery – will keep you inspired in the coming weeks. I'm sure you'll be spending every minute of your holidays reading your set texts for next term, but if you have a spare moment see if you can solve the Dogon Sirius conundrum. Good luck! If you succeed, then I'll give you the Trinity term off!'

2

The lodgings belonging to the warden of All Souls were a grand suite of oak-panelled rooms overlooking the beautiful fellows garden, with its flower-filled herbaceous borders and immaculate, centuries-old moss lawn. At sixty-five years of age, the warden was a veteran of university life. He was an energetic, grey-haired man with a large nose and bushy eyebrows. His whole demeanour instantly commanded respect. As well as being in charge of the everyday administration of the college, he was an eminent philosopher and logician.

Today, however, he found himself in the unhappy position of being the bearer of dreadful tidings. A Thames Valley police officer had just informed him that Professor Kent, a fine colleague and good friend, had been found dead on the mountainside at Machu Picchu in Peru. The cause of death was a heart attack; however, it seemed the attack had almost certainly been brought on as the result of attempted suicide. But the officer had said it was best not to go into details at this stage as it was too early in the investigation. The Special Branch liaison officer in Lima was following up with the Peruvian police.

Sitting at his large old oak desk with his shoulders stooping and his head bowed, the warden cupped his forehead in his left hand and slowly massaged his brow. Sighing deeply, he found himself, for the first time in as long as he could remember, completely uncertain as to how best to deal with events.

What can I possibly say to Catherine? The professor was like a second father to her.

At that moment there was a knock at the door.

'Come in.'

Catherine was looking as radiant as ever and, seeing her youthful demeanour, the warden was again struck by a pang of remorse – why did it fall to him to break this awful news? Already her face was a mask of apprehension and concern.

'Please, warden, what's happened?'

'My dear girl, I am very sorry to say that Professor Kent is dead.'

Catherine collapsed into the nearest chair, her face ashen. Then she collected herself.

'How? When?'

'Apparently he died two nights ago in Peru – at Machu Picchu . . . near the Inca ruins. The police paid me a visit – they've just left. I sent for you straight away.'

Catherine's eyes held the dulled expression of someone in a state of deep shock.

'I don't believe it! I mean, what happened? There must be some mistake. The professor told me he was going to Mexico – he was due to get back late yesterday evening.'

The warden tried as best he could to be diplomatic.

'We're not sure just yet. However, the Peruvian police have concluded it was suicide.'

In an instant Catherine's face changed from shock to disbelief. She sat bolt upright in her chair.

'No! Impossible. Never – this is all a terrible mistake.'

The warden stood up and walked around his desk. Not knowing what else to do he poured a glass of water and took it over to her.

'My dear, I am very sorry. The police have it all in hand . . . I think you should try to relax.'

Catherine was shaking her head. She looked up at him.

'Professor Kent had no one. His only sister died three years ago. There isn't even anyone to tell, no one to arrange the burial. It is all too tragic . . . But I want to know more. There has been a mistake. I can guarantee you that. It is quite impossible that the professor committed suicide ... I want to talk to the police myself.'

The warden smiled at her gently.

'Catherine, my dear, I understand entirely. But let's wait to see the full report from Peru. I am quite sure that the British police liaison office in Lima has got it all in hand. If you would like, once the report is in, I will come down to the police station with you. There is not much I can do today, I still have quite a few meetings to attend this afternoon – I just can't cancel them, much as I would like to.'

A look of determination crossed Catherine's youthful face.

'No, I understand. Thank you for telling me straight away. You did the right thing. I must make sure everything is all right. He was my closest friend in this country. You know that. I must go home and work out what to do.'

'Yes, of course, my dear. It's a dreadful day. Quite awful ... Professor Kent was a fine scholar and, more importantly, an extraordinarily good man. I'm so, so sorry.'

Catherine got up from her chair, picked up her bag and walked over to the door. As her hand gripped the door handle the warden spoke again.

'One last thing . . .'

She turned to look at him. It seemed to her his tone

of voice had changed somehow . . . or perhaps she was just upset.

'Was there anything the professor said to you the last time you saw him? Or did he perhaps give you anything?'

Somewhere deep in Catherine's subconscious, an alarm bell rang.

'I'm sorry, what do you mean?'

The old don eyed her steadily.

'I just mean that perhaps there was something he was working on that he told you about – or perhaps he gave you something? I could pass it on to the police . . . maybe it would help.'

Keeping her composure, she repaid his unwavering gaze in kind.

'No – nothing I can think of . . . the last time I saw him was about ten days ago, I had tea with him out at his farm in the Cotswolds. No gifts or anything. And I can assure you, he was in his usual high spirits.'

As she opened the door and stepped out into the hall she heard the warden's dry voice behind her: 'Terrible business – absolutely terrible.'

Catherine shut the door firmly. Her heart was pounding. She looked up and down the corridor and then, absolutely certain there was no one around, she opened her bag: the letter from Peru was still there.

3

Catherine headed straight for Professor Kent's rooms. She had a key of her own, as she often used his study and well-stocked library when he was away on his travels. In fact, even when he was in the country he tended to work from home – an isolated Oxfordshire farmhouse that was the perfect base for his research. It was a typically charming Cotswold building with a colourful garden surrounded by dry-stone walls and gently rolling fields. She had spent so many happy hours there, and now she thought of it standing empty, never to welcome the professor again.

She walked out into the quad and across to the medieval passage that led to the professor's staircase. As she walked around the square grass lawn, memories flooded her mind. The tragic news was simply too much to bear . . .

'Can I help you, my dear?'

It was the voice of the college porter. Catherine felt

his hand on her arm and, as she suddenly came to her senses, she realized she was standing in the quad with tears rolling down her cheeks.

'I'm sorry, Fred. I'm just a little bit confused.' She tried to smile and did her best to wipe away the tears.

'Can I get you anything?'

'No – I'm sorry, I'll be all right now . . . I'll just go to Professor Kent's rooms and have a little sit down.'

A minute later she had let herself into the professor's book-lined rooms. At a loss as to what to do she sat down in her favourite armchair by the fireplace and tried to make sense of what was happening. Here she was, in the peace and tranquillity of the professor's cosy study in Oxford while thousands of miles away he had died a terrible death on some lonely mountainside. It couldn't possibly have been suicide . . . what were they talking about? It was all just too horrible to contemplate . . . it didn't make any sense at all. Her mind raced, and she tried to think if he had said anything the last time she saw him or given any clues that he was thinking in this way.

But there was nothing. She had visited him at the farm only two weeks ago. He had been as warm and eloquent as ever. They had talked about college matters and he had shown her a rare orchid he had been sent by a friend. He had placed it by the kitchen window, hoping it would blossom and thrive. He had said he looked forward to seeing her again after his trip, that he wanted to introduce her to an old friend of his who was interested in her field. Then they had parted.

She pulled her bag onto her lap and, taking out the envelope, examined it again carefully. Yes, it was definitely the professor's handwriting. Why on earth hadn't she told the warden about it? What had stopped her?

Nervously, Catherine tore it open. Inside was a plastic sleeve that contained a sheaf of maps. On top of the maps was clipped a small white piece of paper about the size of a postcard. On it she could see some writing.

Feverishly Catherine slid her hand into the plastic pocket and pulled out the piece of paper and turned it the right way up. When she saw what was written on it her blood froze.

In case I don't return.

Eureka

40 10 4 400 30 9 30 70 100 5 200 30 10 40 1 80 5
100 400 40 10 50 10 200 300 100 8 70 9 1 50 300 10
20 800 10 300 10 200 0051172543672

What is going on? What on earth does all this mean?
Catherine stood up and walked quickly over to the writing desk. Pushing all the professor's papers to one side, she placed the collection of maps on the desk.

There were seven of them in all. Her lucky number, she thought sadly. Spreading them out, she began to study them more closely. Three were computer-generated maps – the kind you see in an atlas. The other four were clearly copies of earlier documents. The originals were obviously very old maps, possibly pre-medieval, showing different locations around the world.

She couldn't immediately recognize the places that any of them represented, but they were obviously bona fide maps and not just creative illustrations: they showed coastlines, river systems, mountain ranges and islands. The paper quality was inconsistent, as was the quality of the copies.

As Catherine read the note again and stared in incomprehension at the mysterious maps, a sense of absolute panic began to take hold of her.

But what do these maps represent? And what does the professor's note mean?

4

James Rutherford looked at the clock in the corner of his laptop screen – 12.55 p.m. Hurriedly he swept the books on his desk into his bag and shut down the computer. He had to leave the library immediately. He had an appointment to keep with Professor Kent, one of the university's leading minds, and he was not about to miss it.

Rutherford had met Professor Kent for the first time only two weeks before. The professor had been a dinner guest of one of Rutherford's colleagues. By chance Rutherford ended up sitting next to him. They had immediately fallen into deep conversation as the professor was very interested in ancient mythologies. He was unusually interested, in fact, given that it had nothing to do with his field of expertise – or so Rutherford had thought – but what amazed him was the breadth of Professor Kent's knowledge. They had talked for three hours about nothing else.

James Rutherford was one of the university's top experts on world mythology. Although everyone in the university knew the old professor was a polymath, he was famous for being an ecologist. But ecology seemed a long way away from Rutherford's world of ancient texts and his study of strange, fabulous myths and legends. And this was what puzzled him.

It was two days after their dinner-party conversation that the professor had contacted him, pretty much out of the blue, to arrange a meeting. Rutherford had just returned to his spacious flat in north Oxford, the city's most academic suburb, after a long run in the University Parks. When he entered his apartment he discovered his cleaner, Anne, busy hoovering the floor.

James collapsed exhausted into a big chair. At thirty-eight, he was slim and fit and had a full head of close-cropped dark hair. He was careful what he ate and drank and was told he looked years younger than his age, but a ten-mile run was a ten-mile run.

'You had a visitor.'

Rutherford perked up.

'Unfortunately, it wasn't a young lady.'

It was Anne's opinion that James should marry, settle down and have a family instead of wasting away his hours 'studying old books', as she put it.

'Oh well, I'll keep hoping . . . So who was the visitor, if it wasn't the woman of my dreams?'

'It was Professor Kent, from All Souls.'

Anne picked up an envelope that was lying on the kitchen table and handed it to Rutherford.

'He gave me this note to give to you.'

Jumping out of his chair, James took the envelope from Anne and went out onto the spacious balcony that had a view of college playing fields and the rolling hills behind. Here, in privacy, he began to read.

Dear Dr Rutherford,

I very much enjoyed talking to you over dinner the other day. At the risk of trying your patience I would like to continue our conversation about ancient mythologies.

I think I may have made a monumental breakthrough. I believe that I have discovered, hidden in all the disparate myths and religions of the world, a terrifying message from the past. This message, which I have succeeded in decoding, is a warning from a long-vanished people – a warning to us so that we might in turn avoid the cataclysm that destroyed them.

It is of vital importance for the survival of humanity that we make this message known or the same cataclysm will befall us and our planet too. The ancients knew that humanity would rebuild itself from the ruins and that, one day, it would be able to understand the contents of the message. There are forces at work, however, that want the message suppressed, and I believe I've uncovered why.

It would be my great pleasure if you would come to my college rooms for coffee sometime the week after next. How does 1 p.m. on Tuesday sound? Unless I hear to the contrary, I shall look forward to seeing you then.

With my warmest regards,
Prof Kent

Rutherford could scarcely believe his eyes. Professor Kent's claims were staggering. Here was a leading academic – a scientist no less – and a cautious man, claiming to have uncovered evidence that not only shattered current preconceptions about the history of human development, but also proved that mankind was in mortal danger.

It all sounded extremely outlandish but Rutherford had trained himself over the years to keep an open mind. He took the motto of the Royal Society as his own: *Nullius in verba* – Take nothing on authority.

5

Catherine felt numb. What on earth should she do now? She looked around the professor's study, at the familiar bookshelves and furniture, and her eyes began to fill with tears. Everything reminded her of the fact that she would never see her old friend again.

She remembered the first time she had visited the professor at his farmhouse – it was many years ago now. She had been a Yale undergraduate on a Rhodes scholarship and, as he was a close friend of her parents, Professor Kent had offered to look after her during her stay in England. Even then he had sported his trademark white beard.

'Oh, my life as a scientist hermit wouldn't suit very many people,' he had said, laughing. They had been walking in the garden, a garden rich in flowers and low shrubs, with a small pond at the centre, and then they had set out across the sunlit fields to the edge of one of the two large woods that adjoined the property. The landscape was stunning in a gentle English way and Catherine could quite understand why Professor Kent found it so inspiring.

'Of course, I don't need thirty-five acres. I'm not a member of the landed gentry. I only bought so much land because of what happened in my last village. In the ten years I lived there I saw it destroyed as thoroughly as if it had been laid to waste by Genghis Khan. Its heart was pulled out when the post office and pub went, the village school too, and then the pretty countryside surrounding it fell into the hands of big business. When I first arrived, the fields and meadows in the summertime were the pride of the county with bright red poppies and vivid blue cornflowers growing side by side among the golden wheat. On a summer's day under a cobalt-blue sky there probably wasn't a more awesome and incandescent sight this side of Jupiter! But long gone are the meadows of wild flowers and in their stead are vast swathes of high-yield grass and soulless business parks.'

The professor had an elegiac way of speaking, thought Catherine. He talked of an ancient tie that bound the people to their soil and to the seasons, and of the brutal loss of that tie. It made some of the other fellows scoff. When he attracted followers from the green movement in Oxford, who cycled out to see him, the senior tutor called him the college guru and laughed about it at high table. But Catherine had always found him to be a very quiet and kindly man.

They had gone down to the river and sat on the bank, listening as the waters gently burbled. She remembered the professor had taken off his shoes. She had found it almost comical, seeing this eminent don wiggling his toes in the water.

'Everywhere you turn on the planet the outlook is the same. Forests are being cut down, wetlands drained. Pollution is endemic. Every day species are made extinct, the earth's magnetic field is being changed, with no one knows what possible consequences. The ozone layer that protects all living things from the sun's ultra-violet radiation is being rapidly depleted, and the very air that we breathe has less and less oxygen and more and more carbon dioxide – a poison that is gassing us and heating up the planet. Why are we doing this? Because we are committed to the idea of economic progress, and our social institutions are totally incapable of recognizing the problem for what it is and tackling it head on. It simply requires too much imagination and sacrifice. Why don't you try the water, my dear girl? It's very lovely.'

So, smiling, Catherine had taken off her shoes and socks and dangled her bare feet in the water. He was right, it was lovely to feel the water on her skin. And she was, of course, the visiting American, she said, so it was important to size up the local customs.

'Absolutely! You'll find they make perfect sense. A beautiful hot day like this in Britain – you have to make the most of it!' said the professor.

'But to answer this question,' he continued more soberly, 'we have to see that our industrial society, with its ever-more powerful institutions, its fascination with growth and technology is more and more losing sight of what life's goals should really be. We must wake up and realize that it is the very structure of our society that allows these great agglomerations of power to occur – agglomerations that take on a life of their own, that are more than the sum of their parts. Our objective today in the twenty-first century should always be to ensure that power is dispersed, that the great destructive vortices of power are never allowed to develop. If they do, they will suck us all in, and destroy us. But I am not optimistic; power has its own rationale and it knows how to appeal to the worst aspects of human nature.'

Catherine, sitting with her feet lapped by cool water, staring out over a vista of fields, took his point.

'But I've been boring you,' said the professor, 'and we really should get you some tea. Terrible thing, to lure a new student to your house and then talk shop endlessly without even offering refreshment!'

They had walked in bare feet through the long grass at the edge of the meadow and arrived back in his garden laughing and carefree.

'This sure isn't what I expected when they told me I was going to Oxford. Thank you, professor.'

Catherine was jolted back from her happy memories to the terrifying reality of the present: someone was knocking loudly on the study door . . .

6

In a panic, Catherine stuffed the note into her bag and swept the maps into a pile on the desk and quickly hid them under some papers. Then, taking a deep breath, she walked over to the door and opened it. Standing patiently in the hall was a tall, dark-haired, handsome young man. He smiled at her and stuck out his hand. His voice was warm and reassuring: 'Hi, I'm Dr James Rutherford – we met once at the warden's drinks party. I'm a classicist at Brasenose College.'

Catherine was disoriented. She *did* recall his face – there weren't many dashing young dons at the university, after all – it was just that she was still in shock and wasn't prepared for a normal friendly conversation. Not knowing what else to do, she swung the door open and Rutherford stepped into the room. He looked concerned and before Catherine had time to say anything he spoke again, 'I've just heard the news from the porter – I'm very sorry. I can't quite believe it's true.'

Instantly Catherine's guard dropped a little. She sighed and shook her head. For a moment she forgot about the note and the maps.

'Yes – it's absolutely awful. I . . .'

They fell into silence for a second before Rutherford explained the purpose of his visit.

'I'm sorry. I don't mean to intrude. The porter told me you were here and I just wanted to ask if you knew any more about what happened. Is there perhaps something I can do to help?'

Catherine walked back to the desk. She noticed the corner of one of the maps was sticking out from under the pile of paperwork. She tried to position herself so she was standing in her visitor's line of sight.

'No, but thank you. It is a horrible shock and, even though I was one of his closest friends, I don't know any more than you. It's a complete mystery; it doesn't make any sense at all.'

Rutherford was still standing awkwardly just inside the door:

'I was meant to be meeting him, you see – we had only recently arranged it. I hardly know the professor – I mean I know him from TV, of course, and I've read his books, but I only met him once. I was quite flattered because he sent me a note proposing this meeting and saying he wanted my professional opinion on something

. . . Look, I'm sorry, I'll be on my way. It's just so strange, he seemed to be such a happy man.'

He turned to go. But Catherine was thinking, *Perhaps James Rutherford might be able to help. Perhaps he might recognize the ancient maps. He is a leading classicist after all.*

Her mind, hungry for a solution to the mystery, jumped at the possibility. It was worth a chance. What did she have to lose?

'Look – actually perhaps you *can* help me.'

'Of course – I'll try – what can I do? Would you like me to contact some of his friends in the faculty and break this dreadful news to them?'

She hesitated a moment. *Can I trust him? Is it simply a coincidence that he had a meeting with the professor this morning of all mornings, or is something more sinister going on?*

Before she could show him the maps and the note, she had to know why the professor had wanted to meet him today.

'Do you mind telling me what exactly it was that the professor wanted to discuss with you?'

As Catherine asked this question she studied her visitor's face for anything that might tell her more about him. Rutherford shrugged his shoulders.

'No, not at all – let me show you the note he left me.'

Delving into the inside pocket of his jacket, Rutherford pulled out the message the professor had left with Anne. He walked over and handed it to Catherine. She scanned it quickly, a dark frown appearing on her face.

She looked up.

'These are bold claims for the professor to make. Do you know anything more about them? Had you spoken to him about these ideas before in previous conversations?'

Rutherford cast his mind back.

'Well, for a start, we only ever had the one conversation. But I always admired him greatly. I believe what he says about what we are doing that will lead us to our own destruction . . . But he didn't know me – we just happened to be sitting next to each other on the same table at a Balliol college dinner. As soon as he learnt my main interest is classical mythology, we talked for the rest of the meal. Or, more precisely, he asked questions and I tried to answer them.'

'What sort of questions?'

'Well – he was most interested in stories of ancient cataclysm. He clearly thought they were in some way relevant to his work. Like, for example, the story of Noah's flood in the Bible. He saw Noah's flood as a real environmental disaster that happened in ancient times.'

'What do you mean? Are there other myths from

around the world that talk of the flood that can corroborate this theory?'

'There certainly are.' Rutherford couldn't resist a wry laugh. 'There are about seven hundred and counting.'

'That many! So Noah's story is not unique?'

'That's the understatement of the year. You can go anywhere in the world and find the very same tale.'

'Anywhere?'

Rutherford, grateful for the opportunity to be of help, began to speak enthusiastically, 'Yes. Take China for example. They have a myth about the flood that is almost identical to our own. Their story tells how men became arrogant and ignored the gods and how the gods took their revenge by turning the whole universe upside down and shaking it like a child's toy so the stars and planets and the earth tumbled through the heavens. Rain fell and all the land was covered with water.'

Catherine's eyes widened in surprise, but before she could press Rutherford for more detail he was off again.

'Closer to us, in Europe, the Greeks have a great flood myth – they even have their own Noah – he's called Deucalion. And so do the Celts and the Vikings . . . and the Indians. Let me tell you about their version. Manu, the hero in the story, sees a tiny fish in a puddle next to his house. The fish is actually the god Vishnu who asks Manu to protect him from the dangers of the world and promises him that his reward will be great if he does so. Manu picks him up and puts him in a larger puddle, but the next day the fish has grown so much that Manu has to move him into a lake. Quickly he outgrows the lake. Finally, Manu has to put the fish in the sea. In thanks, Vishnu warns Manu of a coming flood and tells him to build a strong boat, orders him to collect seeds from all the plants of the world as well as two of every animal, and then climb on board himself. When the flood comes, Manu is saved and Vishnu drags the boat over the oceans and deposits it on a mountain in the north. Manu, Deucalion, Noah – it's the same person or mythic figure, I should say. Do you want any more examples?'

Catherine smiled in silent encouragement. She was impressed.

Rutherford spoke again, this time with a deeply pensive note to his voice, 'I think Professor Kent, as well as believing that all these myths had at their heart a true event, thought they were used to convey a secret message – the *same secret message* – and that our ancestors, through these myths, are warning us, from across the chasm of time, of an impending disaster.'

'So that's why he said in the note that he thought he had deciphered the ancient secret message.'

'Yes – I suppose so. I was really looking forward to finding out. Breakthroughs often come from newcomers to a field of research and this promised to be the biggest breakthrough of all time. I was hoping the professor might be like Heinrich Schliemann.'

'Who was he?'

'Schliemann was the archaeologist who in 1871 discovered the site of the ancient city of Troy. He was an amateur. He had been a very successful businessman and when he turned fifty he had already made his fortune. He realized he would never have to work again, so he went back to university and did a degree in classics at the Sorbonne in Paris.

'There he studied the *Iliad*, which is the story about Troy. He thought that at some level it wasn't just a myth, it was actually true, that the poet Homer was describing a real city and a real war and that Achilles and Helen of Troy were real people, not just poetic inventions. Needless to say, no one believed him and he was laughed out of town by the academic community, but after three years of searching around the Aegean he found the ruins of Troy and proved them all wrong.

'I thought Professor Kent might be another Schliemann . . . you know, a newcomer to the field who makes an astounding breakthrough because he or she is not limited by received preconceptions – someone who follows their intuition.'

Catherine was lost in thought. Something told her

that the professor's esoteric research was somehow related to the strange maps and her intuition told her that James Rutherford was trustworthy, but she still had her doubts. She looked deep into his eyes and breathed in slowly. Her mind was made up. She would show him the maps but keep the note a secret for now.

'I want to show you something important. This is going to sound strange but it is related to what's happened today. You're a classicist – do you know anything about old maps?'

Rutherford was taken aback.

'Er, yes, a little.'

Catherine turned to the desk and retrieved the maps from under the papers. Laying them out again, she was more convinced than ever that they were of real places.

'I want you to look at these and tell me if you recognize them or if they mean anything to you. However strange this may sound, it *is* relevant. I was sent them by Professor Kent just before he died.'

Rutherford walked over to the desk and began to scrutinize each one carefully. After a minute or so he looked up at her, his expression serious.

'I'm afraid I can't help you.'

Catherine's heart sank.

Then, he smiled. 'However, there is someone who can. Dr Von Dechend, Emeritus Professor of geography. I've been to a couple of his lectures – he's quite brilliant.'

Catherine's eyes lit up.

'Of course! Von Dechend – why didn't I think of him? He's here, at All Souls.'

Rutherford looked surprised.

'Do you know him?'

'Yes I do – it just didn't cross my mind – we never talk about work, but I always chat to him in the common room.'

Rutherford's expression had become solemn. He didn't want this to be the end of his meeting with the beautiful and intriguing Catherine Donovan. It was all too exciting. And it was a far cry from his everyday academic routine.

'Would you like me to come with you? Maybe I can still be of help – although I haven't done much so far.'

Catherine wasn't sure what to say. What on earth was she getting herself into? One moment she had been delivering her final lecture of the term, and the next she was trying to understand her dear friend's tragic death and the fact that he had clearly been engaged in some very strange research. And now, she seemed to be about to follow his footsteps into the dark . . .

She looked at James. She was grateful for his calm, reassuring presence; as she contemplated facing the dark mystery of the professor's death alone she felt fear rising in her stomach . . . But, feeling positive for the first time since leaving her lecture, Catherine made a decision.

'Yes. I'd like that very much.'

PART TWO

PART TWO

7

The iconic building housing the United Nations in New York stands like a sentinel at the junction of 46th Street and First Avenue, right on the banks of the East River, where it commands a fabulous view over the whole of Manhattan. From the upper storeys of the building, Central Park can be seen to the west, and to the east is a view of the sprawling suburbs of Queens and Brooklyn and the eye-catching network of bridges that connect the island of Manhattan to its eastern shore. The building was designed in the aftermath of the Second World War and construction of the thirty-nine storeys was finished in 1962. The world-famous General Assembly debating chamber, which has a seat for one representative from every nation on earth, is situated on the third floor, at the very heart of the structure.

It is a little-known fact that the United Nations building, in addition to soaring into the heavens, also descends deep into the earth. In total, eleven basement levels of steel reinforced with concrete are sunk directly into the mud of Manhattan Island. Three levels contain garage space to house the many diplomatic vehicles that ply a constant course between the various foreign embassies and the UN headquarters. Another level hosts the enormous plumbing and air-conditioning systems that are required to run a building of this size. But beneath all these layers of functional utility, there are still further sunken floors, designed with great foresight in the days before the Cuban missile crisis, to house the entire assembly in the event of a major attack on New York City. Accessible from a separate elevator system situated in the north-east corner of the building, all the crucial facilities of the upper storeys are replicated down below, as is the case for any critical US federal or military facility: there is a large canteen; there are three floors of office space; and a whole floor given over to accommodation. But most importantly of all, there is an exact replica of the famous General Assembly Debating Chamber for use in the event of an unforeseen global disaster.

This back-up chamber, situated on the seventh basement floor, has never been used to host the General Assembly. Directly after the attacks of 9/11 in 2001, the secretary-general of the UN did briefly entertain the idea, but concluded that it would send out the wrong message to the world at large. Consequently, the entire emergency facility is meant to be kept entirely empty, secured under lock and key.

It was a Tuesday morning in March, 7 a.m. Eastern Standard Time, and the two capacious elevators that went down to the subterranean levels had been in constant use for the last hour. Since 6 a.m. a more or less unbroken line of limousines and BMWs had been pulling up outside the front of the UN building and disgorging passengers onto the forecourt. All were male, all arrived alone, all were wearing expensive business suits. The majority were Caucasian but there seemed to be representatives of every race on the planet. Without looking right or left they strode up to the enhanced security cordon that has stood in front of the main entrance to the building ever since the events of 9/11 and, briefly showing their credentials, were ushered through the enormous revolving glass doors where they were swallowed in the refracted angles of sunlight.

Beyond the glass doors it is a short walk across the marble atrium to the corridor that leads to the north-east corner of the building and the elevators to the lower levels. None of the staff of the UN building, security or otherwise, batted an eyelid at the stream of well-dressed arrivals. The UN building receives more visitors a year than almost any other public facility in the world and in any case, every single one of the early-morning visitors appeared to have the correct security clearances. It was quite normal for smartly dressed middle-aged men to be roaming the marble floored corridors of power.

All the visitors knew exactly where they were going and all had been issued with key passes for the elevators. By 7.15 a.m., the seventh basement floor was a hive of activity. The pristine back-up General Assembly room was playing host to an entirely unscheduled and extremely sinister meeting. By 7.30 a.m. an audience of over 300 was gathered in the underground chamber sitting comfortably in the horseshoe of tiered blue seats. The meeting of the Corporation was about to begin.

At the front, behind the speaker's table, where the UN secretary himself would normally sit, a sallow, dark-haired, sixty-year-old man waited patiently, his hands folded together on the table top, his eyes staring out over the hall.

This was Secretary Miller and as secretary of the Corporation it was his job – on the rare occasions that it was required – to convene the meetings of the global governing council. Today was one of those occasions.

At 7.40 a.m. precisely, he pushed his chair away from the desk and stood up. He was about 5 feet 7 inches tall and, in common with all the other men in the room, he looked like a successful Wall Street banker or a high-powered lawyer. His only outstanding feature was his dark, heavy-lidded eyes, which scoured the room from behind a pair of thick-lensed spectacles.

He seemed agitated. Under normal circumstances he would have been exchanging pleasantries with the arriving guests and pressing the flesh but today his equilibrium was disturbed. He slipped out of the debating chamber and began to pace slowly up and down in front of the elevators, his face wearing a dark frown of concentration.

It was most unusual for the ultra-secretive board of the Corporation to ask him to convene a meeting of the global governing council. There had not been such a meeting since the final collapse of the Soviet Union. What did it all mean? What did the board have to say? Whom would they send as their representative?

But before Miller could ponder any longer, the silence of the corridor was broken by the pinging of the lift bell. The representative of the board had arrived. As the elevator doors slid open, Secretary Miller's blood turned cold. There, standing alone in the tomb-like space of the elevator, was Senator Kurtz.

Secretary Miller could barely mask his shock. Senator Kurtz was a prominent and well-known politician. He was a close friend to many of the president's inner circle and as such often appeared on television chat shows.

His solid support base among the religious community of his southern constituency meant that he had the backing to rise to great political heights. His private interests in the security and arms industries were an open secret, as was the fact that he was widely tipped to become the next Secretary of Defense.

Although the Corporation could boast two dozen retired senators and congressmen in its ranks, in addition to politicians of every ideological hue from all around the world, it was unprecedented that such a senior member of an incumbent administration should be active on the board.

Secretary Miller himself was a fine example of the type of man who formed the backbone of the Corporation. He was a financier who, in his own realm, wielded the kind of power a Roman emperor would have envied. He had inherited from his father control of Grippen AG, a private Swiss bank, in addition to having many vast and diverse holdings in natural-resource companies and he employed thousands of people all round the world. But he was an eminence grise – in no way the kind of man who sought the limelight.

He was a faithful servant of the Corporation and his loyalty to it had been rewarded a thousand times over, but he was not privy to the ultimate source or arrangement of power at board level. He did not even know how board members were elected. Indeed, he did not even know how many board members there were at any one time. But he did know it was most unusual for a serving politician as senior as Senator Kurtz to be so openly involved. In fact, there were many people in Senator Kurtz's own administration, including the president of the United States himself, who would be scandalized by the true extent of the Corporation's power.

Stepping forward, Secretary Miller swallowed hard.

'Welcome, Senator. It is a pleasure to have you here today.'

The senator strode out of the elevator. At 6 feet 1 inch, he looked just as fit and vital as he did on television. He had been a successful college athlete in his younger days and clearly still worked out. His once black hair was greying at the temples in a distinguished manner, but he was still an attractive man in a masculine, patrician way. He thrust out his hand.

'You must be Secretary Miller.'

'Yes, sir, that's correct. Welcome. I must say, it is truly an honour . . .'

The senator's dark eyes scanned the corridor. His Secret Service bodyguards were waiting up on ground level. There could be no exceptions, not even for a serving member of the United States Senate.

Secretary Miller spoke nervously: 'Everything is prepared. I have convened the Corporation's governing council as the board requested.'

Pleasantries dispensed with, Senator Kurtz spoke again, a note of steel in his voice: 'Are you quite sure we are beyond detection here?' He glanced around and then continued gruffly, 'Ironic as it may be to use the United Nations headquarters as the launching pad for our final ascent to power, it would be most inconvenient to draw attention to ourselves needlessly at this late stage.'

The secretary, looking a little affronted, indicated with a sweep of his arm the way to the main hall, as a page might motion to a king.

'The venue was not intended as a joke. The United Nations building provides the perfect cover for our comings and goings. The land is owned by the Port Authority of New York City, which we in turn control. But as ever, it will be our first and last meeting at the site.'

The senator relaxed a little and smiled warmly.

'Good. Good work. Very soon, there will no longer be any need for all of this . . .' He waved his left hand in an expansive gesture. 'Our super-government must continue to exist in extra-legal conditions for a few days more, that is all. On Monday morning, at the dawn of the spring equinox, we can dispense with this charade.' He paused and then addressing the secretary curtly as if he was half expecting him to lie, he asked, 'And the professor?'

Miller's eyes narrowed imperceptibly. He felt most uncomfortable under the scrutiny of the senator's gaze. Every nerve in his body informed him it was not a good place to be. But why, when they were on the very point of final success, was the senator so obsessed with the professor and the eradication of all evidence of his work? What possible threat could now be posed by a collection of old maps? Secretary Miller could only assume the board had their own obscure reasons – to him the entire business was opaque. He looked the senator squarely in the eye and, swallowing hard, he nodded his head.

'It has been done.'

Senator Kurtz grunted approval. A frown corrugated his brow.

'It's a bad business, Secretary, a bad business. But what was it Shakespeare said? "Needs must . . ."'

Then suddenly, he turned and slapped the secretary on the back.

'Don't feel guilty, Secretary. We're at war, and the professor was a direct threat to the interests of the Corporation. Wars are complicated and messy – there are always casualties.'

The tiniest hint of a smile flickered around the corners of the senator's mouth. But almost as quickly as it appeared, it was gone, replaced by a frown of suspicion. The senator's hard eyes once again focused on the secretary. His tone had swung back from the jocular and reassuring to the cold and suspicious.

'Let me remind you of something, Secretary, something of the utmost importance. There is nothing on this earth more dangerous to our cause than personal initiative. Nothing. The professor is a case in point. One of the blessings of our constitution is that we allow people a certain amount of leeway, a certain amount of freedom. Some might say too much freedom.'

The secretary stood frozen to the spot.

'And this of course is a good thing,' Kurtz continued. 'But the problem is that people get ideas into their heads. This is because they are in no position to see the whole picture – only we are in a position to see that. And I am sorry to say it, but we cannot afford to take any risks. If this means people have to be silenced, then that is the price we must pay. Show me a war where there have been no casualties and I will show you a speedy defeat ... Always bear in mind the bigger picture. The Corporation has to be allowed to complete its work for the sake of humanity. What is good for the Corporation is good for America. God put the resources of the natural world at our disposal, we must exploit them before someone else does.'

The pair began to walk away from the elevator, towards the meeting chamber. Senator Kurtz placed his hand on the secretary's shoulder, much as a coach might do to one of his players escorting him onto the sports field.

'If people had any idea what lay in store for them in the very near future, our government would lose its grip overnight. The disaster in New Orleans would look like a picnic in comparison, and all our efforts would be undone in an instant. I do not exaggerate. There would be riots on the streets, civilization would break down completely. Rape, looting and anarchy would ensue. Murder would become commonplace. The time for such chaos has to be of our choosing.'

The secretary muttered his assent. They were approaching the door to the main debating chamber. The senator stopped again, as if struck by a particularly unpalatable thought.

'But we must get on,' he said. 'The board requires that you keep the professor's erstwhile associates under observation. The priority now is to locate and destroy the rest of the maps. Anyone who has so much as been in the same room as them will have to be dealt with. Have the relevant agents been apprised of this and sent to his college? I am assuming you have already burnt the one map that fell into our hands in Peru.'

'Yes, Senator, of course – as you requested.'

Senator Kurtz straightened his tie and drew a deep breath before addressing the secretary privately one last time: 'Good. All is in order. What the Corporation does is in the public's interest, but it must remain behind closed doors . . . That is the way of the world. Now, introduce me to the meeting. It is time I broke the good news. Only six days remain until the dawning of the spring equinox and then our hour will have finally come . . .'

8

Catherine and James climbed the final flight of stairs, emerging onto the top landing of staircase twelve. Catherine, a little breathless, gasped in satisfaction: 'Phew! He's free . . .' The only wooden door on the landing was ajar. 'He's not sporting his oak.'

Rutherford frowned. 'He's not what?'

'Oh, it's an old expression. All the sets of rooms have two doors. An outside door made of oak and an inner door. If you shut the outer door, it means you are in no mood for visitors – you're "sporting your oak". Come on.'

Rutherford paused at the top of the stairs, his hand resting on the banister, and looked at Catherine.

'Do you think we should tell him about Professor Kent's death if he hasn't already heard?'

Catherine was full of purpose now. Her earlier confusion had been replaced by a steely resolve.

'No – I don't think so . . . if he doesn't know about

it yet, then we shouldn't bring it up. We're only here to ask him about the maps.' She knocked firmly.

After a long minute, the heavy oak door creaked on its hinges and swung open, revealing a small dark anteroom and a short, plump figure. Dr Von Dechend was in his early sixties with greying hair and a wild, fading, ginger moustache. He was dressed in a fine, slightly worn three-piece herring-bone-tweed suit. He leant forward and peered at them from behind a pair of thick spectacles. The odour of fresh pipe smoke filled the air. A second or two later, his face lit up.

'Catherine! What a delightful surprise. Come in, come in at once and have some tea! And who is this with you . . . a new boyfriend perhaps?'

Catherine felt herself blush.

'No – This is a colleague of mine from Brasenose – James Rutherford. James is a classicist and an expert on the ancient world.'

Dr Von Dechend ushered them into his cosy study, aware that this was not a social call. Catherine seemed unusually tense. As soon as the pleasantries were dispensed with and tea had been organized, and they were all sitting comfortably in leather armchairs around the empty fireplace, he got straight to the point.

'So what's troubling you?'

Catherine looked nervously over at Rutherford and then began.

'We were wondering if you could perhaps take a look at some maps for us and see if you recognize them.' She placed the envelope carefully on the table.

Von Dechend lit his pipe, swapped his thick-rimmed spectacles for a pair of reading glasses and proceeded to extract the documents from the envelope, carefully spreading them across his desk. He could sense an eagerness in his two young guests that went beyond mere academic curiosity. *I do hope I recognize what these things are,* he thought, *otherwise I'm going to have two very disappointed people here.*

Angling the desk lamp directly down onto the first map, Dr Von Dechend began to examine the documents before him.

'Hmmm. Very, very interesting. Very interesting indeed.'

He looked at Catherine over the top of his spectacles.

'Where did you get these maps if you don't mind me asking?'

For a split second she hesitated. She glanced across at Rutherford. He raised his eyebrows as if to indicate it was her decision.

'From Professor Kent.'

'Ahhh! Kent, eh! Now why on earth would he be interested in *these* maps?'

'Well, perhaps if you told us a little about them we might be able to work it out.'

'Very well, but prepare yourself. These are no ordinary maps. These are what one might call the most disturbing maps in history.'

9

Secretary Miller stood up and tapped the microphone in front of him on the desk. Gradually, the mutter of voices in the enormous debating chamber fell silent. Clearing his throat, he said, 'Gentlemen, I give you Senator Kurtz.'

He respectfully placed the microphone in front of the senator and sat down. There was a low rumble of approval from the audience as Senator Kurtz rose from his chair. Taking the microphone he began to speak: 'Thank you, Secretary Miller, and thank you, gentlemen, for coming today. I still believe that even in the age of video conferencing, nothing can replace actually meeting and talking face to face – and maybe even having a beer together. I hope the secretary will let us do some of that later.'

A ripple of appreciative laughter rose up from the hall. Senator Kurtz looked down at the secretary and gave him a patronizing smile before continuing.

'Now, some of you folks have come a long way for this meeting and so I want to start by assuring you that any effort you have made to get here will prove to have been worthwhile. Today we are about to pass the point of no return.'

The audience listened in rapt attention.

'On Monday morning, at 8.05 a.m., events will unfold that will result in the complete destruction of the global status quo and our ascension to worldwide power. I am talking now about the final coup de grâce.'

A murmur of anticipation rose from around the room. Secretary Miller surveyed the crowd – already they were putty in the senator's hands. There was no doubt he was an expert speaker. It would not be difficult to imagine him on television, alternately terrifying and then forgiving a nationwide audience.

The secretary looked at his watch and, slipping quietly out of his chair, stole over to the door. No one noticed. Everyone was transfixed by the senator's speech, listening to the unfolding of the plan. A burly security guard pulled the door open as he approached and silently stepped out into the corridor.

Despite his own private reservations about the persecution of the professor and his associates, he had work to do. The professor's maps were still unaccounted for – someone, somewhere, might even be looking at them right now. It was time to activate the agents in England.

10

Dr Von Dechend pointed to one of the maps on the table. Catherine and Rutherford stared blankly at it. It was so worn they could only faintly trace the outlines of land and the occasional river and island.

'Western empirical knowledge is like a huge dam built from piling up many, many individual bricks of knowledge,' the old man began. 'Occasionally scientists come across a piece of knowledge that simply will not fit into its allotted place in the dam. The Piri Reis map, this map before us, is the prime example of this. No one, and I repeat *no one*, knows how to explain the odd-shaped brick that is the Piri Reis map.'

Dr Von Dechend adjusted his glasses and continued.

'It was made in Constantinople in 1513 by Piri Reis, the admiral of the Turkish fleet, and drawn on gazelle skin. It maps the eastern coast of South America, the western coast of Africa and the northern coast of Antarctica – when it was a tropical paradise, before it became covered in ice. Piri Reis of course did not make the survey himself. He says that he used many different maps from the Ottoman imperial archives.

'Now, we can be fairly certain that the coast of Antarctica was only without ice from about 14000 to 4000 BC. Before *that*, we had the Ice Age and Antarctica was completely buried under billions of tons of ice, as it is today.

'So you can see the problems this map causes. It is impossible the coast could have been mapped at any date *after* 4000 BC – because it was covered in ice and has been right up until the present day – and yet the period *before* 4000 BC is known as the Stone Age.

'In short, this simple map seems to undermine the foundations of world history, as we know it now.'

'But that's incredible,' said Catherine. She shot a glance at Rutherford, who was looking similarly startled.

'Precisely. That is why I regard it as the most disturbing map of all time. In the corridors of this university, indeed throughout the universities of the western world' – Dr Von Dechend waved his hand through the air, gesturing to the walls of his room and beyond – 'civilization begins at Sumer in 4000 BC. The last ice age ended properly in about 8000 BC, and as the ice retreated, moisture was released into the atmosphere and life returned to earth. The Neolithic hunting peoples who had struggled through the long winter of the ice age suddenly found that life got a little easier and this led, in Sumeria and the lands of the fertile crescent, which are in what is now Iraq, to the development of the first settled agricultural communities. Prior to this, according to orthodox history, mankind, until 4000 BC, was "backward" – certainly not capable of accurately mapping the world. Since then "civilization", and I use that word with my tongue firmly in my cheek, has evolved to the present day, with its progress marked by nuclear bombs, spaceships and world wars.'

Clearly not a devotee of progress, thought Rutherford. *But this really is surprising. How did the professor get hold of these maps? And what was he proposing to do with them?*

'As you can see,' Von Dechend concluded, 'there is absolutely no way that this version of history can accommodate the Piri Reis map and so it is simply left out.'

'But how come the conventional version of history still prevails?' asked Rutherford. 'Why don't you tell everyone about this map?'

Dr Von Dechend looked at him laconically.

'My boy, the world-renowned physicist Max Planck once said the following' – Dr Von Dechend cleared his throat in a theatrical manner – ' "A new scientific truth does not triumph by convincing its opponents and making them see the light, but rather because its opponents eventually die, and a new generation grows up that is familiar with it." '

If that were true, Catherine thought, *then the past was awash with forgotten truths, long erased. And equally certain people might simply be killed off so that the world view of the murderers might prevail.*

That idea startled her and her thoughts turned to the professor. *People aren't murdered for ideas, are they?* Greatly disturbed, she forced herself to focus on Von Dechend, who had risen to his feet.

'Let me show you an interesting letter while we're on this curious subject. I have it somewhere around . . . Let me see . . . It is a letter that Lieutenant-Colonel Ohlmeyer of the United States Air Force wrote to a Professor Charles Hapgood of Keene College, New Hampshire, a fellow connoisseur of ancient maps. This Professor Hapgood had asked him to compare the Piri Reis map to his work in surveying Antarctica – a task that had never been done before. The response from Ohlmeyer speaks for itself.'

Von Dechend hobbled over to his bookshelf and reached up and pulled down a file containing a sheaf of letters. He laid it out on the table for both of them to read.

6 July, 1960
USAF
Westover Air Force Base

Dear Professor Hapgood,

Your request for evaluation of certain unusual features of the
Piri Reis map of 1513 by this organization has been
reviewed. The claim that the lower part of the map portrays
the Princess Martha Coast of Queen Maud Land Antarctica,
and the Palmer Peninsula, is reasonable. We find that this is
the most logical and in all probability the correct interpreta-
tion of the map. The geographical detail shown in the lower
part of the map agrees very remarkably with the results of
the seismic profile made across the top of the ice-cap by the
Swedish–British Antarctic Expedition of 1949. This indicates
the coastline had been mapped before it was covered by the
ice-cap. The ice-cap in this region is now about a mile thick.
We have no idea how the data on this map can be reconciled
with the supposed state of geographical knowledge in 1513.

Harold Z. Ohlmeyer, Lt-Colonel, USAF

Rutherford could contain himself no longer. 'But
this is extraordinary! How come we've never heard of
this map? Why hasn't it generated more interest?'

He stood up in bewilderment and paced the room.

Catherine noticed his strong, broad shoulders, and the way his hair fell untidily onto his collar. Von Dechend nodded his head sagely and continued, 'Well, funnily enough, when Hapgood first made his discovery, courtesy of the US Air Force, he contacted Albert Einstein. He must have thought if he needed endorsement, why not get endorsement from the father of modern physics himself.'

'Einstein! Wow! Hapgood really wasn't messing around,' said Rutherford.

'Exactly. And he chose the right man. Einstein, like all truly great thinkers, was always receptive to new ideas, even if they might be profoundly out of kilter with the thinking of the scientific establishment of the time. Take a look at this – it's an extract from the foreword that Einstein wrote to one of Hapgood's books.'

Von Dechend dragged another book from his shelves, opened it to the right page and pushed it towards them.

I frequently receive communications from people who wish to consult me concerning their unpublished ideas. It goes without saying that these ideas are very seldom possessed of scientific validity. The very first communication, however, that I received from Mr Hapgood electrified me. His idea is original, of great simplicity, and – if it continues to prove itself – of great importance to everything that is related to the history of the earth's surface . . .

A. Einstein

Catherine and James glanced at each other. Von Dechend was well into his stride. He was leaning back on his chair, with his eyes tightly shut.

'Our Professor Hapgood,' he continued, 'was interested in the Piri Reis map because he thought that it helped to prove his theory about earth-crust displacement. He believed that, every so often, the entire crust of the earth slides around. You are probably familiar with the idea of the tectonic plates shifting?'

They both nodded.

'Where they join there is normally a lot of volcanic activity,' said Catherine.

'That's right. The San Andreas fault line that runs through California is an example of where two plates join. California consequently suffers from regular earthquakes. Anyway, Hapgood believed that not only did the individual plates bump and rub against each other, but that sometimes, all the plates moved together. Imagine the earth's crust, the lithosphere, as being like the shell of a giant egg. At some points the lithosphere is only thirty miles thick. Beneath it is molten rock, metals and all sorts of gases and liquids oozing around. Now, theoretically, there is no reason why Hapgood couldn't be right. He argued that the reason that Antarctica had previously been unfrozen was because it had once been in a completely different place – about thirty degrees further north. Interesting, eh? And what's more Einstein went along with it – he also believed that the Piri Reis map was real. However, neither Hapgood nor Einstein attempted to explain who could possibly have been around before 4000 BC who could have had the skill to do the actual mapping. It remains a mystery.'

Catherine and Rutherford stared as Dr Von Dechend scrutinized the rest of the maps. Muttering to himself in an amused and excited fashion, he nodded his head earnestly and then stood back.

'He has them all!' the geography professor announced in amazement.

'What do you mean?' asked Catherine urgently.

'Kent has managed to collect together copies of all the strangest maps in the world. Look!'

Von Dechend was now shuffling excitedly back and forth around the table peering at each map in turn.

'Here we have a map drawn by Mercator, the greatest map-maker of all time. His map also shows Antarctica as it was before the ice and accurately represents its geographical features. And here we have the great Buache map. This is particularly inexplicable! Buache published his map in 1737, claiming that he used many ancient maps that have long since disappeared. He shows ice-free Antarctica in fact being two continents, divided by a channel of water. Once again, it wasn't until the twentieth century that this was proved to be correct when a huge survey was undertaken.'

Catherine and Rutherford looked at each other in astonishment. They were both intrigued – the implications of the maps were profound. Like the Dogon mystery Catherine had been describing only a few hours before, the maps seemed to pose unanswerable questions, only in this case it wasn't just an academic game. This extraordinary collection of maps was the only clue they had as to why the professor was dead.

11

There was a knock at the door and Dr Von Dechend spun round. A diminutive Filipino maid entered carrying a tray on which sat a large pot of tea, a jug of milk and three cups and saucers.

'Ahh – Molly. Tea. Splendid!'

Von Dechend leapt up and pushed the maps to one side of the desk. The maid deposited the tea and left.

'Lapsang souchong. Any takers?' Catherine and James both nodded and thanked him as he poured.

Sipping his tea and feeling immediately revived, Rutherford felt he ought at least to try to put up a fight on behalf of the conventional view of history.

'But maybe these lands were mapped by prehistoric, migrating peoples? Perhaps, as they travelled around the globe in 5000 or 6000 BC they recorded what they saw?' he said.

Von Dechend looked at him mischievously.

'Yes – I can picture them now! Floating along in their cowhide boats, as the fifty-feet high South Atlantic waves crash about them. I can see them searching for their compasses and pens and paper. Oh dear, I forgot. Pens, paper and compasses hadn't been invented. Well, maybe they used bark or shells or stone tablets and scratched the maps on them. But still – tell me – how did they know where they were? I mean according to the contemporary version of history we are talking about primitive, Stone Age peoples with zero technology or knowledge. How, among all that terrifying water, did they even know where they were?'

'I'm sorry – I don't understand.'

'What do you two know about latitude and longitude?' Von Dechend asked.

'Not a great deal,' admitted Rutherford.

Catherine, whose expertise in astronomy made her quite knowledgeable in this area, couldn't see why they were discussing it.

'I know what they are, but I don't see the connection,' she said.

'Well – perhaps you could explain longitude and latitude to our friend here. I assure you, it is very important that he understands.'

Catherine looked at each man, expelled a deep breath and began: 'OK. Longitude and latitude are the imaginary fish net that surrounds the globe. The horizontal lines running east–west are called latitude and the vertical lines running north–south are called longitude. Are you with me so far?'

'Yup. I've seen them drawn on world maps,' said Rutherford confidently.

'Now, imagine I wanted to tell you where I was in the world, I could give you my coordinates on this grid and you would then be able to locate my exact position.'

'Makes sense.'

'First we would need a prime meridian. A degree zero from which we can take all our measurements. This could be any longitudinal line, running north–south, we care to pick – as long as we both use the same one. It so happens that thanks to Britain once dominating the high seas, the line of longitude that runs north–south through the Royal Observatory in Greenwich is currently accepted as being the degree zero. So, if you are in New York you are seventy-four degrees west of Greenwich and if you are in Hong Kong you are a hundred degrees east of Greenwich, and so on. Are you with me?'

'Yes. Clear as crystal so far.' Rutherford smiled at her.

'Now, this is where it becomes more tricky. I am not going to try and explain why, as it is very complicated and we simply don't have time, but to establish your longitude you need to be able to keep a log of the time at the point of departure, and be able to maintain your timekeeping *throughout* the journey – and you need to be very exact about it.

'This might sound like a simple task but it is not. Even as late as the eighteenth century the very best timepieces would lose a minute an hour. This was hopeless when even a few minutes could put the captain's calculations out by tens of miles – he might miss land altogether. Imagine how far off seafarers would be after a few days, let alone a few months. As most timepieces had pendulum mechanisms, they naturally didn't work very well on the high seas being tossed this way and that, and that's not to mention the variations in the speed of the timepiece due to fluctuations in temperature and humidity. Throughout the entirety of human history, mariners have dreamt of a time-keeping device that could overcome this problem. So finally, after two thousand sailors perished in an epic shipwreck, the Board of Longitude, a British government department, offered the king's ransom of £20,000 to anyone who could invent a naval chronometer that could maintain an accuracy of thirty nautical miles over a six-weeks voyage to the West Indies. Up stepped a man called John Harrison. It took him over forty years to finally alight upon the design of his successful chronometer, but when he did he had cracked it!' said Catherine.

'Amazing. And what date was that?'

'About 1760.'

Catherine glanced at Dr Von Dechend. He nodded encouragingly.

'Anyway – I think the point that Dr Von Dechend is making is that prior to this invention, no one, not the Romans, the ancient Chinese, the Sumerians or indeed any other civilization—'

'That we know of,' interjected Dr Von Dechend.

Catherine raised her eyebrow and continued.

'That we know of – had the ability to determine longitude with any accuracy at all.'

Von Dechend sipped his tea and then eyed them impishly.

'How on earth do we then explain the fact that the geographic features so faithfully described by Kent's maps are placed at exactly the right longitudes and latitudes?'

Catherine again felt the same feeling of mild dread.

Oh no! Not more dismantling of received history.

But Dr Von Dechend was enjoying himself.

'Yes. A very good question it is too. All these maps accurately place the lands they describe. Even the Zeno map, which was drawn in about 1380, and which maps

Greenland and the seas of Iceland, manages to place tiny islands, marooned in the wastes of the Arctic seas, at exactly the right longitudes and latitudes. How is this possible?'

The doctor was now strutting around the room in a fit of inspiration brought on by contemplating the early map makers.

'You've probably seen many different maps of the world. Some where all the countries look very tall and thin, others where they are more spread out. All maps represent a sphere – or a portion of a sphere – on a piece of flat map paper. This is very difficult. In fact it is impossible to do without a knowledge of complicated and advanced mathematics, as well as one of the sophisticated time-keeping devices Catherine described.

'When these maps were made – which must have been after 14000 BC and before 4000 BC – conventional history tells us there were no advanced civilizations capable of anything like the level and sophistication necessary to do this. Hapgood wanted some clarification here, so he approached Professor Strachan at the Massachusetts Institute of Technology.'

Dr Von Dechend turned to face them both and stared at them hard.

'Strachan declared the accuracy and effectiveness of the maps meant they could only have been made by a highly advanced civilization with a knowledge of spherical trigonometry as well as instruments for accurately measuring longitude and latitude. So how else can we explain these perfect, exact maps that have come to us out of the darkness of prehistory? The evidence is indisputable. There was in remote times, before the rise of any of the known cultures, a truly advanced civilization. Furthermore, however advanced it may have been, this civilization somehow disappeared.'

Catherine was dumbfounded.

'But this is impossible! For a start, why aren't there any remains, any ruins of this civilization?'

Von Dechend shrugged his shoulders. 'I don't know. I merely explain to you the truth behind the maps. I am just a humble geographer.'

They all fell silent. And then Von Dechend spoke again: 'Imagine this society was so advanced that it did not need to mine for metals and drill for oil fuel . . . Imagine it used wind power and the renewable energy of wood. Imagine if it consciously decided not to harm the earth in the ways we do, then what would be left? Very little, I should think.'

Catherine was speechless.

All I wanted to do was find out why the professor had these maps and I've stumbled on something completely bizarre and terrifying.

She needed at least one practical answer.

'But why did Professor Kent have these maps in the first place?'

'That is a great mystery, one that I'm afraid I cannot shine any light on at all.'

12

Clutching the envelope of maps in her hand, Catherine emerged from Dr Von Dechend's staircase and into the sunlight of the main quad. She felt more panicked than ever. Her whole universe seemed to be collapsing around her. Rutherford followed her out, his head spinning from all they had learned. Dr Von Dechend's explanation of the maps had particularly unsettled him – he couldn't help thinking of the note the professor had written to him. There seemed to be no escaping the conclusion that the maps were directly related to Professor Kent's claim.

If there really was a message being sent from long ago, then it was logical to conclude that there must have been, in the very distant past, before recorded history, a great civilization. And the maps seemed to be hard evidence of this long-lost civilization that had vanished into the mists of the past. *Maybe the professor really had uncovered a warning, travelling through history, a warning from this hyper-civilized people to the children of the future that the same dreadful fate was about to befall them too*, Rutherford thought.

But it just seemed so outlandish.

Catherine sighed heavily, not sure what to do. She still couldn't bring herself to tell Rutherford that the professor had clearly known he was in danger. It wasn't that she didn't trust James, it was that she could hardly bear to face up to the implications; if she showed him the note and told him of her suspicions, indeed if she told anyone, then there would be no turning back.

Sounding almost desperate she began: 'James, I have another odd question for you. You're a classicist – can you tell me what you know about the word "eureka"?'

Rutherford was taken aback. *There's something Catherine's not telling me about what's happening.*

He wanted to help her so he smiled sympathetically.

'Eureka, eh? Well, I suppose there's no point me asking why you want to know about it?'

Catherine looked apologetic. 'No – but trust me. It's important.'

Rutherford laughed and shook his head, as Catherine continued, 'All I know is that it was Archimedes who said it first. He sat down in his bath and suddenly realized how a body's mass displaces an equivalent amount of fluid. He then cried "Eureka" which means

"I've got it", jumped out of the bath and ran naked down the street, jumping for joy.'

Rutherford looked at her thoughtfully.

'I'm afraid you have just told me the plagiarized version.'

'What do you mean?'

'Well, it wasn't Archimedes who first said eureka, it was Pythagoras, upon his discovery of the relationship between the square of the hypotenuse in a right-angled triangle to the sum of the squares of the other two sides. The version featuring the naked Archimedes and his bath water is a later invention much loved by schoolmasters.'

'But how do you know it was Pythagoras and not Archimedes?'

'Shouting eureka only really makes sense if Pythagoras said it. Pythagoras had a sense of humour!'

Catherine was confused. *What has a sense of humour got to do with anything?*

'What do you mean?'

'Pythagoras was interested in gematria: the unlocking of secret messages.'

Gematria? thought Catherine, turning over the word in her mind. She had never heard of it before.

'How can you have a secret message in a single word? It must be a short message.'

'Yes – in this case it is – it's more of a pun actually. Let me explain. But I'll need a pen and paper.'

'OK – but if you don't mind, I'd quite like to get out of college, I'm beginning to feel a little claustrophobic,' replied Catherine. 'Could we go back to your place?'

Rutherford paused, but one glance into Catherine's deep, earnest eyes told him that, for whatever reason, his explanation was of grave importance to her. He nodded decisively.

13

A tall, slender man in his early forties, wearing a black felt fedora and dressed in a dark blue cashmere overcoat over an elegant grey suit, was standing in All Souls lodge, half swallowed by the gloomy shadows.

His name was Ivan Bezumov. He had been standing there for half an hour, barely moving, hardly even breathing, waiting patiently like a bird of prey, his dark eyes scanning every person who crossed the quad.

As Catherine and Rutherford walked towards him, Bezumov strained his ears to hear what they were saying.

At last! It is her. I can't afford to fail. She is the only link to the professor's research.

When they were about five yards away, Bezumov drew in his breath and stepped out into the quad. Trying to appear as relaxed and friendly as possible, he smiled broadly and removed his hat.

'Hello! I'm Ivan Bezumov. You must be Catherine Donovan.'

Completely ignoring Rutherford, Bezumov shook Catherine's hand warmly and continued, 'I've heard so much about you from the professor.'

Bezumov's Russian accent was unmistakable. Catherine was looking confused. Rutherford stepped forward forcefully and stuck his hand out.

'James Rutherford.'

'Ahh good – I see.' Bezumov turned straight back to Catherine. 'I was a colleague of the poor late professor. It is a terrible tragedy, and I'm so very sorry,' he added. 'I've been waiting for you in the lodge – I thought you might eventually come through. I understand it is not the best time, but it is important I talk to you. Perhaps I can buy you a cup of tea?'

Who is this strange man? thought Catherine. *Surely his work isn't so important that it can't wait until after Professor Kent's funeral? It seems somehow disrespectful that he should be barging in here asking to talk to me.*

'I'm afraid you're right, Mr Bezumov, this really isn't a good time. But perhaps in a week or so – are you in Oxford for a while?'

Bezumov started to look quite anxious. He reached abruptly into the inside pocket of his cashmere overcoat. Instinctively, Catherine and Rutherford stepped away from him.

'Here – this is a letter of introduction from the professor.'

He thrust under Catherine's nose a single piece of paper. On it, written in green ink, was a brief note in the professor's handwriting. Without taking it from Bezumov's hand she read it suspiciously.

Dear Catherine,

My colleague Ivan Bezumov is arriving in Oxford from St Petersburg. We have been working together on a project recently – please give him all the help you can while he is in Oxford and provide him with anything he may need.

Thanks,
Kent

That's odd, she thought. *It's so unfamiliar and formal, not like the professor's normal voice at all.*

Before she could take it all in the Russian was off again: 'Dr Donovan, I was wondering if you had been to the professor's rooms yet? You see, the professor and I were working on something very important before he died.'

Bezumov glanced down at the envelope of maps that Catherine was carrying in her right hand.

'I wanted to see if I could retrieve the relevant notes.'

Catherine instinctively held the envelope closer to her. Bezumov picked up on her reaction and, while continuing to talk, could not prevent his eyes being drawn towards it.

'Again, I am very sorry to bother you at a time like this but did he leave anything? Documents or notes? A folder perhaps?'

Bezumov's lips parted again in a thin, pleading smile. His gaze was now fixed on the package Catherine was holding. She was starting to find the man's whole manner extremely creepy. She thought of the note Bezumov had produced.

The professor never called himself Kent to me. Was he – her throat tightened – *being forced to write it? Did he even write it at all?*

After the strange events of the morning she wouldn't be surprised if Bezumov had forged it. Her head whirled. She was suddenly feeling quite tired and sick.

'Look – why don't you go and see the warden? I am sure he would be happy to help you. And I would be glad to speak to you in a few days' time.'

As Catherine glanced around the quad, looking for a way out, she was startled to see the warden watching them from the window of his library. Before she could fully register this fact, his head had disappeared again from view.

Bezumov was becoming desperate.

'Dr Donovan, please – let me be honest with you. I have to have the documents. It is more important than you could possibly imagine – I demand that you help me.'

Rutherford stepped forward again, placing his strong athletic frame between Bezumov and Catherine.

'Mr Bezumov, Dr Donovan doesn't know anything about the documents that you are talking about. I suggest you do as she says and talk to the warden – and it might be wise to be a little more sympathetic towards people who are still suffering from the loss of a loved one.'

With that he began to usher Catherine around the frantic Russian. In a last bid Bezumov fumbled in his jacket pocket and pulled out a card.

'Wait! I'm sorry.' He took out a fountain pen and removing the top he scribbled on the card. 'This is my mobile number. Call me. I can help. And Dr Donovan, please, if you do have the documents, guard them well. Others will come for them too. They may not be as polite as I am, but they will come.'

Catherine took the card as she walked past. She slid it into her pocket and without looking back at Bezumov, she and Rutherford ducked through the low door of the lodge and out onto the High Street. Bezumov watched them go with a look of pure anguish on his face, his hands crushing the rim of his hat. He would have to take another approach.

14

As Senator Kurtz stepped out of the lift and made his way briskly back across the marble foyer to the front entrance of the UN building, he looked over his shoulder at Secretary Miller.

'Was it a good speech, Secretary?'

The secretary's brow was furrowed.

'Yes, Senator, it fitted the occasion perfectly. But might I just ask, was it wise to announce the details of the plan before we action it? It is only Tuesday morning. Can we trust all the foreign delegates? Monday morning is still six days away.'

The senator laughed derisively.

'It really doesn't matter. There is nothing anyone can do now to stop us – even if I did tell them the truth.'

The secretary swallowed hard. The senator smiled mysteriously and paused before the great glass doors of the front entrance, turning to face him as if to emphasize his point. The steady flow of people coming and going through the doors passed to either side of the men.

'Your job now is to brief the delegates on their individual duties, coordinate their actions.' The senator paused and, with narrowed eyes, he continued, 'Be very careful. Our time is drawing near.' He looked through the glass doors and out towards the bustling city. 'We will meet again in Cairo, on Sunday afternoon, but we will talk before then. In the meantime, make sure that there are no more repercussions from the professor's discoveries.'

With that he turned and, accompanied by his security guards, disappeared out through the doorway and into the noise of the day. The secretary hovered by his side, following him through the doors, unsure what to say next. As the limousine pulled up in front of them, the senator lifted his head up to the sky and smiled.

'The end is coming, Secretary. I advise you to prepare your soul.'

The secretary watched in stunned silence as the senator slid into the back of the waiting limousine. The car pulled away and disappeared into the traffic on UN Plaza and, as it did so, Secretary Miller felt nausea rising in his stomach. Thoughts of the dead professor needled him. What possible threat could an old man with some maps have been? And why had the senator advised him to prepare his soul? They were strange words for the head of the world's most powerful secular brotherhood. Strange and totally inappropriate. Who was this senator really? Nothing seemed to add up any more, nothing seemed to make sense.

The only thing that was still certain was that in six days' time – by Monday afternoon – the world would be changed for ever and he, at least, intended to be on the winning side.

15

The door to Rutherford's flat swung open and Rutherford motioned for Catherine to enter.

'Please – go ahead.'

'Thanks. This is a lovely apartment,' said Catherine, feeling distracted and trying to reach for social niceties. 'My, you have even more books than I do!'

'Yes – well, I find the more books you have the more intimidated your students are! Can I get you anything?'

'Er – a glass of water would be lovely, thanks.'

Rutherford darted past her and into the kitchen. Catherine made herself comfortable on the main sofa and stared around at the yards and yards of books – half of which seemed to be Latin and Greek and other ancient languages. She took out a collection of Catullus's verse, in translation, and was leafing through it, not really reading the words, when Rutherford returned. He sat down next to Catherine and placed her glass of water and a pen and paper on the table in front of them both.

'Where was I? Gematria. Hmm . . .' Rutherford scratched his head, paused for a moment in thought and then began very earnestly: 'Gematria is in many ways like a game. An extremely clever and cunning game. But it is also more than that – it is deadly serious. It is a secret code that was used by the seers of the old world and it was believed to be endowed with magic properties. But first, before we get into the mystical side of it let me explain its literary base,' he said. 'The philosophers of the old world didn't divide knowledge up into disciplines as we do, for they thought that underneath everything all subjects were connected by secret formulae on which the whole cosmos is based. They would have been appalled at the way we teach subjects in separate compartments because they thought that one of the main purposes of education was to show the unity of knowledge. By observing nature, they noticed that certain numbers kept coming up again and again – in the notes on the musical scale and in the movement of the planets, the same handful of numbers and formulae underpinned everything. By working out which numbers and which formulae were critical, the laws of the cosmos could be extracted and then communicated in a clear and simple way.

'Now, it was often the case that these numbers and ratios, which express the hidden workings of the universe, were hidden in written languages. Each letter in the ancient Greek alphabet as well as in the Hebrew and Arabic alphabets has its numerical value. Stories, poems and religious texts were all composed using letters and words of specific values. So what appears to be a simple story on the surface is in fact also a kind of receptacle of the deeper knowledge of the formulae that explain the nature of the universe.'

Catherine listened with fascination.

'So you mean there are old books that have secret messages disguised within the very words of their stories?' she asked.

'Yes, exactly. That's exactly what I mean.'

'Would I know any of these books? Can you give me an example?'

Rutherford couldn't stop himself smiling.

'Have you ever heard of the Bible?'

'The Bible! Really?'

'Absolutely. The Bible was originally composed in Greek. Most people don't realize it but whole passages are constructed using gematria, enabling those who understand what is going on to get an insight into the real message that lies behind the story. For example, it is definitely the case that the writers of the gospels chose the names of the characters and key phrases so that their gematric numerical value would have a specific meaning. They were passing on knowledge in a coded form.'

'So – you're telling me that the story of Jesus's life, death and resurrection isn't just about his life, death and resurrection?'

'Well, that is oversimplifying it – but yes.'

Catherine couldn't believe it. 'But if this is really true then the Bible would be filled with words that have deeper meanings.'

'And it is. Let me give you some examples. But first let's go back to your original example: Pythagoras's exclamation "Eureka" or "ευρηκα" in Greek. It actually refers to the sides of the right-angled triangle five, three and four that he used to prove his theorem.' Rutherford quickly drew the Greek alphabet on the paper, with a number beneath each letter.

α	β	γ	δ	ε	ζ	η	θ	ι	κ	λ	μ	ν
1	2	3	4	5	7	8	9	10	20	30	40	50

ξ	ο	π	ρ	σς	τ	υ	φ	χ	ψ	ω
60	70	80	100	200	300	400	500	600	700	800

'If you use the numerical values of the letters that I have just written down and add them all up to get a total, then you will find "eureka", or "ευρηκα" as it is in Greek, adds up to 534. Coincidence? I think not.'

Rutherford grinned at Catherine as he saw the look of wonder cross her face.

'You see, Pythagoras just wanted to display his

knowledge in an easily memorable way and also make a pun! And this is absolutely typical of the way people worked back then. The whole history of the world would be very different if people stopped taking myths and religions entirely literally and instead found the hidden meanings.' Rutherford scribbled furiously as he spoke. 'One example is as follows: Jesus "Ιησους" 888 plus Mary "Μαριαμ" 192 = the holy ghost "το Πνευμα Αγιον" 1080. And 1080 is also the exact radius of the moon in miles. This is, of course, no coincidence. The moon resurrects itself every twenty-seven days and is therefore the perfect symbol of the resurrection. Equally, Mary is also symbolized by the moon and rebirth.

'Or take the number 1746; it is the New Testament's signature number. No one knows why, but the gospels are littered with key phrases that add up to this. For example, a grain of mustard seed "κοκκοσ σιναπεωσ", or the treasury of Jesus "ο θησαυρος Ιησου". I could go on.'

Catherine's body was tingling with excitement.

'So do you mean the Bible story is made up to fit around the numbers?'

'Certainly not!' Rutherford replied. 'I myself am a regular at college chapel. The gospels are full of divine wisdom, if we allow them to express their teachings of love and peace. All I mean is that the gospel writers may well have chosen the names of the central characters as well as certain phrases to fit in with the gematric scheme. In this way, they are also passing on other messages about the nature of the universe, and the numerical systems which govern it.'

'But why hide these messages?'

'Well – assuming these ancestors of ours were highly intelligent, and they must have been, then they would have anticipated that over the years, certain overzealous supporters of Jesus's ideas might actually lose sight of the truth. So they took the precaution of burying it in the text itself so that the real message could survive – hidden.'

Catherine's head was spinning. She was looking at these bizarre lists of numbers and words, all of them written out in James's neat script.

But there wasn't time to think about the implications of Rutherford's comments right now – something told Catherine she did not have time to waste.

She was certain: gematria was the key she needed to unlock Professor Kent's strange and cryptic message.

16

Catherine inhaled decisively and turned to look Rutherford squarely in the eyes.

'James, I want to show you something important. It's the reason I asked for your help.'

Catherine removed Professor Kent's note from her bag and put it on the table.

'Something terrible is going on. I have known Professor Kent since I was a young girl. My parents were academics at Yale and the professor was a great friend of theirs. He was like a member of my family and we were very close.

'James – the warden told me they thought it was suicide. But he was in no way suicidal. Such an act was anathema to him. And then, when I opened the envelope with the maps, I also found this note. Here – look.'

She handed the note to Rutherford.

In case I don't return.
Eureka

40 10 4 400 30 9 30 70 100 5 200 30 10 40 1 80 5
100 400 40 10 50 10 200 300 100 8 70 9 1 50 300 10
20 800 10 300 10 200 0051172543672

'I am telling you all this because he obviously trusted you – and I do, too.'

Rutherford's first thought on reading the note was that at last he finally understood why Catherine was so interested in gematria. But he couldn't stop looking at the first sentence. In case I don't return.

Rutherford swallowed hard. He wasn't at all sure if he wanted to be drawn into this. What a moment ago had seemed like an enticing intellectual adventure had suddenly taken a truly frightening and sinister turn.

The discoveries, the invitation from the professor, the bizarre maps and now this cryptic note that suggests, quite clearly, that he thought he was in danger. Catherine needs help – she has turned to me – and maybe the professor was on to something, something of value to humanity. But this is bad, very bad.

As he stared at the note, turning over the events of the morning in his mind, Rutherford suddenly realized what Catherine was also thinking. Without even saying anything to her, he lay the gematric code on the table next to the note and proceeded to run Professor Kent's numbers in the message through the reverse sequence.

As soon as he plugged in the first numbers to the

conversion table they both knew their instincts were right. The code produced a name: Miguel Flores.

Feverishly, Catherine grabbed a pencil and translated the rest of the numbers back into words.

Miguel Flores Lima Peru Ministry of Antiquities 0051172543672

Rutherford watched with growing astonishment.

My God – it all works. The professor is communicating from beyond the grave.

Catherine sat up straight and exhaled, staring forward, lost in thought.

'But what does this mean? And why doesn't the end of the code translate – it just comes out as gibberish.'

Rutherford spoke, an expression of mortal fear on his face.

'It's a phone number – it's a phone number in Peru . . . I think we're meant to ring it.'

17

They both stared at the phone sitting on the desk. Rutherford turned it onto loudspeaker and dialled. They held their breaths and listened as the ringing sound began. Then there was a click – the click of a connection being made across the thousands of miles.

'*Holá. Buenos días.*'

Catherine, who knew some Spanish, leaned forward.

'*Holá! ¿Habla inglés?*'

'Yes. I speak English – who is this?'

'Good morning, Señor Flores – my name is Dr Catherine Donovan, I'm phoning from Oxford, England. I am here with my colleague James Rutherford. We are sorry to ring you out of the blue – I wanted to talk to you about Professor Kent.'

There was a long pause and then the voice answered in tones of deep suspicion, 'Who gave you my name?'

'Er . . . we found it – we are friends of Professor Kent.'

'What is going on? Who are you? Where is Professor Kent?'

Rutherford and Catherine looked at each other in shock. Not knowing how else to put it Catherine continued, 'Señor Flores – Professor Kent is dead.'

There was a terrible silence.

'Señor Flores – please help us – we need to talk to you about Professor Kent. Were you working on something with him?'

There was no answer.

'Señor Flores, are you there?'

'Did you say your name was Catherine?' said Flores.

'Yes, yes I did.'

'My God, the professor said one day you might call.'

There was another pause and then the Peruvian spoke – the undercurrents of fear clearly audible: 'We must not talk on the phone. This concerns things too dangerous. Our work is not ready.'

'Can we meet you?'

'Come to Lima. Call me when you get here. Please do not mention me to anyone else.'

With a click the line went dead.

Rutherford looked at Catherine.

'That was very, very weird.'

'And he sounded so afraid. This is getting more dreadful by the moment.' Catherine shook her head, her voice was trembling, but she seemed determined.

'Well, there is only really one thing we can do – if Flores won't talk on the phone, we have to go and meet him face to face in Peru. Are you with me?' she asked.

Rutherford, his brow furrowed, looked back. In the space of only half a day he felt as though he had known Catherine for years. A wave of affection flooded over him as he studied her strong troubled face.

She was looking at him calmly.

'I'm definitely going,' she continued, 'and I will go alone, if I have to. I understand if you don't want to get involved. You probably had other plans for the holidays.'

James was thinking that in the real world he was a busy don with a lot of work to catch up on. *But Catherine needs help – I can't let her disappear off on her own. And if she's brave enough, then I can't just run away.* He gritted his teeth.

'When do we fly?' he said, not quite believing what he was saying. 'I quite fancy a South American holiday – I've been working so hard recently I haven't been abroad for two years.'

Catherine's face lit up with a huge smile.

'Let me go online and then I'll tell you in one second – pack your bags, soldier!'

18

Deep in the bowels of the UN building Secretary Miller walked quickly back towards the General Assembly meeting chamber. As he approached the doors, a smartly dressed man called him from the other end of the corridor.

'Sir, there is an urgent phone call for you.'

The secretary turned on his heel and followed the young man into a spacious open-plan office filled with dozens of empty desks and vacant computer terminals. On one wall were four giant plasma screens, obviously intended for conference calls, and on the opposite wall was a huge map of the world. Over the top of the gigantic map were emblazoned the words:

BACK-UP UN GLOBAL COMMS HQ

In the far corner was a spacious glass-walled room that contained a large conference table. Secretary Miller strode swiftly over to it and, shutting the door behind him, walked over to the table and picked up the phone. The assistant quickly transferred the call across to him. Impatiently, he snapped into the receiver: 'Yes?'

It was the warden of All Souls College.

'I am very sorry to disturb you, Secretary, and I only do so because you instructed me to call you if I found anything even the least bit suspicious.'

A look of mounting irritation crossed the secretary's face.

'Go on. Get on with it.'

'The professor had a friend. A close friend. She is another fellow at the college.'

'And?'

'Something tells me that she suspects.'

'People always suspect. Does she have any evidence?'

'That I do not know yet. But one of your agents has just informed me that she has booked herself and an associate on a flight to Peru. She's probably just going to retrieve the academic's body, or talk to the police – she was very upset. I just thought I ought to mention it, just in case.'

There was a long pause. The secretary stared at a huge map of the world adorning the wall. He had so much to do, so much to prepare – the trivial and annoying business of these academics was beginning to try his patience. But the words of Senator Kurtz came rushing back: 'There is nothing more dangerous to our cause than personal initiative.'

A pained expression crossed the secretary's face. He rubbed his brow with his free hand and stared hard at the portion of the map that depicted South America. How could one person, no matter how committed, undo the board's plans for the new world order?

Even though he trusted him less and less, he deferred to Senator Kurtz's wisdom: 'We will have to deal with these loose ends in Peru. There can be no mistakes.'

Sighing with impatience, he turned his attention back to the phone call.

'Make sure she is closely watched until she gets on the aeroplane. And keep track of everyone she talks to. Contact me if anything else comes to your attention.'

'Absolutely, Secretary.'

But he had already gone.

The fate of the academics wasn't the only thing that was on the secretary's mind. The more he thought about what the senator had said as they left the building, the more suspicious he became. What was really going to happen on Monday?

The takeover would be a violent and bloody business – that was unfortunately inevitable. But it wasn't meant to bring the end of the world. Far from it: it was to be the beginning of a new era. The old corrupt, demagogic forms of government would perish and the direct rule of the Corporation would prevail. At least that had always been the plan.

Something was badly wrong and the secretary had to make a decision. Perhaps Senator Kurtz was operating alone? Perhaps he should attempt to contact the board behind Senator Kurtz's back? No. That would be utter folly – he wouldn't live to see the end of the day, let alone next Monday.

There was however one other avenue that still remained open. In his conversation with the senator, he hadn't been entirely truthful . . .

Very slowly, Secretary Miller lifted his gaze from the desk and turned to look at the corner of the room where stood an elegant teak cabinet; behind its locked doors was the squat and ugly presence of the secretary's personal safe. No, he thought to himself. Not yet. It was too risky. It would have to be his last resort. He should first try to find out more about the senator – try to find out what really motivated him.

19

As the plane broke through the clouds high above Peru, Catherine was just waking up. The drone of the engines confused her for a moment. She rolled her head one way and then the other, half asleep, wondering where on earth she was. But then she registered the voices of the excited British backpackers who were sitting in the row behind her and with a rush of adrenalin she was brought back to full consciousness. There was a crackling sound on the cabin intercom and then the captain's voice came on air: the aircraft had been diverted slightly to the south of its flight path in order to avoid turbulence in the north of Peru, but they were now travelling north again, thirty miles or so inland from the coast, and would be landing in under an hour.

Catherine closed her eyes again and breathed slowly. She had been dreaming of Professor Kent. She tried to block out the noise of the aircraft and its passengers so she could claw back the memory of the dream before it dissolved for ever.

She had dreamt that she was back in the professor's farmhouse. They were sitting in the kitchen together, talking and laughing just as they always used to do. He was still wearing mud-spattered trousers and a big pair of green wellington boots. It was his uniform when he was at home in the country.

She had called round to see him for their weekly lunch. There was a smell of roasting chicken coming from the oven, and he had just uncorked a bottle of red wine and put it on the sturdy oak table, in preparation for their feast. He seemed particularly inspired that morning and, as ever, Catherine was enjoying his company. One of the greatest pleasures of her friendship with him was that she always felt she learnt something whenever they met. She never got the sense that he was preaching, just that he was at every moment alive and engaged with the world around him.

In the dream, she had recalled a conversation that they had once had about labour-saving tools. The professor with his usual talent had explained to her the real significance of these so called technological advances.

'Plato,' said Professor Kent, 'the father of the Western tradition, said that the hand is an *organon*, which in English means tool. To call the hand an *organon* is simply to say that it is a tool of the owner. Plato said the hand is an *organon*, the hammer is an *organon* and the hammering hand is an *organon*.

'However, the electric juicer that one finds in many kitchens today is something much more sinister. It masquerades as an *organon* but it is in reality something quite different. It is one of the many manifestations of the gigantic system that is devouring our world.'

Catherine feigned disbelief, because she sometimes liked to play devil's advocate.

'Come on! Surely it's just a harmless device to speed up a boring task – to make more time in the day. And the end result is a healthy drink – aren't we *meant* to be buying juicers?'

He smiled at her. He liked her to discuss anything with him. He had a gentle way of arguing, but he didn't mind being forced to state his case. He enjoyed convincing people, or trying to, with his reasoned arguments, always centred in the holistic world view from which he could never be moved.

'Well, Catherine,' he said, 'like it or not, the age of tools has passed and the age of systems is here. Let's put it this way: you juice your oranges and make a delicious healthy drink. Wonderful! But if you observe the juicer more closely its more disturbing aspects can be noticed. The electricity to power the juicer arrives via a network of cables and overhead power lines, which are fed by power stations that depend on water pressure, pipelines or tanker consignments, which in turn require dams, offshore platforms and derricks in far-off countries. The whole chain only guarantees an adequate and prompt delivery if every one of its parts is staffed by armies of engineers, planners, financial experts, who themselves can fall back on administrations, universities, indeed entire industries – and sometimes even the military, as we have seen again and again.

'Whoever thinks they are merely using a juicer is wrong. The juicer is a disguise; it is not a convenient tool at all but the final element of just one of the millions upon millions of tentacles of the great system that is wrapping itself around this world and every day tightening its grip.'

'My goodness,' interjected Catherine, having forgotten that she was trying to play devil's advocate, 'that sounds pretty worrying.'

The professor shook his head. A sad smile crossed his face.

'Yes – and so through such insidious disguises as the blender, the washing machine, the car and so on, these tentacles enter our daily lives and force us to service the system that will in fact one day, in the not too distant future, destroy us. The opportunity to opt out has long since passed. It is in the nature of systems that they grow and take on a life of their own, eventually creating their own goals, different from those they were meant to serve. Look at organized religions. Today they are vast global systems with ambitions that are now a long way from the good words of their prophets. The goal of our current global system is to force more and more people to depend on the energy it provides. By using the system we are writing it a blank cheque.'

He walked to the table and poured out two glasses of wine.

'And remember, nature is the bank on which ultimately all cheques are drawn. But let me get you some lunch, dear girl. A friend from the village brought me a chicken from his organic farm. They are always delicious – I do hope you'll like it!'

Bleary-eyed, and deeply saddened by the realization that there were to be no more such conversations, Catherine lifted the window shutter to let in the morning light. Below them the Peruvian Alto Plano stretched out as far as the eye could see. It was an awesome view. But then to her bemusement, her eyes started to play tricks on her. Looking down, she thought she could see a strange shape laid out on the ground thousands of feet below. It looked like the outline of a giant hummingbird.

Catherine rubbed her tired eyes and took another look, expecting the hallucination to have disappeared.

It was still there, and next to it was some kind of enormous flower. A little further on were more huge designs: a massive fish, a majestic condor, what seemed to be various geometric shapes, and then two parallel lines. They were dead straight and seemed to go on for ever.

Am I seeing things? These are incredible!

She turned to Rutherford and shook his arm.

'James – you've got to see this. What on earth are those pictures drawn on the ground?'

Rutherford looked over and out at the astonishing site.

'Oh my God! I've got no idea.'

On Rutherford's left, sitting in the aisle seat, was a smartly dressed Peruvian gentleman of about sixty. He had a nut-brown complexion and a classic Inca nose. He had overheard their conversation, and said in heavily accented English, 'Those are the famous Nazca lines. Welcome to Peru!'

Rutherford was puzzled.

'The Nazca lines? I've never heard of them!'

Catherine wanted to know more.

'Nor have I – how can they be visible from way up here? They must be absolutely enormous. Those lines alone must be half a mile long! And they're so straight!'

The Peruvian smiled, his eyes twinkling in the bright sunlight.

'Señorita, they are even longer than that. They are more than five miles long and are perfectly straight – they go up and down hills, across gullies and never once stray.'

Catherine was amazed.

'But what are they for and when were they made?'

'You've obviously never been to Peru before, señorita.' The old man grinned. 'You will have to get used to hearing this during your stay, but I'm afraid no one knows!'

20

A few minutes later, Catherine turned to Rutherford having consulted the guidebook. Earnestly, with a frown on her face she said, 'The Nazca lines are the crop circles of Latin America. There are hundreds of gigantic designs and no one really understands how they were done. As well as pictures of identifiable animals and fish, there are many perfectly made geometric shapes. What's really bizarre is that they can only really be appreciated, or even recognized for what they are, when looked at from the air – as we are doing now. At ground level, due to their huge size, it is almost impossible to get a handle on their overall dimensions and as there are absolutely no high points in the land around Nazca – it is uniformly flat – why they were made before we invented man-made flight seems all the more incomprehensible.'

She paused for a second. Rutherford was deep in thought. She barely needed to ask – but did: 'Are you thinking what I'm thinking?'

Rutherford nodded. His strong, handsome face wore a frown.

'If you mean it reminds you of the professor's theory,' he said, 'of the ancients leaving messages for the future, then yes, I am definitely thinking what you're thinking. It's extraordinary.'

Catherine looked back out of the window and down at the strange patterns passing majestically beneath them. A huge bird and then a massive empty parallelogram drifted by. She let the book drop into her lap. She felt a lump rise in her throat – it was all becoming too much.

How is it you can go through your entire education – high school, university, a doctorate and finally an academic career and then in the space of twenty-four hours, the whole basis of your comfortable world view is torn apart? Why did no one ever tell me about these things before – the maps, the Nazca lines, the fact that the Bible is really a secret code for transmitting ancient wisdom?

She felt Rutherford's consoling hand on her arm.

'Catherine? Catherine – are you OK?'

The warmth of human contact and the sound of his voice drew her back to the present moment. She turned her head to look at him and tried to force a smile but the pressure was finally getting to her.

His expression was serious.

'Catherine – we have to stay calm. We must not be

afraid. Remember the professor – he went down this path and we must follow him. We have to trust in the truth and ignore everything we thought we knew until now.'

This time she smiled sincerely. She was very glad he was there.

'James, thank you. I'm sorry – it's just that, well, a lot seems to have happened in such a short time. A lot seems to have changed . . . for me at least.'

'I know – I agree. I have no idea where this is going and if I think about the implications, to be frank, it rather frightens me. We have to try not to look too far ahead, just go forward and see what we discover.'

Catherine glanced back down at the surreal landscape of the plateau. It was still there, taunting her with its mysterious hieroglyphs. With renewed purpose, she reopened the book and read aloud: 'Many people have attempted to date the Nazca lines but it is an impossible task. There is no organic material used in the designs, so radiocarbon dating is out. All there is to go on are pottery shards that have been discovered embedded in some of the man-made ruts and trenches. The pictures themselves also beg questions. For example, why are so many of the creatures depicted foreign to the Andes? There is a condor, but apart from this there is a whole collection of inappropriate animals, including a whale, a monkey, odd species of birds and, strangest of all, a perfect representation of an extremely small and rare jungle spider that only lives in the depths of the Amazon rain forest.

'The spider is of particular interest because astronomers have calculated that its position and the position of the straight lines adjacent to it serve as a model of the Orion constellation and surrounding stars.'

Catherine closed the book. As an astronomer that settled it for her.

'James, whoever made these designs one thing is for sure – they were definitely from a high civilization. To understand the heavens and to map the Orion constellation like this requires an enormous amount of sophistication.'

Rutherford shook his head in incomprehension.

'Yes – and what about the fact that half the animals are not even Andean?'

Catherine suddenly had an idea. She leaned forward and addressed herself to the Peruvian gentleman again. He was immersed in his newspaper.

'Excuse me, señor, can I ask you a question?' The old man lowered his paper and smiled encouragingly.

'What do Peruvian people say about these lines?'

His dark eyes scrutinized her face carefully. Catherine felt as if his response was going to depend on what he thought of her character. She looked at him beseechingly.

'Señorita – we already *know* who drew these lines. It was the Viracochas, the demigods who first ruled Peru. They came from the sea many, many thousands of years ago. They made the laws and taught the people many things. American archaeologists and the Spanish before them thought that when we talk of the Viracochas we are talking of myths, but we are not. There are no written records of these people but we know they came.'

He nodded firmly, then returned to his paper.

Rutherford, his eyes wide with wonder, leaned closer to Catherine and whispered, 'I think you've just discovered what it is we should be focusing our attention on. Who were these Viracochas – and could they possibly have existed?'

Catherine nodded and whispered back, 'Yes – you're right – they might well be the key to this part of the mystery. Perhaps the Viracochas are the people who left the warning message in the myths of the world. Perhaps the lines are part of that message.'

Rutherford, staring past Catherine into the endless blue of space, muttered almost to himself, 'Yes! Exactly. It is extraordinary . . .' He turned to look at her. 'I have a feeling that our friend Miguel Flores is going to have a lot to say to us about all this.'

21

Lima airport was in fiesta mood. As they came through the swinging double doors that marked the exit from the Peruvian Customs Authority, their senses were instantly assaulted. Most striking of all were the people. After Heathrow airport with its smartly dressed business folk, holiday makers dragging their neat luggage behind them and the general feeling that one was being moved around like a ball-bearing in a pinball machine, the chaos of Lima airport was refreshing. The noise was immense, the heat sweltering and the thousands of Peruvian Indians, many in the traditional poncho and felt hat, all contributed to the feeling that they had stepped into a tropical market place.

Battling past the touts Catherine and James made their way to the taxi rank and, after a brief wait, managed to slide into the calm interior of a cab. It was a spacious yellow American-style cab driven by a friendly looking man in his early twenties. Breathless from their exertions, Catherine instructed the driver to take them to the city.

The driver grinned and gunned the engine into life. The taxi pulled out – making all sorts of strange noises as it went – and drifted onto the dirty, busy main road that went to Lima City. As they left the airport perimeter, the buildings at the side of the road began to deteriorate: everywhere the shanty town sprawled.

Rutherford stared in amazement at the terrible sight. It was like a parody of an American or European city. Everything was man-made but rather than being used for its original purpose had been adapted for another, more basic, one. A car bonnet was the roof of a house, an empty oil drum was a bath. Groups of grubby children were playing with rubbish dumped in the streets.

So these are the notorious slums of South America, he thought.

Catherine was transfixed. It was an apocalyptic vision after the serene beauty of Oxford. *How can people have a good life in these wretched conditions?* She turned to Rutherford. 'I don't think the Viracochas would be very happy if they could see the country today.'

'No – definitely not. It's depressing.' He looked on appalled as they passed row upon row of makeshift dwellings. 'I say we go straight to the Ministry of Antiquities and find Flores. We can worry about a hotel afterwards – what do you think?'

'Good idea. I could do with a strong cup of coffee, though. I didn't sleep much on the flight.'

Rutherford rummaged through his rucksack and pulled out his diary, in which he had written the address of the Ministry of Antiquities. With a smile he handed it to Catherine and nodded at the driver.

'I think you'd better do this, otherwise who knows where we will end up!'

Catherine laughed and spoke to the driver. Then she laid her head back on the headrest and closed her eyes. *Soon we will know the secret Professor Kent and Miguel Flores shared. And we will be one step closer to understanding why the professor died . . .*

The Ministry of Antiquities was a huge, imposing, neo-classical building on the north side of the grand and chaotic Plaza Mayor situated in the heart of Lima, at the crossroads of four of the capital's busiest roads. Consequently the plaza was filled from dawn to dusk with a sea of assorted vehicles all eager to get to their destinations; lorries from the country, local buses and private cars, all trying to nose their way through – all seemingly oblivious to road signs and traffic policemen.

After struggling round the square and weaving in and out of traffic, the taxi finally jerked to a halt at the foot of a flight of massive steps. Catherine paid the driver while Rutherford wrestled the bags from the boot. Eager to get indoors and escape the pollution and noise, they scrambled up the steps. At the top was a huge pair of iron doors, both of which were open. Beyond was a set of glass doors shielding the interior of the ministry from the din of the traffic and the stench of diesel fumes. Above the iron doors was a bronze emblem depicting a giant condor with the words 'Ministerio de Antigüedades' embossed underneath.

The atrium was a gloomy, badly lit cavernous hall with an aura of sepulchral calm. The floor was marble, as were the walls, and the ceiling was of a cathedral-like height. There was virtually no furniture except for the reception desk and an accompanying sofa. One receptionist sat behind the desk, but apart from that the Ministry of Antiquities looked and felt deserted.

They walked over to the reception desk and Catherine cleared her throat before addressing the diminutive black-haired receptionist.

'*Buenos días* – we've come to see Miguel Flores, please. My name is Catherine Donovan and this is James Rutherford – we're from Oxford University.'

The secretary looked very upset and started talking very quickly in Spanish.

'Can you understand her?' Rutherford asked Catherine.

'No,' she replied. 'She's talking too fast – hold on . . . she's calling someone.'

The secretary spoke rapidly into her phone and then thrust the receiver at Catherine.

'*Holá – habla inglés?*' Catherine asked.

Sure enough, the man on the other end answered in English, in suave and reassuring tones.

'Hello – this is the deputy minister for antiquities. I gather you have come to see Señor Flores?'

Catherine turned to Rutherford and gave him a conspiratorial smile. He watched as she listened to the voice at the other end. Suddenly all colour drained from her face, and her hand, still holding the receiver, dropped to her side. She turned to face him. She was no longer smiling – her eyes were filling with tears. She had a look of pure fear on her face.

'Flores was hit by a car this morning on his way to work. He's dead.'

22

The crisp clicking noise of shoes on marble warned them of the approach of the deputy minister. Striding towards them from the far end of the hall was a short, dark, moustachioed man wearing a black suit and tie. He looked to be in his forties.

As he approached, Catherine's instincts took over. She whispered quickly to Rutherford, 'Don't tell him why we're here.'

The man strode straight up to Catherine and shook her by the hand, then turned to Rutherford and did the same, all the time beaming with an insincere, ingratiating smile. He had gold rings on his fingers and one gold tooth. His accent was thick and he exuded a much practised charm.

'Welcome, welcome. I am so sorry to break the news of this tragedy. I am Raphael Mantores, I work in Señor Flores's department. You just spoke to me on the phone. Please – have a seat.'

Rutherford and Catherine were almost glad to be told what to do. Shell-shocked, they moved over to the sofa and sat down.

'Please, Señor Mantores, can you tell us what happened to Señor Flores?' asked Catherine.

He let out a sigh. It seemed theatrical to Catherine, but perhaps she was just feeling particularly frightened and suspicious.

'Oh, it is terrible. Every day he gets out of the bus on the other side of the plaza and then walks through the traffic, instead of going round. Today he was hit by a car.'

Rutherford couldn't believe what he was hearing.

'Did the vehicle that hit him stop?'

'Stop? Ha! This is Lima! No, it didn't stop, it drove off.'

'Were there any witnesses?'

'In Lima people do not stop. It was an accident – what could anyone have done? The police arrived some time later – a half hour or so. It is a very busy area . . . they are not the NYPD. They took him to the hospital, but it was too late.'

Catherine, still hardly able to process the information, said, 'But that's awful – no one bothered to say what happened or report the number of the car?'

'What good would it do, señorita? It's probably an unlicensed vehicle like most vehicles in Lima – the police wouldn't be able to trace it. But you came here to see Señor Flores? I am so sorry your visit has been ruined. Can I help you? We don't get many people from Oxford here – it is an honour.'

The practised smile had returned to his face. Catherine glanced at Rutherford – paranoia was taking hold. She answered for both of them: 'No, thanks. Please don't worry. We wanted to talk to Señor Flores about the Incas, but it is not important. We will get a guide from the hotel.'

Mantores pressed his help on her.

'But, señorita, perhaps I can persuade you to visit some of our more modern attractions? Peru is more than just the Inca heritage, you know.'

Looking around the cavernous atrium, half expecting some unknown enemy to appear from behind one of the doors, she stuttered, 'No, no, thank you very much. We will be fine.'

'Well, if there is anything I can do to help during your stay, please don't hesitate to call. Here is my card. I am sorry your visit has begun this way.' He glanced at their rucksacks which still had the airline luggage tags attached and smiled broadly at them. 'I very much hope things will improve.'

'Thank you, Señor Mantores, I am sure they will. I am sure they will.' But Catherine wasn't at all convinced.

23

Rutherford and Catherine stood at the top of the steps outside the huge double doors and surveyed the sea of slowly circling traffic filling the square below. Horns honked constantly; the din was almost unendurable, the smell of diesel fumes overpowering.

Rutherford dropped his rucksack to the ground and stared out over the mayhem of Plaza Mayor. Standing in full view of the vast plaza, he suddenly felt hugely vulnerable and his instincts cried out to him to hide, to get back in the building, to disappear.

Catherine was shaking her head, her mind racing. *Flores must have been murdered – it's just too much of a coincidence that he should get run over twenty-four hours after our phone call. But how could anyone have known that we contacted him? Was the phone tapped? And if it had been – by whom and why? Whoever it was must be very well organized – internationally organized in fact – and also hell-bent on stopping whatever it was that the professor and Flores were involved in. Flores had said on the phone that they weren't ready. Ready for what?*

Then cold logic delivered her deep into the realms of fear. A feeling of horror overtook her. *But if they killed Flores for merely talking to us, then surely . . .*

She looked around in panic; she felt like bursting into tears, she wanted to hide . . . and then she thought again of the professor, a humane, compassionate man, murdered in cold blood for reasons she didn't yet understand. Anger struggled with fear as her resolve began to grow anew.

We are not going to be brushed off that easily. We won't be frightened into submission.

She tried desperately to think of the next course of action.

'Would there be any point in talking to the police . . . or the British Embassy?'

'No,' said Rutherford firmly, looking up at her. 'What evidence do we have?'

Catherine sat down on her bag. She simply didn't know where to turn next. She could sense a gulf growing between them. She hardly knew James Rutherford and James Rutherford had hardly known the professor.

Poor James. He must be wondering what he is doing here. But somewhere, there must be a solution – or at least a clue as to how we should carry on.

Rutherford was pacing around the flagstones at the top of the gigantic steps.

'Catherine, I really think we should head back to the airport. I mean, we tried . . . Someone else should take it up. The CIA. MI6. I don't know. People who understand these things.' He paused and turned to address her directly. She was lost in thought.

Suddenly she leapt to her feet.

'Could you wait here a second and watch my bag? It has the professor's maps in it.'

Rutherford spun round.

'What! What are you doing? Hey – why are you going back in? Wait . . .'

But it was too late. Catherine had disappeared through the gap in the huge iron doors, back into the darkness of the atrium.

Alone at the top of the steps, Rutherford felt as though there was a noose tightening around his neck.

24

Señor Mantores walked briskly down the corridor to his spacious office on the third floor. Gone was the oily charm of a few moments ago. He dipped his hand into his jacket pocket, drew out a handkerchief and mopped his brow. He put the handkerchief back, drenched in sweat. With a look of dread on his face, he walked slowly up to his door and then, pausing for a second, turned the handle. Taking one last deep breath, he walked in.

Sitting in the comfortable, high-backed leather executive chair behind his desk, was the man who had killed Professor Kent. The murderer was dressed in a black suit and white shirt. His short but muscular arms were folded across his chest in a highly aggressive manner. Over by the window, a second, sinister, black-clad westerner stood peering through the blinds onto the plaza below. It was the small man's accomplice from that dark night above the ruins of Machu Picchu. There was something military about the two men – their close-cropped hair, their lean weather-beaten faces. The small man glowered at the terrified figure of Señor Mantores before firing a question at him.

'So – is it done? Can I tell Secretary Miller that this is the end?'

The Deputy Minister of Antiquities was reduced to a quaking wreck. All the confidence he had exhibited to Catherine and Rutherford in the lobby had vanished. His voice trembled. 'Yes, señor. I spoke to them. I told them absolutely nothing except that Flores had been killed in a traffic accident. They were very shocked. I do not think they will stay long in Peru.'

'You *think* they will not stay long or you *know* they will not stay long?'

A look of panic swept across Mantores's face. His voice became pleading and high pitched. 'Señor – the trail is dead. They can find nothing. They will go home, I am sure of it.'

Suddenly, the accomplice, who had up until that moment been preoccupied with the view from the window, spun round. 'The girl's coming in again. Alone.' Then he turned back to the window and with his fingertips re-parted the blinds.

His seated colleague snarled, 'Mantores, why the hell is she re-entering this building?'

Mantores was at breaking point.

'Señor, I don't know. Please, I will talk to her – let me go down again . . .'

The seated man glowered at him.

'No. This is too important.' With that he pushed the chair away from the desk and stood up. 'Our orders are clear. We will make sure this does not get any further out of hand. Come with us.'

Two minutes later Catherine reappeared through the doors, brandishing a piece of paper with some writing on it in her right hand. She had a smile on her face.

'What's that?' demanded a confused Rutherford.

'This is the address of Flores's family. I told the receptionist I wanted to send some flowers.'

Rutherford couldn't believe his ears. She was actually planning to continue their journey. But he couldn't help being impressed by her nerve.

'It was that easy?'

'Well – it's true.' Catherine grinned. 'In fact, I want to deliver them in person. Come on, let's go.'

Catherine walked over to her bag and heaved it onto her shoulder. Rutherford watched as she ran down the steps to hail a cab. She got to the bottom and then turned to look back up at him. She saw he was hesitating, and she could understand it. *But I need you to come – please, James.*

She sighed and then called up to him, 'Listen, James – please let us see Flores's family. We can go to the airport after that, I promise. I can't go home without following this lead – I will never be able to live with myself.'

Rutherford took one look at her pleading face and his common sense melted away.

'OK – we go over to the Flores house now and then we go straight back to the airport – understood? And let's keep it short.'

25

It was now approaching midday on Wednesday and the streets of Lima were filled with cars. The sun was hidden, as it is for ten months of the year, behind the infamous coastal fog that rolls in from the Pacific and blankets the city in a white haze. It is called the *garoupa* by the locals, which means the donkey's belly, and its oppressive force adds to the stifling effect of the pollution and heat.

Their route took Rutherford and Catherine through the old colonial city centre. It was a picture of faded grandeur. They passed beautiful wooden villas and large stone palaces that had mainly been converted to government use as ministerial buildings and museums.

Old Lima is small and within minutes the taxi was driving through the filthy crowded streets of the modern city with its dreary concrete buildings and dilapidated roads. Signs of poverty were visible everywhere and, as the car edged through the traffic jams, hawkers of everything from plastic clothes hangers to cigarette lighters swarmed around the slow-moving vehicle.

Twenty minutes later, having stopped at a flower shop so Catherine could buy some lilies, the taxi nosed its way round a tight corner and down a narrow deserted alley, deep in the heart of one of the residential districts. The driver craned his head this way and that, letting the vehicle gently roll along the grubby street.

'Aha! It is here,' he announced finally. 'That door – the green one.'

Catherine and Rutherford stared warily at a two-storey concrete house jammed into a row of others all of the same grim design. Catherine handed the agreed fare over to the driver and got out of the car. The empty street made her feel nervous. She glanced around and then turned back to the driver.

'Can you wait here till we're ready to leave?'

'Sure thing, señorita. You take as long as you want.'

The Indian driver turned off his engine, clicked on his radio and leaned his head back, pulling his baseball cap down over his eyes with a contented smile. Catherine and Rutherford walked over to the door.

Rutherford stepped back a pace and glanced up and down the street as Catherine rang the bell. The silence unnerved him. After about thirty seconds, there was the sound of a key turning in a lock. The door opened a fraction. A woman's face looked out through the gap. Her eyes were red – probably from crying, thought Catherine.

The woman had strong attractive Inca features – a heavy brow, firm nose, high cheekbones – and her skin was very dark. Catherine guessed she must be about thirty-five.

'*Hola, señora – habla inglés?*'

The woman remained inscrutable. Catherine pressed on: '*Nosotros somos amigos de Miguel Flores.*'

At the mention of Flores's name a flash of recognition crossed the woman's face. She instantly looked more open and at the same time more vulnerable.

'*Ustedes conocían a Miguel?*' – You knew Miguel?

Catherine felt terrible for intruding on the woman's grief.

'*Sí*, señora. We are very sorry for your loss . . .'

Rutherford watched in silence as what was clearly a very delicate scene slowly unfolded.

Finally, after a pause of almost a minute, the chain came off the door and the woman, looking anxiously into the street as she did so, ushered them into the house. Shutting and locking the door behind them, she called out into the depths of the house in Quechua – the language of the Incas, still spoken in various dialect forms by the Indians of the Andean provinces of Peru.

Out of a doorway further down the corridor emerged a short handsome Indian man, also in his mid-thirties. He was drying his hands on a cloth. His face wore an expression of great anxiety. His voice was urgent and intense, and he spoke quick, fluent English.

'My sister tells me you knew our brother. Who are you and what do you want?'

Catherine wasn't sure what to say.

'Er – we are very sorry to intrude at this time. It is only because it is so important we talk to you that we have come.'

The Indian looked very unhappy, but after scanning Catherine up and down and peering past her at Rutherford he eventually spoke: 'OK – but you cannot stay long.'

They followed him into a large room that contained two sofas as well as a large library of books on Inca history, culture and art. On the walls were photographs of breathtaking vistas of Peru, clearly taken from all over the country: in the jungles, on the coast and, most impressively of all, in the Andes mountains.

Catherine offered the lilies they had bought to the inscrutable man.

'These are for you. I have to be honest, we did not know your brother. We only spoke to him once. My name is Catherine Donovan and this is James Rutherford. We are from Oxford University. We arrived in

Peru this morning. We were hoping to meet your brother today. We didn't even have an appointment.'

The dark eyes of the Peruvian flicked between the two westerners. His suspicion was palpable.

'Thank you for the flowers. Please sit down.'

He handed the flowers to his sister and pulled up a chair. He wasn't giving anything away. He looked very uncomfortable indeed.

'If you didn't know my brother then why were you coming to visit him?'

Catherine swallowed nervously.

We have to get something from this man – however awkward it is to be here, however insensitive it is to trespass on their grief – we absolutely have to get something.

'A friend of ours in England – Professor Kent – had been working with your brother on something just before he died.' Catherine paused to see how the Peruvian reacted but he just stared at her with his deep dark thoughtful eyes. She continued, 'Look – I know this won't make much sense to you but your brother's name was found in code among our friend's papers after his death. I called him but he didn't want to talk on the phone; he told us to come here.'

The Indian suddenly stood up and Catherine stopped talking. He walked slowly over to the fireplace and then turned to face them.

'Señorita, the last time I saw Professor Kent he was

sitting exactly where you sit now – but that is another matter. I cannot help you. I think we must end this conversation. I don't want to know anything more about you. Please – we would very much like you to leave.'

But Catherine was reeling.

'You *knew* Professor Kent?'

'No, I have met him only twice, both times here in Miguel's house. My brother brought him back so they could discuss their work in private. Now, I must really ask you—'

Rutherford interjected, 'Señor Flores – I am sorry indeed about your brother's death. But something very bad is happening here. You can't just ignore it. We need your help – Professor Kent was murdered, we think, and we need to know what he and your brother were doing. We must not let their deaths be in vain.'

The Indian was clearly being pulled in different directions. Rutherford could sense he wanted to talk but fear was holding him back. Rutherford pressed on: 'Would we be offending you if we asked you questions about his work with the professor? Did your brother ever talk about it to you?'

The Indian looked at him and smiled a sad smile.

'You could not be less in danger of offending me. Miguel's work was of great importance to me as well. That is not the point . . .' The Indian's voice trailed off

– he was unsure what to do and then, as if deciding finally he couldn't simply bury his head in the sand, he turned to look at them both and shook his head.

'I am sorry,' he waved his arm in the air, 'Miguel told me yesterday that if something happened to him I should speak to no one. We are very frightened – it has been a very bad day. Very bad.'

Catherine felt a surge of empathy for the poor man.

'Señor Flores – we are sorry to intrude. We just want to understand what is happening. The professor was like a father to me, I too have lost a loved one.'

The Indian sighed. 'It is complicated. Their work was secret. But where do I begin?' For a moment he was lost in thought, then he began again, 'Despite our name, we are a full-blooded Quechua family from Cuzco, the ancient Incan capital up in the Andes. Our grandfather took a Spanish name. We are unusual for rural Indians, fortunate in that we both had a high-school education and Miguel studied at Cuzco University. He became an archaologist and historian and I worked until recently for an aid organization in Cuzco state. Our life's work, in fact our whole life, is our people, the Quechua – the descendants of the Incas.'

Catherine let out a sigh of relief. *He's talking . . .* In a deep, serious tone, Flores continued. He spoke slowly and deliberately, every word carefully chosen. All the time his eyes flicked between Catherine and Rutherford.

'We know the history of our people. We know the stories from the past and since we were small boys we have wandered among the ancient ruins of Cuzco, of Ollantaytambo and Tiahuanaco – the city of the Viracochas – near Lake Titicaca.

'We know the history of our country in a way that a Spanish or American academic sitting in their office surrounded by their books never will. But we have the books too – as you can see. We are not ignorant of contemporary scholarship. We just disagree with it.'

The Indian's face was radiating purpose now. With his newfound resolve he continued, 'For generations after the conquest, the Spanish and particularly the Catholic church did everything they could to wipe out all evidence of our civilization. Monuments and religious centres were vandalized, religious books were burnt, priests were massacred and people were converted by the sword. In a couple of generations there was virtually nothing left and even today our children are taught the orthodox version of our history – the Catholic version. Professor Kent understood this injustice. We did not have to tell him that before the Incas there was another civilization even greater still. I don't know how, but he already knew this and wanted to find proof. We have that proof.

'Professor Kent was a very learned man; he told us

the truth we had revealed to him would help reveal an even greater truth that may save mankind.'

Listening to Flores's revelation, Catherine had already decided what they must do next.

'Señor Flores – can we too learn the true history? We want to carry on the professor's work.'

'Señorita – please call me Hernan. I am sorry for my initial unfriendliness, but we are not safe here. If we want to carry on talking, or even thinking about these things, then we must leave Lima immediately and travel to Cuzco.'

At that moment Hernan's sister reappeared in the doorway. She looked as if she was on the point of bursting into tears. She started to jabber frantically in Quechua and pointed accusingly at the two westerners. Hernan looked embarrassed and at the same time very upset by his sister's grief. Using soft words and speaking very quietly, he took hold of her hands and slowly calmed her down and ushered her out of the room.

Rutherford barely noticed. He was preoccupied by very different thoughts.

There are now two dead men. What does Flores think happened?

Hernan reappeared, shaking his head. Before he could begin speaking again, Rutherford, trying as hard as he could to be delicate, said, 'Señor Flores, there is one thing I would like to ask you. Do you have any idea who could be responsible for the deaths of Professor Kent and your brother?'

Hernan shook his head ruefully and then glanced at his watch.

'No, I am afraid not. But it doesn't matter exactly who they are. What is important is that they exist. They are powerful and they are prepared to do anything. I am not being paranoid. We are now all in danger – believe me.'

The expression on his face became blank again. Catherine studied his high cheekbones and dark eyes. Somehow, despite the terrible tragedy of his brother's death, the man still managed to maintain his dignity.

'Hernan – thank you very much indeed for your help. Would you mind if James and I conferred?'

'No – please go ahead. I must go to the hospital now, but if you are coming to Cuzco, the flight leaves at five thirty. If there is anything you need, then don't hesitate to ask.'

Hernan left the room. Catherine was bursting with new enthusiasm – it seemed their trail was very much alive again. She turned to Rutherford with a smile on her face and her heart sank. She could immediately tell, from his grim expression, that he had come to a very different conclusion.

26

Catherine looked imploringly at Rutherford. She was desperate for them to carry on.

'James – I really think we should go with Herman—'

Rutherford, his voice sounding incredibly tense, cut in before she could go any further: 'I'll tell you what the facts are. These maniacs – whoever they are – have already murdered both Miguel Flores and Professor Kent. They will kill us without a second thought; we are nothing to them. They do what they want anywhere in the world, you know that. And we don't even know what it is we're looking for!'

Rutherford jumped to his feet and began to pace up and down in front of the fireplace.

Catherine didn't know what to say. Tentatively, she began: 'That's not true. We do know what we are looking for – an ancient secret hidden in the myths of the world. If we keep following Professor Kent's trail, then I feel sure we will find out more.'

She was worried. It was the first argument they had had. She realized again how much she needed his support. But she was desperate to carry on and angry that he was suggesting otherwise. Standing by the fireplace, however, his arms folded, Rutherford was looking more defiant than ever.

'Catherine – to say this is dangerous is the understatement of the year. The professor knew full well just how powerful and ruthless these terrible people, whoever they are, could be – why else did he write the note? Wouldn't we be insane to continue down this track?'

Catherine couldn't bear to listen to what he was saying.

'I understand your point, but I can't turn back. I intend to go on until I find out what all this is about, regardless of the danger.'

There was fire in Rutherford's eyes.

'And what about our safety – aren't you worried the same thing will happen to us?'

'I am prepared to take that risk.'

Rutherford, his forehead carved by a deep frown, exhaled slowly. He turned away from her and looked out of the window at the back yard of the house.

He suddenly realized he could not bear the thought of not seeing her again. She had walked into his life less than forty-eight hours earlier and turned it upside down and he was damned if he was going to let her walk out. Decisively, he turned to face her again.

'Well – I am not prepared—'

Catherine didn't want to hear any more. Her heart sank. In a voice cracking with emotion, she said, 'I understand. It's been so kind of you to come this far. I'll always be grateful.' But underneath her pragmatic words she was in agony. Even though they hardly knew each other, she didn't want to lose him – and it wasn't just because she would have to face the dangers alone.

Rutherford was smiling at her – a resigned smile.

'Let me just finish, Dr Donovan. I'm not prepared for you to take that risk alone. So it looks like I'll have to come along with you.'

27

Catherine and Rutherford spent the afternoon holed up in the house making use of the Flores family's library. At four o'clock they left in the waiting taxi for the afternoon flight up to Cuzco.

As the car pulled away from the Flores house and drove off down the dusty road, another car emerged from the shadows of a narrow side street. It was a silver Mercedes. The driver was a thickset Indian, wearing dark glasses. Next to him, in the front passenger seat, sat the menacing westerner in black. Behind, on the back seat, were his stocky accomplice and Señor Mantores. Beads of sweat were pouring down Mantores's forehead. In silence, they watched the other car move off down the road.

The westerner in the front passenger seat swivelled his whole torso round so he could better see Mantores and, with a growl of anger, said, 'Now where the hell are they going? So much for getting rid of them.'

Turning back to look out of the window at the rapidly disappearing vehicle, he muttered, almost to himself, 'I knew we should have dealt with the whole of Flores's family at the time.'

Mantores's eyes were wide with fear – he tried to speak but no words came out. The murderer took a phone out of the inside pocket of his jacket and dialled a number in North America. Three rings and the phone was answered.

'Sir – we took out Flores as you requested but unfortunately, the academics have made contact with his brother . . .'

There was a pause as the voice on the other end spoke. The short man listened attentively.

'Affirmative. Understood. We will make sure of it this time. Yes – yes, sir, this will end in Peru.'

28

The flight to Cuzco is an incredible experience. As the plane takes off from Lima airport and travels away from the coast, the first foothills of the Andes immediately rear up on either side. The plane climbs and climbs and still the mountains rise up all around, until finally the aircraft breaks through the clouds and soars away into the thin air. In the distance the higher peaks pierce the clouds and dot the horizon like islands in a sea of white foam.

Catherine was in no state of mind to enjoy the view. As the gravity and implications of the two deaths began to sink in, she found the sense of fear and panic beginning to well up inside her once again. Were they even safe up here among the clouds?

She scanned her fellow passengers. Like Hernan, sitting one row in front, all were Indians. Could one of them be in the pay of this dark enemy?

She was so glad to have James with her. The calm and practical way he had handled their extraordinary adventure so far made her realize he was a very special man. A normal person would have got straight back on the aeroplane, on learning of Flores's death. In fact a normal person wouldn't even have come in the first place. Despite his reservations, he seemed made for the challenges they were facing. The life of libraries and old books now seemed too small for him, too limiting. Although she didn't want to admit it to herself, with every hour that went by, she found him more and more attractive.

The ancient cobbled streets of Cuzco reminded Rutherford and Catherine of Oxford. The air was superbly clean after Lima and for a moment they both felt the sense of grim foreboding leave them.

As Hernan drove them in a hire car to the old city, he talked at them non-stop about the ancient civilizations of the Andes. With one hand on the wheel, he guided the jeep through the narrow streets, while with the other he gesticulated wildly to emphasize the points he was making. As he did so the jeep swung this way and that.

'The Incas were not originators – that is the first thing you must understand. Though their wonderful artworks are scattered across the museums of the world, they were really only custodians of a far more ancient culture. The Incas themselves admitted this. A few enlightened Spanish travellers who witnessed the total destruction of the Inca civilization were moved to try and record its traditions even as they were vanishing into the mists of time.'

The jeep veered dangerously across the middle of the road, narrowly avoiding a small, colourfully painted and jam-packed bus trundling towards them in the other direction.

Rutherford grabbed hold of the back of Hernan's seat. *As if our journey isn't dangerous enough!*

Catherine shut her eyes for a split second as the minibus whizzed by, missing them by a fraction. She glanced at Rutherford and raised her eyebrows. Hernan caught her movement in the rear-view mirror.

'Oh – I'm sorry, I will be more careful – you are not used to the Andean way of driving yet!'

He slowed the jeep to a more sedate pace, as he continued his introduction to his people. 'I don't think the Spaniards really believed the stories and traditions they recorded from the mouths of the old priests. They probably thought they were too bizarre to be true – but they are true. One of the main traditions throughout the Andean peoples – and this is the one that interested Professor Kent – is that a great civilization existed thousands and thousands of years before our own Inca civilization. But don't worry – you will see for yourselves the proof . . .'

As Catherine and Rutherford listened to Hernan they were steadily transported into another world, a world of Inca princes and Spanish conquistadors and the tragic collapse of the Inca civilization. They stared through the car windows at the brightly clothed peasants they passed, the descendants of that once great people, and marvelled at the cleanliness of the air and the sheer remoteness and other-worldly beauty of the Andean landscape.

Finally, after they had driven through the suburbs of Cuzco and entered the charming cobbled streets of the old city, Hernan pulled the car up at the entrance to a particularly narrow street. He jumped out and opened the passenger door so Catherine could get out.

'OK – so finally we are here. I will go and drop your bags off at my cousin's house and in the meantime you can do a little sightseeing. I am going to tell him you are friends of mine. Whatever you do, you must not mention Professor Kent or even Miguel. I do not want to put anyone else in danger. We will go to the house at nightfall and you can sleep there, but we must leave at dawn – I cannot risk you being seen up here.'

Catherine climbed down from the jeep.

'Don't you want us to come with you and meet them – won't that be more normal?'

Hernan was looking worried again.

'No – I really think it is better to minimize your contact. You may as well take a look around. But my advice is to keep a low profile . . . If you walk up that street there' – he gestured at the entrance to another narrow roadway – 'and continue in a straight line you will come to the main square – Plaza de Los Almabos. I will meet you there, at the entrance to the cathedral, in half an hour.'

Rutherford stretched his arms in an expansive gesture.

'Phew – we seem to have been travelling non-stop for the last twenty-four hours. I would love to stretch my legs.'

Hernan smiled at him.

'Well – have a walk around. If you get lost, just ask anyone where the cathedral is and they will show you the way.'

With that Hernan got back into the jeep and gunned the engine into life. The vehicle rumbled off and disappeared round a corner. As soon as he had gone, Rutherford and Catherine noticed how peaceful it was standing in the midst of the cobbled lanes of Cuzco.

Their first impulse was to take great lungfuls of fresh air. The sky was crystal clear and for the first time since Catherine had learnt of Flores's death she started to feel a little more positive, a little less claustrophobic. She turned to Rutherford, who was examining the masonry of a large and ancient wall that ran along the left-hand side of the road.

'Do you think we are safe up here in the Andes?'

'About as safe as we can be, but I agree with Hernan – I don't think we should stick around. Come and have a look at this extraordinary wall.'

Instead of being made from bricks, the wall was made from gigantic, many-sided blocks of granite, some of them ten feet square.

Catherine stared in wonder.

'How on earth did they manage to make that? Is this Inca stonework?' She went up to the wall and ran her hand over a particularly enormous block. 'Look, this huge one here has ten sides and it's the size of a dinner table. How incredible – it fits exactly with all its neighbours!'

Rutherford stood back, marvelling at the crafts-manship.

'I really don't know. It must be Inca, it's definitely not Spanish or European anyway. Imagine even try-ing to move these beasts – some of the big ones must weigh over ten tons. Come on, let's go and find this cathedral.'

Trailing her hand along the wall, Catherine followed Rutherford up the gentle incline of the street, in the direction of the main square.

To think that only a day ago I was delivering my last lecture of the term, thinking about my holidays. It's only Wednesday evening but Oxford feels an age away. I have fallen through a hole in my old comfortable life and tumbled into another world . . . a world of danger.

Her gaze alighted on Rutherford and she watched him as he walked on ahead, looking this way and that as, ever inquisitive, he studied the Cuzco stonework. His presence reassured her.

As Hernan had promised, the little street ran into the main square, which, after Lima's Plaza Mayor, resembled a ghost town. The square was the size of a large English village green. It was surrounded on all sides by stone buildings and was the meeting point for six cobbled streets. Catherine caught up with Rutherford and they strolled around the edge of the square, enjoying the sense of space and tranquillity and relieved to be away from the unpleasantness of Lima. By the time they had reached the far side they could see the figure of Hernan approaching up the adjacent lane.

'Hi!' he shouted. 'Beautiful place, isn't it?'

Catherine smiled at him.

Rutherford grinned and shouted back, 'You can't really go wrong with a backdrop like this – you'd have to build something really ugly to ruin this view.'

Hernan laughed as he walked up.

'Yes – yes, I suppose you're right.'

The three of them surveyed the square and behind it the rooftops of the old city descending into the distance.

With a playful look in his eyes, Hernan turned to them and, with a smile, posed a question: 'Here in Cuzco the Incas built a temple for Viracocha – it is called the Coricancha. Can you see it?'

Rutherford and Catherine gazed around trying to locate a suitable-looking Inca structure. There weren't any that suggested themselves to be of fitting majesty to be a temple.

Hernan pointed directly at the church.

'It is there. The Spanish built the cathedral on top of the temple in 1533 so as to suppress our religion. They say that one of the last Inca princes was walled up alive when they built it; one day we will let him out. Do you know who Viracocha is?'

Catherine thought of the old man on the aeroplane.

'I heard the word used to describe the people who drew the Nazca lines,' she said.

Hernan looked at her out of the corner of his eyes,

slightly surprised. 'That's right, it was the name given to a people. But Viracocha was also one man – he was the leader if you like. "Viracocha" means "foam of the sea". The people who came with him were called Viracochas. I am glad to see you haven't been brain-washed by the travel guides. This was his capital and above all other deities he was worshipped here.'

Catherine made what she thought was an educated guess. 'Was he an early Inca king?'

Hernan shook his head firmly.

'No – and this is the important thing: he came a long time *before* the Incas. We do not know when; there are no written records. There is no proof so Western scholars ignore the Viracocha legends and regard them as myths. But ignoring Viracocha is a mistake. He has left his mark throughout the Andes. He wandered all over and all the peoples of the region tell stories about him and his great deeds. He was responsible for the stonework and the prodigious feats of civil engineering. You will see ruins of buildings up here in the Andes that will astound you.'

Rutherford was puzzled. 'But wasn't it the Incas who built—'

Hernan interrupted him. He had a severe look on his face, as if he was talking of something of the grav-est importance. 'No. The Incas built some of them –

but they inherited the skills from Viracocha and his followers.'

'But where was he from? And when did he come?'

The Indian slowly cast his eyes around the entire square before replying. 'That is the mystery. There are many oral accounts of his coming. Even the Spaniards in the sixteenth century mentioned these accounts. They all say Viracocha came from the sea with his followers, and had travelled along the mountain route, heading north, working miracles, teaching agriculture and building temples and even the great stone city of Tiahuanaca – then he moved on.

'He was also a healer, like Jesus is in Christianity, and wherever he went he gave sight to the blind and cured the lame and cast out evil spirits. One Spanish conquistador was told Viracocha was "a tall, bearded man with blue eyes". Elsewhere, he is described as having a long white beard, pale skin and wearing white robes, and bringing a message of peace and love.'

Catherine was being drawn under the mythical spell. She could almost picture the great Viracocha.

'What a strange and benevolent character,' she murmured almost to herself.

Hernan stared at her intently.

'Yes – he was a great man and a civilizer of my people. The Incas said that until he came people lived in a most primitive fashion. They had no domesticated animals, no crops – in short, they were hunter-gatherers. He came and taught the people agriculture and masonry, medicine, music and astronomy. He brought prosperity and he did it peacefully. He never used violence to get his way, like the Spanish did.'

Rutherford wanted to know more.

'But why did the Viracochas come? They sound like colonists – except they didn't stay.'

'That is a good question and one the professor was interested in. All the old stories say that the coming of the Viracochas was linked to the great flood.'

At the mention of this, Catherine joined in.

'You mean there are flood myths way up here in the Andes?'

'Yes. And soon I will show you evidence. There are many Andean tales of a great flood, similar to the story that your Bible tells. After the waters began to recede, Viracocha appeared at Lake Titicaca, which is sacred to the Incas. He built a citadel at Tiahuanaca. The ruins are still there today for all to see. After making his base there, he came down to Cuzco and under his watchful eye the remnants of mankind were rescued from barbarity and began to multiply.'

'So Lake Titicaca is the true centre of the Viracocha story?' Rutherford was fascinated.

'Yes. There is much we need to discuss, but now we

must go and get some dinner. Come on – I'll take you to my cousin's house. Please remember, though, we mustn't talk about these things in front of my family ... as far as they're concerned you are friends on holiday.'

Hernan was pleased. His two guests were beginning to understand the truth behind the history of Peru.

29

At Hernan's cousin's house dinner was being prepared. It was a typical old Cuzco dwelling built from stone, with a communal room containing a large fireplace at one end and an adjoining kitchen. There were more rooms upstairs.

Hernan's cousin, Arun, didn't speak much Spanish and he knew absolutely no English at all. He was of typical Indian build, about 5 feet 5 inches tall and heavily muscled. He smiled a lot and seemed less serious than Hernan. Catherine got the feeling he probably never left Cuzco and had little knowledge even of Lima, let alone the outside world. Hernan introduced them and, with much smiling and hand shaking, they managed to express their gratitude. Hernan then spoke at length to his cousin in Quechua before disappearing into the kitchen with him and returning with some drinks on a tray that he put on the table in the middle of the room.

Catherine took a seat by the fire. As she sat staring into the flames, she thought over all they had learnt since arriving in Cuzco. Rutherford, beginning to feel the effects of jet lag, sank back into another chair and before he could even undo his jacket had fallen fast asleep. Catherine stared at his face, lit up by the crackling firelight. She sighed to herself and turned back to the consoling warmth of the fire.

Later that evening, after a delicious dinner, Hernan helped Arun tidy away the dishes and then got ready to go back to his own house. He was doing his best to keep their spirits up and trying not to talk about the evil that lay behind them.

'Well, I hope you enjoyed our hospitality and have been interested in everything we have discussed. Before I forget, I think you might find this useful.' From his bag he produced a book, *Andean Mythology* by Cudden. 'It's a good basic guide to all the myths of the Andes. I prefer to call them stories myself – calling them myths suggests they are not true – which as we know is wrong. Happy reading. I'll come by at 5 a.m. tomorrow to pick you up.'

With that Hernan vanished into the night. Arun came back into the room and, with a smile on his face, gestured to Catherine and Rutherford to follow him to the back of the house. Rutherford, who was already standing up, walked through the doorway after him and down the corridor into a bedroom. There was a double bed in the middle of the room and no other furniture. The embers of a dying but still warm fire glowed in the fireplace. Arun put a couple of pieces of dry wood on the fire and then turned back to Rutherford. Rutherford didn't need to speak Arun's language to understand this was the only bedroom in the house and they were being asked to share it. He smiled at the Indian and tried to indicate with hand gestures that he could sleep on the floor in the main room, but Arun simply laughed at him and shook his head. Clearly the offer of hospitality was non-negotiable.

At that moment Catherine entered the room. Arun smiled at them both and slipped out of the room.

With a blush of embarrassment, Rutherford stepped backwards into the hall.

'Don't worry, I'll be on the floor in the other room.'

He disappeared down the corridor. Catherine shut the door behind him. The instant she had done so, she rested the palm of her hand flat against the door and bowed her weary head.

30

As promised, Hernan came to collect them at 5 a.m. Bleary eyed, they were driven to the station and deposited on the train with a promise that he would meet them the following day up at Machu Picchu, once Miguel's funeral was over.

The ancient four-carriage train pulled slowly out of the station and began to climb what is one of the most spectacular stretches of railway on the planet. Over the course of the three-hour trip, the snub-nosed engine drags its four short carriages up seventy-five miles of zigzagging track and in doing so passes through farms and villages, struggles up the sides of chasm-like gorges, hugs the sides of cliff faces and finally, with views stretching for miles in all directions, bursts through the clouds to reach Machu Picchu Terminares.

*

The rooftops of Cuzco descended beneath them and even Viracocha's temple, the cathedral, had soon shrunk to insignificance in comparison with the gigantic Andean peaks and the vast valleys.

Catherine was nervous. Since the moment she had woken that morning she had been haunted by the feeling that they were being followed – that a vast machine was being turned against them; cogs were in motion and an entire apparatus was focusing all its energies on hunting them down. She scanned the faces in the carriage. Peasants and tourists. *Nothing to be worried about – not yet anyway.* She looked at Rutherford and let out a small sigh of relief.

He had pulled the copy of Cudden's *Andean Mythology* out of his rucksack and was reading the descriptions of Viracocha he had marked the night before. His eyes skimmed down the page, and all the while his mind was racing. There was something that was familiar – he just couldn't quite put his finger on it.

Viracocha came from far away across the sea. He was a white man. Tall and strong with blue eyes and a long white beard. He brought all the benefits of civilization to us and he did it peacefully. But one day some evil men plotted against him. When he returned from a journey they forced him to leave, sailing down the river out to sea. Someday he will return.

Suddenly he had a breakthrough.

'Catherine! I think I've found something. I think I've worked out what the professor was on about.'

Catherine was at that moment gazing out at the magical view. She looked over at him in surprise.

'What? What do you mean?'

'I think I've found a recurring pattern. In his note, Professor Kent said he had found the secret of the true history of the world buried in old myths and legends. Since then I have been constantly racking my brains as to what exactly he might have meant – what is this secret, this "true history" that he is referring to? If the myths all contain this true history disguised in their stories, then there must be motifs that appear again and again in entirely separate mythical traditions.'

Catherine was looking bemused.

'How do you mean?'

'Listen – we find the flood story everywhere – the professor really did think there was a worldwide cataclysm that destroyed an earlier, advanced civilization. But what other myths are told in slightly different ways over and over again, all around the world? And then suddenly as I was reading about the Viracocha myth I realized—'

'What?'

'That the story it was telling was the same – broadly speaking – as the story of Osiris, the most important ancient Egyptian deity. It is a pattern, a recurrent theme. And it makes sense. All cultures have many, many minor stories but the central myths are the strongest. They last for centuries, even millennia. Hide the true history in those myths and it won't get lost. I am sure I have spotted a direct parallel between Viracocha and Osiris the Egyptian deity – and there must be other such grand central myths that occur all over the globe.'

'But that's impossible,' said Catherine. 'There was no contact between the two cultures; they are on opposite sides of the Atlantic.'

'Well – listen to this . . .' Rutherford read the section on the conspirators who overthrew Viracocha and his subsequent departure by boat to the coast and then he immediately began to recount the Osiris myth to Catherine. 'Osiris was the god of resurrection. He came to Egypt with his followers long, long ago and brought all the benefits of civilization. Like Viracocha – and Jesus Christ – he was a peaceful man and never tried to force anyone to adopt his ways but persuaded people and led by example.

'After some time, Osiris decided to go abroad so he

could bring civilization to other savage peoples. He told the Egyptians he would be back soon and left his brother Seth in charge during his absence. But Seth had already become jealous of Osiris and quickly realized this would be a good opportunity to plot against him. He persuaded others to join him and soon he had assembled a group of seventy-two conspirators. When Osiris returned from his travels they were ready. They held a huge feast in his honour and the centre point of the feast was a game. All the guests had to try their luck by climbing into a wooden box that had been specially made for the event. The person who fitted into the box perfectly would win. But Seth had made sure the box was constructed to fit only Osiris. After the other guests had tried, it was Osiris's turn and he climbed in and lay down. Immediately the conspirators slammed the lid shut and sealed the box for ever. They threw it into the Nile, where it sailed off down to the sea, eventually landing at a place called Byblos. The links are there for all to see,' Rutherford continued. 'Even the story of Jesus Christ has echoes: the bearded man who comes in peace, walking on water, and who is then conspired against and entombed. And in all three stories we are told that sometime in the future they will come again.'

'You're right, it is uncanny.'

'Uncanny! It's more than that – it's more than coincidence as well. Viracocha and Osiris are the same figure, that's for sure. It is in myths like this that the code must be hidden. The fact that the same basic story has survived in two totally unconnected cultures over who knows how many thousands of years shows that they are perfect vehicles for an ancient message.'

'But can you see what it is they are both saying?'

'No – not yet. But at least we now know where to begin.' Rutherford sank back into his seat, lost in contemplation of the mythologies of the world.

As the train climbed slowly up the long and winding track, the sheer scale of the landscape was brought home to them. The steep sides of the valleys were overrun by jungle vegetation and the idea of moving anything, let alone gigantic pieces of stone, up these almost vertical slopes in order to construct a temple in the heart of the mountains seemed insane.

Finally, the train began to wheeze and groan its way up the sloping approach to Machu Picchu Puentas Ruinas – the gateway to the famous ruins. Catherine gazed down at the sacred Inca river the Urubamba that curled back and forth far below them, wrapping itself around the base of the mountains like a green, glistening serpent.

31

The station was sliding into view; there were Indians bustling around on the platform and everyone in the carriage was picking up their bags and packages, preparing to leave the train. Suddenly Catherine couldn't quite believe her eyes. As she looked up the length of the crowded little platform, her heart stopped for one terrifying moment. She shut her eyes, took a deep breath and looked again. There was Ivan Bezumov, dressed in a white linen suit. She inhaled sharply and sat back as the train creaked and moaned its way down the track past him.

Catherine stared at Rutherford, wide-eyed.

'You're not going to believe it, but I'm sure I've just seen that weird Russian, Bezumov. He's on the platform – he's walking towards us. What can he possibly be doing here? My God, James, what can we do? Where can we run to?'

Rutherford almost jumped out of his skin.

'He's here? He can't be.' But even as he uttered the words, he caught sight of the Russian striding purposefully towards their carriage, accompanied by two thickset Indians.

Just then, the train finally jerked to a standstill amidst a cacophony of screeching steel and hissing steam. With adrenalin pumping through his veins, Rutherford tried desperately to think of a way out. There was only one exit through the gate at the other end of the platform – but Bezumov and his henchmen were blocking the way.

Darting across the carriage, Rutherford opened the door on the other side of the train and gasped in horror. The door swung open on its hinges, flapping in thin air above the vertiginous scree slope that plunged hundreds of yards straight down to the river far below. One more step and he would have tumbled to his death. Regaining his balance he spun around. Catherine was frozen to the spot. It was too late – the man in white was now right outside their carriage.

Time seemed to come to a standstill as they looked on in horror. Ivan Bezumov stepped up to the train and opened the door. In his thick Russian accent he addressed them: 'Dr Donovan and Dr Rutherford. Welcome to Machu Picchu.'

Rutherford was speechless. Disjointed thoughts flashed through his mind.

Is he going to shoot us? How is he involved in all this? Did he kill the professor? At that he felt his body prickling with disbelief and horror. *But if he isn't going to kill us, then what on earth is going on?*

Bezumov spoke first, smiling broadly at them: 'Please don't look so unhappy to see me. I'm very sorry about our last meeting, I was insensitive and forgot my manners. Allow me at least one chance to redeem myself.'

Anger overcame Rutherford's feeling of fear:

'Bezumov, what the hell are you doing here? How did you know we were coming to Machu Picchu? How did you even get here?'

'I am sorry – I don't mean to stalk you like a maniac, it's just that I absolutely have to talk to you. I went to see the warden and he told me where you had gone.'

A chill ran down Catherine's spine. *How on earth did the warden know I was going to Peru?*

Bezumov continued, 'Given my intimate knowledge of the professor's work I suspected you'd come here sooner or later. I flew on the next plane after you and came straight from Lima. I have been waiting for you – hoping that you would come here soon. When I saw you both I was very relieved – but forgive me, I didn't want to startle you in any way.'

Acting like a latter-day Inca nobleman, Bezumov ordered the two Indians to take Rutherford and

Catherine's bags. Rutherford immediately stood in the doorway of the train to block their way. Catherine stepped up to join him, her face wearing a frown of angry incomprehension. Bezumov offered her his hand and, with a charming smile, said, 'Please – allow me to take you to my hotel.'

Catherine was unimpressed with his attempts at chivalry. She had liked him little enough on the first meeting and now he was here was one hundred times more disturbed by his presence, his thin eager face, his evident nerves.

'No thanks, we'd rather not. We'll find our own.'

Bezumov shook his head sadly.

'I'm afraid the bus will already be full with backpackers and my hotel is the only one with rooms. I have a car waiting outside. Let me offer you both a lift. We can drop your bags at the hotel and then go for a stroll in the ruins. I'll wait for you.'

Bezumov turned and headed briskly down the platform. Catherine and Rutherford hopped out of the carriage and watched him go. Rutherford stared after him in amazement.

'Who is he? We didn't even know that we were coming here until after we met Hernan . . . Do you think he is on the side of the professor's enemies, whoever they are? And why is he so obsessed with talking to you? It's totally incredible – he's flown halfway round the world on the off-chance he could track you down.'

Catherine was thoughtful.

'I don't know. I am totally confused. But I'm afraid of him.'

She turned to Rutherford and looked him in the eyes.

'Well – what shall we do? Shall we try to run? He'll find us, won't he? If he is dangerous he won't do anything until he's found out what he wants to know. Perhaps we should talk to him, try to establish what his connection to the professor was without telling him anything. Then we have to get out of here as soon as we can. What do you say to that idea?'

Catherine put her hand out, took hold of his forearm and gave it a gentle squeeze. Rutherford paused for a moment, then put his hand over hers and nodded.

32

Bezumov's driver held the door of the car open as first Catherine then Rutherford got in. Bezumov was sitting in the front seat and Catherine could see him watching her intently in the mirror. Despite her fear of the strange Russian, she was still fuming. A brief smile flickered across Bezumov's gaunt face.

'Dr Donovan, I am sorry to have been so mysterious. When we first met I thought you were just another academic, so I didn't want to talk to you about what the professor and I had been working on. Now you have come here, I know you know something so we can be more open.'

Catherine and Rutherford were both staring at him. The driver gunned the car into life and headed up the dirt road away from the station and up to Machu Picchu. Bezumov continued, 'I am from St Petersburg Academy of Sciences in Russia. I am a geologist by training but, like the professor, my work has drawn me a long way from my original studies. I became a specialist in Antarctic rocks and, in 1989, I led an expedition to what you in the West call Prince Harald Land – it is a coastal province of Antarctica – and made a discovery of huge significance: I found evidence that tropical flora had grown in Antarctica in the late Palaeocene or Eocene period. This meant of course that the climate had once been tropical ... To cut a long story short, the Soviet Union broke up, my department lost its funding and no one was interested in my research, except for Professor Kent. He first contacted me in 1998 and ever since then we have been working on questions concerning the recent geology and climate of the earth.'

Bezumov hooked his seat belt out of the way and turned round to face them.

'When I say recent, I mean since the beginning of the last glaciation – that is the last 100,000 years.'

Catherine looked sceptical.

'So why didn't you say so in the first place, and why have you chased us halfway round the world?'

Bezumov smiled a thin smile and looked at her with a curious, unreadable expression.

'My dear girl, more than fifteen years of work was coming to a conclusion and suddenly I discovered the professor was dead – you can understand that I was worried about the fruits of our labour.'

Rutherford was unconvinced.

'If you were working together, why didn't you have copies of the research as well?'

Bezumov maintained his smile, but now it seemed a little patronizing, almost dismissive.

'John – I'm sorry, it's James, isn't it? – two days before the professor died, he telephoned me to say he had discovered crucial supporting evidence that the climate in Antarctica prior to 4000 BC was benevolent – that it was fit for life and not an ice desert. Since my original trip I have never been able to go back to Antarctica and no one is interested in supporting my theories. My life's work, my breakthrough, is in danger of being lost to science and to the world. I have to know what the professor discovered.'

Catherine was thinking of only one thing: *The maps. The evidence the professor was referring to must have been the collection of maps. He must have thought he had the last piece of the jigsaw, or he must have decided now was the time to let Bezumov in on his findings.*

'So why me? Why did you want to track me down?' she said.

Bezumov grinned ruefully.

'Because, Catherine, you are effectively the professor's next of kin. Who else is going to sort out his affairs in England if it isn't you? You will have access to everything.'

Catherine was stunned.

Perhaps Bezumov did know Professor Kent reasonably well after all. How else would he know how close I was to him? But why do my instincts still tell me not to trust him?

33

The fabulous ancient ruins of Machu Picchu are located on the spur of a mountain that juts out into a vast, deep, jungle-clad valley. Access is by way of a path that threads its way northwards, through the lichen-covered rocks of the mountainside and out onto the dramatically situated spur. As the path winds its way down through the boulders and undergrowth, the slopes of the surrounding mountains occasionally disappear behind rolling, boiling swirls of cloud. No one who has walked out into this surreal landscape can ever forget the sight.

As Catherine, Rutherford and Bezumov scrambled down the path, Machu Picchu came into view below. Catherine stared in awe at the most beautiful spectacle she had ever seen. Whoever had built the stone works had placed them perfectly among the surrounding landscape of mountains and valleys and terraced pastures so they were just as important as the sculptured megaliths. Everything was balanced; all was in harmony. Rutherford, who was a few steps behind, caught up and gasped in amazement.

In his thick Russian accent Bezumov proceeded to expound enthusiastically on the Incas' achievement.

'The Incas thought they were living in the fifth age – that there had been four worlds before this one but they had been destroyed in terrible environmental cataclysms brought about by an angry god. As you can see . . .' The Russian stopped to catch his breath and then waved his hand over the awe-inspiring sight, 'they were not exactly primitive. However, it does seem that despite what Viracocha taught the peoples of the Andes about living in peace, they did carry out frequent human sacrifices. They appear to have sacrificed people, and lots of them, on altars lined up with Inca versions of ley lines. Do you know what ley lines are?'

Glad there was something in all this he actually knew about Rutherford broke his silence.

'Yes – I have studied them.'

'Perhaps you could explain them to Dr Donovan?'

Rutherford glanced at Catherine. He didn't want to help the Russian, but Catherine was waiting for the explanation. Slightly grudgingly, he began: 'Ley lines are the system of natural energy lines supposed to link up all the great archaeological sites in England. In the 1920s a man named Alfred Watkins looked out over the countryside and discerned a gigantic web of lines that linked together all the ancient sacred sites of British history. Amazed by what he thought he saw, he got a one-inch Ordnance Survey map and had his vision confirmed. Perfectly straight lines could be drawn across the maps of England, joining these holy places together. In some cases the lines stretched across the entire country, going through the heart of site after site.'

Catherine was absolutely intrigued. 'What sort of sites? You mean like Stonehenge?'

Rutherford nodded, unable to restrain his natural enthusiasm.

'Yes, exactly. That is actually a particularly good example. Stonehenge, St Michael's Mount at Land's End, Salisbury cathedral are all exactly in line. That sort of precise lining up would be extremely hard to do even with modern surveying techniques, let alone thousands of years ago.'

'What are they for?'

Rutherford smiled.

'Ah – well, no one really knows. It's not just a coincidence or the result of statistical probability. Watkins himself, an eminently practical man, had a theory that they were originally trade routes.'

Bezumov interjected, sounding suddenly impatient.

'Yes – but there are other theories. The ley lines are often aligned to the positions of particular stars on certain days of the year. In any case,' he went on, 'the Incas had something exactly comparable to ley lines, called *ceques*. These were the reflections on the ground of the major constellations and stars. They were all centred at the Coricancha temple in Cuzco and from there they radiated out like the spokes of a wheel. One of the longest lines starts in Cuzco and then travels five hundred miles, straight as an arrow, through Machu Picchu, Ollantaytambo, Sacsayhuaman before finally crossing Lake Titicaca and striking Tiahuanaca – the city in the clouds.'

Rutherford had never heard of other systems of lines.

'Do they occur anywhere else?' he asked, his curiosity overcoming his dislike of Bezumov.

Bezumov had become quite animated, as though they were discussing his favourite topic.

'Oh, yes. The Chinese have dragon lines. They are the basis for their art of feng shui: the correct positioning of objects in the landscape. They thought of lung mei as being a global version of the acupuncture lines that run through the human body – the buildings and sacred sites were like acupuncture points – and are a way to access the flow of energy. The aborigines in Australia have song lines, the Irish have fairy lines and there are many, many more examples. These lines wrap around the whole world. I have my own theories as to what they are for—' Bezumov suddenly stopped himself. 'But that's another matter. Where were we? Ah yes: Machu Picchu. My point is very simple. The sacrificial altars, as well as other buildings, even the actual placement of the overall site itself are all positioned so they are in line with various stars and constellations on various critical days of the year. For example, the spring solstice or midsummer's day.'

Bezumov held the palm of his hand above his eyes and surveyed the site for a moment in silence before continuing.

'Now, Dr Donovan, you at least are familiar with astronomical computer software like Skyglobe?'

Catherine nodded. 'Yes – I have used it a lot over the years.'

'Well, as you know, Skyglobe allows you to see exactly how the sky has looked on any given date in the past.'

Rutherford was impressed.

'How does it do that?'

'Well, the stars, planets and other heavenly bodies all move in entirely predictable ways and speeds. Skyglobe can show you how the sky would have looked at any date in the past and from any position on the earth's surface.'

'Really? That's like looking back in time.'

'Yes, it is very powerful. Now, in the case of Machu Picchu this is very helpful. If we were to come back this evening, and try to line up the altar with any particular stars or constellations, it would appear the site is not related to the heavens at all.'

'How do you know?' Rutherford asked.

'Professor Kent and I have already tried – on several occasions.'

Catherine had a clear grasp of what the professor and Bezumov had been trying to do.

'So presumably, you used the computer program to find out at what date there was alignment between the site and the stars?' she said.

Bezumov fixed her with a gimlet look.

'That's exactly right.'

'And what did you come up with?'

The Russian paused – staring at them both with an unreadable expression.

'We discovered the original layout of Machu Picchu must have taken place not five hundred years ago, as contemporary archaeology claims, but rather sometime between 4000 and 3000 BC.'

They stood in stunned silence for a moment, and then Rutherford murmured, 'Which means this wasn't originally an Inca site at all.'

Catherine continued the thought: 'Everything points to the same conclusion. There *was* an earlier civilization . . .'

Bezumov was looking very pleased with himself.

'Yes. So now you know what the professor and I were working on. Come and have a closer look.'

After more than two hours, Catherine and Rutherford finally climbed the steps that led away from the site and back to the hotel. Bezumov had returned an hour earlier, leaving them to explore the ruins alone and, as they wandered back into the hotel lobby, Catherine had decided what she wanted to do next.

'Things are finally beginning to make a bit more sense. I think we should show Bezumov the maps – he has kept his part of the bargain and, anyway, it might throw some new light on everything.'

'Talking to him is one thing, but if you show him the maps we lose our only bargaining chip. Who knows what he will do once he knows he doesn't need us any more?'

Catherine walked over to him, took his right hand in both of hers and squeezed it gently.

'James, trust me, if you are right and the Russian isn't being completely honest with us, then his reaction to seeing the maps might really tell us something. We know

know there was an ancient civilization, but I am convinced there is more to learn and Bezumov might just be the man to help us – even if he does so unintentionally.'

Rutherford looked down at her and, feigning indifference at the physical contact, shrugged his shoulders.

'I still think it's a bad idea. We are totally alone up here. If something goes wrong . . .'

Catherine dropped his hand and started back up the path.

'We have to try,' she said, in a determined tone.

James watched her go and then turning one last time to look at the magical view he sighed deeply, shaking his head.

I don't like this one bit . . .

As they entered the hotel dining room they saw Bezumov already sitting at a table. A waiter was pouring him a glass of water. The moment he saw them, he leapt out of his chair and with an expansive wave of his arm gestured for them to be seated. He radiated an over-friendly warmth as he beamed at them. Then he saw Catherine was carrying the envelope containing the maps. His eyes instantly lit up.

'Ahhh! I see you have something for me, no?'

Catherine walked up to his table with Rutherford just behind her and laid the dossier down.

'Yes. Professor Kent sent me these maps from Peru just before he died.'

Bezumov's eyes widened further and his mouth opened in a greedy grin. Grabbing his napkin, he began to wipe his hands furiously. His Russian accent suddenly became more pronounced as his poise left him.

'Maps, you say! But this is fantastic . . .'

Catherine proceeded to open the envelope. Bezumov's hands flapped impatiently in the air. The maps slid out onto the table and Catherine stepped away, to allow the Russian free reign over the treasure trove of documents.

Like a man possessed, Bezumov's eyes seemed about to pop out of his head. Reverentially, as if they were as delicate as ashes, he drew the maps towards him over the table. He scrutinized each one closely before putting it aside and moving on to the next, all the while muttering to himself in Russian.

Rutherford, standing a little back from the table, had noticed the transformation. *So – this is the real man that lies underneath the suave exterior. Greedy somehow, almost ravenous. And he is clearly hunting for something in particular . . . What is it that he's looking for?*

Then quite unexpectedly Bezumov stopped dead in his tracks.

'I knew it! The pyramids of Giza, of course!'

Rutherford and Catherine leaned over to better see what was causing Bezumov's excitement. It appeared to be a normal map of the world but in its top right corner it bore the legend 'Implied Prime Meridian of Piri Reis Map – Property of US Air Force'. The map's line of zero longitude, instead of running through the Greenwich Observatory in London, ran through the desert, just adjacent to Cairo.

Bezumov was salivating with joy, running his hands up and down the edge of the map.

'Giza! Why didn't I trust my instincts?'

Catherine and Rutherford looked at each other in bewilderment.

Catherine was the first to speak: 'What does it mean?'

With a wolf-like smile the Russian turned to her.

'It means, my dear girl, that some kind soul in the American military has gone to the trouble of calculating where the original creators of the Piri Reis map located their degree zero, their equivalent of Greenwich Observatory, and it was Giza . . .'

Rutherford was still baffled.

'But what's so amazing about the fact that Giza was the ancients' prime meridian?'

Bezumov fixed him with a very dark look. The force and strangeness of his gaze was such that Rutherford almost stepped back.

'It means that Egypt, or the Great Pyramid at Giza to be precise, lay at the centre of the last world. That is monumentally significant.'

Bezumov's eyes were ablaze; he was staring into the distance, preoccupied, talking almost to himself.

'These monumental works of art and architecture – the Nazca lines, Angkor Wat in Cambodia, Kathmandu, the ancient city in the Himalayas, and the mysterious sacred isles of the Pacific Ocean: Nan Medol, Yap and Raiatea – they're all connected to one another, part of a great machine and the centre, the brain, of that machine must have been in Giza, at the pyramids. This was the apex of the old civilization. And in four days' time, on Monday, at sunrise, it will be the spring equinox. I must be there! He who controls Giza controls the world . . .'

He seemed to have forgotten they were there. He put his hands on the edge of the table and pushed his chair backwards. He stared upwards for a moment, as if saying a silent prayer or making a resolution, and then looked down at Catherine and Rutherford.

'Ah! All this excitement has left me positively exhausted. Please excuse me. I think alas, the jet lag is coming home to roost. I must just go and lie down.'

With that he bowed stiffly and, turning on his heel, walked briskly out of the hotel restaurant and off into the gloom of the corridor beyond.

Catherine and Rutherford stared at each other, dumbfounded.

'What on earth do you think was going on there? And what was he saying about "a great machine" – he sounds completely insane,' said Catherine.

Rutherford stared at the doorway through which the Russian had just departed.

'I really don't know – but I'm pretty damn sure of one thing: Bezumov has a very specific agenda and it's not just an academic's love of knowledge. And as for his sanity, given what we have just seen, I would say that the jury is definitely out.'

'What were those places he was referring to? How do they fit in?'

Rutherford, a deep frown buckling his forehead, explained: 'They're other ancient sites. Angkor Wat is one of the most spectacular ruins in the entire world. It's in the heart of the Cambodian jungle.'

'Ruins of what exactly? Pyramids?'

'No – not pyramids. It's an enormous complex of seventy-two stone palaces, astronomical observatories and temples. The biggest palace, the centrepiece of the site, has five sacred roads leading up to it and on either side of each road fifty-four gods are carrying the rope-like body of a giant serpent – that's a hundred and eight on each road. It looks like a tug of war, but in fact the snake is wrapped round a milk churn, and they are churning the milky ocean of the milky way.'

'And the others?'

'Well, Kathmandu lies hidden high up in the clouds of the Himalayas. No one really knows when it was first founded. As for the others, they are all tiny islands, marooned in the vast waters of the Pacific. They are home to extraordinary ruins of long-vanished civilizations and they are all sacred sites.'

Catherine nodded her head and looked down at the pile of maps that were now scattered across the table.

'And Bezumov thinks these sites are all connected by ley lines.'

Rutherford's eyes flashed with understanding.

'Clearly what we have just shown him was the final piece of the jigsaw puzzle. And the spring equinox, which is only four days away now, is in some way critical . . .'

34

Catherine gasped in terror. Someone was quietly forcing open the flimsy lock on the door to their hotel bedroom. Lying in bed in the darkness, her sense of hearing heightened, it was absolutely clear to her that someone was in the process of breaking in. A huge wave of adrenalin swept through her body.

Oh my God – it's Bezumov – he's come to murder me!

She heard the door handle turn and she sensed a body enter the room. Was there anything she could use as a weapon – was there a way out?

As she tried to focus through her terror and the darkness, she saw a small, muscular figure coming towards her. Instinctively she made a move to roll out of bed and onto the floor away from the advancing form. But at the first rustle of bedclothes, a voice whispered in the darkness, 'Catherine, don't worry, it's me, Hernan.' His voice sounded urgent, even panicky.

Catherine gasped with relief and almost laughed.

'Hernan! What were you thinking? Are you trying to make me die of fright?'

The alarm clock on the bedside table read 2.37 a.m. Before she could even ask what was going on, Hernan, panting for breath, spoke. 'Sshhhh! You've got to get out of here immediately.'

As the adrenalin rush faded, Catherine struggled to understand what was happening.

'What – why?

'There were two men in Cuzco asking questions about you. I don't know if anyone in the hotel has told them about you being here, but we must leave at once.'

'Two men? But who are they?'

Hernan walked over to the window to check the curtains were completely drawn and then turned on the light on the little desk.

'That's what frightens me. No one knows who they are. They have been visiting the hotels and hostels of Cuzco trying to find out who has been in and out in the last two nights. They are not secret police – I know that much – even though they look military. They're trying to be discreet, but I know everyone in Cuzco. They're after you and James. We haven't got a minute to waste. Sooner or later they will go to the station and discover you took the train yesterday morning and they will know you are here. They may already be on their way . . .'

Once again the increasingly familiar icy tingle of pure fear ran down Catherine's spine.

'Oh my God. What can we do?'

'We'll take you out over the Bolivian border and down to La Paz. From there you are on your own. The main thing is to get you out of Peru and pronto. Give me your air tickets and I will change the departure dates at a travel agent; this will confuse them and maybe buy you some more time. OK?'

Catherine was beginning to register the gravity of the situation and then she remembered the Russian.

Sitting up in bed she said, 'Hernan, we have one problem.'

'What?'

'We've met an acquaintance from Oxford.'

Hernan looked incredulous.

'What? What are you talking about?'

Catherine felt almost embarrassed. 'Listen – I know it sounds ridiculous, but a guy from Oxford who also knew the professor came to Machu Picchu to find us.'

'You're joking. Half the world seems to be here in Machu Picchu. Who is he?'

'He's a Russian scientist. His name is Ivan Bezumov.'

At the mention of Bezumov's name, Hernan tensed up like a frightened animal.

'Bezumov is here – in the hotel?'

Now it was Catherine's turn to be horrified.

'Er – yes. You know him?'

Before she could enquire any further, Hernan grabbed a chair and wedged it under the door handle. He looked over his shoulder at her and with a cold glint in his eyes put a finger to his lips. Then, from the rucksack he was carrying, Hernan pulled out a gun. Catherine was speechless. Hernan crept to the door and pressing his ear against it listened intently for what seemed like an eternity. Finally, he turned and, stealing cat-like across the room, crouched down next to her.

'Pack your bag immediately,' he hissed. 'Which room is James in?'

In an equally urgent whisper Catherine responded, 'Number twenty-three. Hernan – what's going on?'

'I will tell you later. Trust me – Ivan Bezumov is not only a scientist. We must act fast; he is a very, very dangerous man. Do you know which room he is in?'

'I think he's in room number three.'

'Right – stay here – I'll be back in a minute.'

Still holding the gun in his right hand, the muzzle pointing towards the ceiling, Hernan removed the chair with his left hand and opened the door very slowly. Catherine looked on in horror as he slipped out of the door into the pitch black of the corridor.

35

Hernan moved like a trained assassin down the corridor towards room number three. He pulled the hammer back on the revolver and leaned against the door, pressing his ear to the wood panel. With a sudden violent shove using all the power of Hernan's compact and muscular Andean frame he rammed his shoulder against the door. The flimsy lock didn't stand a chance. Within a fraction of a second he was in the middle of the room, his legs apart and his arms outstretched before him, pointing the gun at the bed. But it was empty. The Russian was long gone.

Hernan cursed loudly and uncocked the hammer. Catherine appeared in the doorway behind him, looking wide-eyed. With the adrenalin flowing away Hernan suddenly felt exhausted.

'Catherine – I'm sorry . . .'

Catherine stared in disbelief at the silhouette of the Indian, gun in hand.

Hernan flicked the light switch on and, beckoning Catherine into Bezumov's room, shut the door. Catherine was bursting to ask questions but realized it would be better to let Hernan speak. He gradually recovered his composure and, as his normal breathing returned, he looked at the gun in an embarrassed fashion and smiled apologetically.

'Ivan Bezumov is not just a scientist. It is something that Miguel and the professor only discovered after his last visit: he is a former colonel in Russian naval intelligence. He had misled us all along. He is a dangerous man. He is also highly intelligent. The reason it took us so long to discover his true identity is because he really is a world authority on ancient archaeological sites, Arctic geology, prehistory and many other things as well.' He slid the gun into the belt of his jeans. 'Bezumov walked away from the ruins of the Soviet Union with a dream – one that had been nurtured by Soviet scientists for a generation: to harness the natural energies of the earth, the staggering electromagnetic currents that flow from the sun to our planet. Wave machines and wind power are nothing compared to some of the ideas these Russian scientists had. They wanted to use the orbital motion of the earth itself to create vast amounts of free electricity that could be used to whatever ends they desired. Bezumov became convinced that mankind had in the past already harnessed this enormous power. His desire is to rediscover how this was done and then become the master of these prodigious amounts of solar energy.'

'But that's just incredible!' Catherine exclaimed.

'Yes – it sounds insane. But actually Professor Kent thought he was really on to something – it was just that the professor, as you know, believed all technology leads inevitably to the degradation of nature. He thought Bezumov's plans to harness these new forms of energy would be far worse than our attempts to harness fossil fuels or nuclear energy. If mankind starts to meddle with the actual rotation of the planet or the gigantic flow of energy on its way to and from the sun, the results could be truly catastrophic.'

'Catastrophic in what way?' asked Catherine.

'Who knows? Miguel told me Professor Kent thought that, if the orbital motion of the earth was interfered with, the sudden change in centrifugal force might cause the planet to come apart at the seams or even just spontaneously combust.'

Catherine's jaw dropped. She pictured beautiful blue Planet Earth floating majestically in the endless night of space. A tender ball of life, perhaps alone in the infinitude of blackness, exploding into a billion fragments, shattering like a mirror, gone for ever.

'We have to stop him.'

'You're absolutely right. He's a megalomaniac and

he will stop at nothing to succeed. But right now I am more concerned about your safety – we've got to get out of here. Bezumov isn't the only person in Peru interested in catching up with you.'

PART THREE

36

It was 7.30 on Friday morning in an anonymous building in the financial heart of New York City. Secretary Miller was seated at the conference table with ten other smartly dressed men of diverse ethnicity.

'Gentlemen,' he said, 'many thanks for your diligence and loyalty over the last few years. This will be our final morning meeting; indeed, it will be our last chance to meet at all. There are now only seventy-two hours left until the dawning of the spring equinox. Let us briefly recap.'

He took out a pair of reading glasses and, putting them on, cast his eyes over the pad of paper that lay before him on the desk. The eleven men seated round the table waited in silence. They could have passed for highly affluent, late-middle-aged business executives; like Miller they exuded authority and intelligence. Looking over the rim of his glasses, he began. 'OK – the Middle East is being taken care of directly by Senator Kurtz and the board. So let's start with Japan.'

He looked over at three oriental men sitting at the far end of the table. The Japanese delegate bowed slightly and then spoke: 'As you know, Secretary, the Japanese Central Bank has been in the hands of the Corporation since the Second World War. When the universal crash begins on Monday morning, the bank will, contrary to official policy, liquidate all foreign currency holdings and sell all foreign and domestic assets. There will be no possibility for the market to recover its nerve. Furthermore, the board has committed to mopping up any drops of liquidity should they occur.' He bowed his head and sat back.

The secretary turned to a Chinese man sitting to his left. The Chinese man nodded and said, 'Secretary, the Japanese action, along with the worldwide sell-off that the board will engineer, will cause a banking crisis in China resulting in meltdown in the financial markets. More than two hundred million people will be made unemployed overnight in the main industrial cities. Huge social unrest will prevail and, within ten days, our currency will be worthless. Our agents in the Chinese military have readied the plans for a simultaneous invasion of the Korean peninsula and Taiwan. We are quite certain that the government, in a bid to distract the legions of unemployed, will follow through with these plans. We already know from our brothers in America that the US navy will also attack the mainland from their fleet of nuclear submarines, before mounting counter-invasions of both Taiwan and Korea. With China hobbled, the way will be clear for the Corporation in the aftermath.'

The secretary nodded. The Indonesian delegate looked across at him.

'At the first hint of US aggression the Indonesian navy will lay mines across the Straits of Malacca, the busiest trade route in the world, which will sink any vessel attempting to go through, thereby bringing international trade to a halt. All food imports will cease. We anticipate revolutionary social unrest within a week, followed by the full-scale invasion of Malaysia and Australia.'

The secretary turned his gaze to the remaining seven delegates, one of whom was African, two Asian and the remaining four all Caucasian.

'And who will speak for Eurasia and Africa today?'

A thin-faced, pale Englishman with the air of an undertaker nodded at Secretary Miller, who indicated that he should speak.

'The universal crash will begin with our agents leading the sell-off. Neither the European Central Bank nor the Bank of England will support the market, ensuring that panic spreads. In addition, bombs will go off in all the capital cities of Europe. The European, and particularly Russian, oil infrastructure will be destroyed but in such a way that when the Corporation seizes power, it can be quickly repaired.' The speaker paused, then continued. 'Just before midnight on Monday a device will be set off outside the Indian prime minister's residence with more than sufficient force to kill him and his family. A Kashmiri Islamic group of our making will claim it as their success, plunging Pakistan and India into a prolonged war. Meanwhile, we can also bring to the cause a Nigerian delta in civil war. For some time we have been arming and funding three rebel militias. Oil exports from the region will fail. Aid and food imports will cease. Starvation and war will become ubiquitous across the continent.'

'Good,' said the secretary, 'I will be coordinating the United States, along with the board members themselves. You will all receive your final orders directly from Senator Kurtz as the board's current representative, but I am confident you are absolutely clear on all the codes and there will be no mistakes. We have all been waiting a long time for this day . . .'

The assembled men nodded in solemn agreement before the secretary moderated his tone, suddenly becoming more cautious.

'I don't think I need to stress to you, gentlemen, that there must now be no divergence from our plans.

The sequence of events is crucial for our ultimate success. Nothing, and I repeat, nothing, must happen until the senator gives the command. Do not act until you receive his final instruction. Is everyone clear?'

The assembled group murmured their assent.

The secretary shuffled his papers and then stood up.

'Thank you, gentlemen, and good luck. Your children and grandchildren will read about you in their history books. A new world order will be born from the ashes of the old. Long live the Corporation.'

As the meeting broke up and the delegates filed out of the room, Secretary Miller returned to his chair. The room emptied until only his most trusted assistant, Agent Dixon, remained. Secretary Miller waited for him to close the door and then indicated that Dixon should have a seat.

The young agent sat down and placed a pile of paperwork on the table.

'Sir, I have done the research you requested on the senator.'

'Go on, Dixon. We're alone.'

The agent looked more than a little uncomfortable. He frequently investigated people's secrets on the secretary's instructions, but never before a member of the board.

'Well, sir, it seems that Senator Kurtz is a member of an extremely radical evangelical church called the

Church of the Revealed Truth. It is headquartered in his constituency and he has been a member since birth. Both his parents come from families that have provided several generations of ministers to the Church.' Agent Dixon paused to see if what he was saying was acceptable to Secretary Miller.

The secretary nodded at him to go on.

'The senator doesn't advertise his membership of the Church of the Revealed Truth, though does admit to it when asked. Instead he refers to himself simply as "a committed Christian". However, the Church's beliefs are considered too extreme by the vast majority of evangelical Christians.'

The secretary's eyes lit up.

'Like what?' he asked, eagerly.

Agent Dixon drew in his breath. 'Well sir, it seems that the Church of the Revealed Truth believes wholeheartedly in Armageddon. They are waiting for the end of the world – in fact they are actively committed to bringing it about. They believe in the literal truth of the Book of Revelations. When the end of days comes, the Church's believers will be swept up to heaven, leaving the rest of us behind to take part in the carnage of the ultimate battle between good and evil.'

The secretary sat bolt upright in his chair. For a moment he found it difficult to breathe. The board could not possibly know of Kurtz's real allegiance.

Although they were working towards global chaos and destruction, the Corporation certainly did not want to cause irretrievable damage – merely to change the balance of power in its ultimate favour.

He realized Agent Dixon was awaiting his response and looking nervously across at him. He collected himself. The time had come to act.

'Thank you, Agent Dixon. As always your work has been exemplary. I am sure I don't need to tell you to keep this information to yourself. Please get my car ready, I will be upstairs in five minutes.'

As soon as Dixon had left the room, Secretary Miller stood up and walked over to the teak cabinet in the corner. Taking a key from his pocket he unlocked the doors and spun nimbly through the numbers on the dial of the safe. The locks clicked and the four-inch-thick steel door swung open. He reached in and retrieved an innocuous-looking brown envelope. Folding it once, he slipped it into the inside pocket of his jacket before shutting and locking the safe.

His heart was pounding. He straightened down his hair. Beads of sweat had gathered on his temples. As he adjusted his jacket, he shook his head in disbelief at the recklessness of his own actions. If anyone should find out what he was doing, or even so much as suspect, he wouldn't live to see nightfall. In fact, unfortunate as it was, he would have to have Agent Dixon disposed of.

Thanks to the thoroughness of his work the young man was now a major liability.

Secretary Miller strode over to the office door and rested his hand on the door handle. The situation was bleak. The only consoling thought was the knowledge that at least by now the two academics would be dead.

37

Hernan had been driving hard for four hours – desperate to get his passengers safely to the Bolivian border before it was too late. They passed around the southern tip of the magnificent Lake Titicaca and marvelled at its enormous size. In all directions, they could see the peaks of the Andes, some draped in cloud, others visible with crystalline clarity against the heart-stopping blue of the sky. Around the edge of the lake the vegetation was sparse. They were a long way above the tree line; the poor soil and almost constant cold were not the best of environments for anything other than the most hardy of mountain plants. Hernan pointed out the seashells on the shoreline and the great green tidemark staining the cliffs around its edge, proof that a great flood had reached right up to the Andean plateau – two miles above sea level.

On they drove at breakneck speed until they reached

the great ruined stone citadel of Tiahuanaca – the lost city in the clouds.

Hernan guided the vehicle to a standstill on the edge of the modern road that runs past the ancient site and turned off the engine. Ahead, only an hour's drive away, lay the safety of Bolivia. On the plain next to them, the ruins of what once must have been a vast city sprawled into the distance. Huge broken stone edifices littered the landscape and great pyramidal mounds of earth stood as testaments to a long-vanished priesthood.

'I wanted you to see this place, if only for a minute. It is our most sacred site. In the middle of this ruined city stands a sunken temple – inside there is a pillar of red rock. Carved into the pillar is a depiction of a man. He has a beard. Whoever this man was, he sure wasn't an Inca.'

Rutherford turned and looked at Hernan quizzically.

'How many Indians have you seen in Peru with a full beard?' he asked.

Catherine nodded her head slowly.

'It's Viracocha, isn't it?'

'Yes! All around this ancient city are carvings of him and his companions. Some of the images depict him with elephants and horses. There have been no elephants in South America for over ten thousand years.

The biggest statue presents Viracocha as a sort of mermaid or merman. His top half is human but from the waist down he is covered in scales – he is wearing a sort of fish-scale cloak.'

Rutherford was intrigued – his mind was whirring.

'Hang on a minute! I've seen that figure before!'

Hernan looked puzzled. Rutherford turned to him and Catherine, his face illuminated. Excitedly, he said, 'Do you know anything about Mesopotamian mythology? The Chaldeans – the world's oldest recorded civilization?'

Hernan shook his head. Catherine did too.

'There is a demigod called Oannes. He is like a man but wears fish clothes and is partly amphibious. He teaches the savage people to read and write, till the soil and establish rational, civilized government. Finally he leaves and disappears over the sea.'

Catherine was stunned.

'But that's amazing! It's like Osiris all over again.'

'And that's not all! You recall the Mayans and the Aztecs and the other ancient civilizations of Central America?'

Catherine had a vague recollection of the Aztecs with their pyramids and sun worship. She shrugged and gestured for Rutherford to continue.

'The Mayans all believed in a figure called Kukulkan "the winged serpent"; the Aztecs in Quetzalcoatl, the plumed serpent – same figure, slightly different name. He was a bearded, white-skinned deity who apparently arrived in Mexico from across the sea, sometime in the distant past. He taught people the arts of civilization. It must be the same person. He even disappeared out to sea on a raft . . . The reason Cortes, the leader of the tiny invading Spanish force, was not immediately killed when he first landed was because Montezuma, the king of the Aztecs, thought that because Cortes had white skin and a beard, he must be the returning Quetzalcoatl.'

Catherine gasped. 'This is extraordinary. We now have four appearances of these strange bearded white men – all in totally different parts of the world.'

Hernan was shaking his head, greatly impressed.

'And there is more fundamental evidence here,' he said, 'that Viracocha lived before the dawn of history. Do either of you know anything about the star alignments of ancient monuments and how, using modern software, the original dates of construction can be calculated?'

Catherine and Rutherford both nodded earnestly.

'Well, the stones and statues of Tiahuanaca all line up perfectly for one date in the past. Many astronomers and archaeo-astronomers have checked this and it is incontrovertible—'

Catherine interrupted, desperate to know. 'Which date?' she demanded.

'Fifteen thousand BC.'

A silence fell over the group as they contemplated the idea of these highly advanced prehistoric people working away with great intelligence and prodigious energy to create the awesome site that now lay before them. Catherine turned back to look at the two men.

'But it doesn't help us understand why the professor thought we were being warned. And most importantly of all, it doesn't help us understand why there are forces out there so determined to keep this knowledge about the past hidden that they are prepared to kill innocent people.'

Rutherford and Hernan were equally puzzled. Then with an anxious look around, Hernan turned the key in the ignition – the engine roared back into life.

'We mustn't delay a moment longer,' he said. 'I am going to deliver you to the Aymara Indians at the border. Round here – on both sides of the border – this is all their land. They will provide you with fake Bolivian tourist visas and take you on to La Paz. With their help you will get out of here alive.'

38

Senator Kurtz climbed down out of the helicopter and into the blazing afternoon sunshine. Ducking under the din of the rotor blades, he strode across the small helipad and onto the enormous lawn of the head-quarters of the Church of the Revealed Truth.

As the helicopter lifted off again, the senator could not stop himself from smiling. There was barely a cloud in the sky, the air was fresh and clear and this was his favourite place on earth. What a release it was to be away from the hustle of Washington DC and the pressures of his work at the Corporation. But it would all be worth it: very soon now the prophecies of the Book of Revelations would be fulfilled and he would be among the few souls carried aloft to escape the torment that would be inflicted on the rest of humanity . . .

One hundred and fifty yards away the brand-new buildings of the Church of the Revealed Truth rose up in splendour, their windows glinting in the sunlight.

As the senator crossed the lawn, he tried to stifle a sense of pride. He could take a large part of the credit for increasing the Church revenues these last few years to the hundreds of millions of dollars a year they were today.

The television studio in the centre of the complex was the beating heart of the Church. It was shaped like a Greek amphitheatre with a horseshoe of seats rising up on all sides and a central podium where the preacher could stand, heightening the intensity and atmosphere of the occasion. The passionate services were broadcast across the nation, donations were requested and miraculous stories of how the Church had changed people's lives told first hand by ecstatic audience members.

Senator Kurtz breezed past the smiling receptionist and made his way down the warren of corridors until he reached a palatial waiting room. Thick carpets and leather furniture gave it the comfortable feel of a five-star hotel. The air conditioning hummed quietly. The only religious imagery, indeed the only decoration at all on the otherwise spartan walls, was a simple wooden cross hanging next to a closed door on the far side of the room. The name plate above read 'Reverend Jim White'. Without hesitating, the senator marched across the room and rapped sharply on the door. A second later there was a gruff salutation barked at him from behind it: 'Come!'

The accent was Texan – the voice energetic.

Senator Kurtz swung the door open and stepped into the room. The pugnacious figure of the reverend greeted him with a howl of approval.

Reverend Jim White was a short, powerfully built man in his mid-fifties with a flat boxer's nose and a strong brow.

'Senator! What a delightful surprise. I wasn't expecting to see you until tomorrow.' The reverend got up from his chair and advanced around his desk, his booming Texan voice filling the room.

The senator grasped his outstretched arm and the two men shook hands warmly and then embraced, slapping each other on the back. The reverend referred to Senator Kurtz by his political title more as an affectionate joke than anything else – they had known each other since they were children. Together they had masterminded the Church's transformation from an obscure sect to a major force in the evangelical movement. They had travelled a long, hard road together and, through force of belief and pure charisma, had persuaded thousands of ordinary Americans to follow them.

Senator Kurtz took a step back and looked his friend up and down.

'It's great to see you, Jim. You're looking very well. Have you been using the pool as I advised?'

The reverend laughed heartily.

'Ha! When I have the time – when I have the time. We've been so busy, recording programmes, broadcasting, introducing important new members to the site . . . there's barely time to think. But please, have a seat. I want to hear everything.'

The two men walked over to a pair of armchairs that faced each other over a small coffee table. The reverend's jovial expression suddenly changed to one of deep seriousness and he clutched his chin with his meaty right hand.

'So, what can you tell me? Are we almost there?'

Senator Kurtz nodded earnestly as very slowly and deliberately he broke the news.

'Jim – I think we've done it.'

The reverend's face lit up again. He could barely contain his excitement.

'Really? You honestly think we are finally about to enter the end time?'

'Yes, Jim – we are. I cannot see how we can be stopped. I could not hope for things to be going better. The dangerous heresies of the British professor have been airbrushed from history. And the Corporation's planned takeover is proceeding. I was at the board meeting myself. Armageddon is just days away.'

The Reverend Jim White's eyes were as wide as saucers. Finally, after so much effort and struggle, it seemed as if they were on the brink of their dream. The senator continued, 'I will fly to Cairo directly, where my base will be. I have coordinated with our agents in Israel and they are ready. We have smuggled a mini thermonuclear device into the Muslim shrine of the Al-Aqsa mosque in Jerusalem, to be detonated in parallel with the Corporation's global crisis. As you know, our agents have already mined the Wailing Wall, via the old disused Roman sewer network. When the wall is turned to dust, the Israelis will automatically order the air force to bomb Mecca. The Middle East will be engulfed in flames. I am sure that Israel will resort to using nuclear weapons and I expect upwards of a hundred million casualties during the first days. All this will take place on my command on Monday morning – at sunrise on the spring equinox.'

The preacher stood up and with his right hand open and fingers outstretched, he reached upwards towards the ceiling of his luxurious room. His wide eyes were glistening with moisture. In his booming voice he cried out in rapturous joy, 'Praise the Lord!'

39

It was 7.35 a.m. at the Ruinas Hotel, Machu Picchu, when a brand-new Japanese four-wheel drive screeched to a halt in front of the entrance. Looking very out of place among the scruffy Andean peasants and the majestic backdrop of the mountains, Professor Kent's murderer and his younger accomplice stepped out of the vehicle and onto the dusty hotel forecourt.

The two men, wasting no time, strode into the hotel lobby. Behind the reception desk sat an old man and in the corner was an Indian woman mopping the floor. Both the receptionist and the cleaner looked up in surprise. It wasn't normal to see people wearing suits and driving brand-new vehicles in Machu Picchu and, in any case, everyone in Peru, from the smallest child to the oldest crone, knew that such people were best given a very wide berth. The old woman propped her mop against the wall and scuttled off down the hall.

The murderer turned to his accomplice and spoke.

His voice was guttural and filled with tones of frustration and disgust. 'I'm telling you, we've missed them . . .'

The accomplice looked worried. He marched over to the reception desk and snapped at the receptionist, 'I want to see your records for last night. Quickly.'

The old man, looking terrified, fumbled with the leather-bound reservations book, his gnarled fingers trying to open it at the relevant page.

'Give it to me, you old fool.'

The young man snatched it from him and started to flip the pages over. Seconds later he was running his right-hand index finger over the names of two of the guests – Donovan and Rutherford. With a sharp curse, he looked up.

'OK, *viejo* – where have they gone? *Dónde están los gringos?*'

The old receptionist's eyes had widened in fear and incomprehension. He shuffled backwards away from the desk and into a doorway. The young man flipped up the counter top of the reception desk and followed him into the room behind the lobby. The old man cowered against the wall of the little room and began to mutter incomprehensibly in an Indian dialect. The young man's temper had snapped. He began to shout, 'Where are Donovan and Rutherford? *Dónde están* Donovan and Rutherford?'

The receptionist had dropped to his knees and was leaning away as if expecting a blow. In broken English he blurted out, 'Señor – the foreign couple left in the night.'

'Where – where did they go?'

'The road to Bolivia.'

The young man stepped up and grabbed the receptionist by the scruff of the neck.

'Were they alone? Who were they with?'

'Yes, señor . . . yes, señor. They were with a friend, someone who's been here before. Señor Flores.'

The murderer had now joined them. He curled his lip in disgust.

'They know they're being followed. We must move fast.'

The younger thug threw the old receptionist to the floor and the two men stormed out of the hotel.

40

After Catherine and Rutherford had climbed out of the car at the Bolivian border and dusted themselves down, Hernan pointed past the hut that was border control, in the direction of a lone four-wheel drive parked just over the border.

'There is your lift. He will have you in La Paz in no time at all. His name is Quitte – he doesn't speak any English. He will take you down to his family house in La Paz. From there you can plan your safe passage out.'

Hernan cupped his hands around his mouth and shouted in the direction of the motionless vehicle: '*Hola, Quitte, estoy aqui con mis amigos. ¡Vámonos!*'

The driver's door opened and a short, grinning Indian descended. He waved at them and Hernan waved back.

Hernan then turned to address them for one last time. His eyes were bright and every muscle and fibre of his body seemed to be urging them on, willing them to succeed in their quest.

'My friends – good luck.' He fixed Catherine with his powerful gaze. 'And be careful.'

Catherine felt a lump rising in her throat. She felt a terrible sense of foreboding.

'Can't you come with us to La Paz; lie low for a few days?'

Hernan smiled and shook his head.

'No, Catherine, I must return to my family, we are still in mourning, I must be with them.'

With that, they embraced and then Catherine stepped away, tears forming in her eyes. Rutherford took Hernan's hand and shook it warmly.

'Thank you for everything. I promise we will do our best to see this through for Miguel and the professor – expose the truth and stop Ivan Bezumov.'

Hernan leant forward and embraced the Englishman.

'James, take care of yourself – and this beautiful woman here.'

James hugged the stocky Indian and then they parted for the last time.

41

Inside the York Avenue building of Sotheby's, the world-famous antique dealer's Manhattan office, an attractive, well-groomed young woman was showing Secretary Miller into a darkened, windowless room. Searching round the door frame with her perfectly manicured hand, she located the light switch and the room emerged from the gloom.

'This is the map room. As you can see, there are no windows, so there is no chance of natural light damaging your item. Please, have a seat. On the walls are some pieces from our collection that might interest you. Mr Silver will be down in one minute.'

The secretary surveyed the large, elegant room. There was a conference table in the middle, surrounded by comfortable leather chairs. Above the table, suspended from the ceiling was a technical-looking overhead light that could be raised and lowered in any direction. The walls were decorated with framed maps.

The young woman continued, 'That one there is the original map made by Christopher Columbus of his first voyage to America. It is quite literally priceless, which is why it is behind bullet-proof glass in a stainless-steel frame incorporated into the structure of the building.'

She flashed a white-toothed smile.

'Can I get you anything? Tea or coffee?'

Secretary Miller grunted a response, 'No. Thank you. As I say, I am not a connoisseur and I believe my item is a copy, not an original. I simply need it to be identified.'

At that moment, the young woman, who was still standing in the doorway, spun round.

'Ah! Here he is.'

Byron Silver, globally acknowledged authority on ancient cartography, walked into the room. He was in his late fifties, but looked older. He was wearing a three-piece pin-striped suit and was almost bald. His thin, pale face spoke of many years spent in the semi-darkness of old libraries studying maps and manuscripts. He stuck out his hand.

'Hello. You must be Mr Miller.'

'Yes. Thank you for seeing me at such short notice, Mr Silver.'

The antiquarian smiled sycophantically, his culti-vated voice sounded as smooth as silk.

'That is quite all right. For someone who recognizes the value of my expertise and is prepared to pay as well as you are, I am happy to work at a moment's notice.'

The young lady left the room, shutting the door discreetly behind her. Silver gestured to the table.

'Shall we? No point standing on ceremony.'

Secretary Miller walked over to the table and slipped his hand into his jacket pocket and removed the brown envelope. Gingerly, he tore it open, pulled out a single sheet of map paper and laid it on the desk. A frown crossed Silver's face. He fished in his pocket for a pair of fold-up eyeglasses and slipped them onto the end of his nose. He then reached up, switched on the overhead light and manoeuvred it into position above the map. Secretary Miller watched him like a hawk, desperate for any sign of recognition. After a minute Silver looked up again and removed his glasses.

'Well? Do you know what it is?'

Silver nodded sagely.

'Yes. It is a copy of the Piri Reis map. Do *you* know what that is?'

Secretary Miller shook his head in irritation.

Silver continued, 'It is a map made by a Turkish Admiral, called Piri Reis, in the Middle Ages. It is based on earlier maps – much earlier maps – or so he tells us, and was intended as a navigation aid for the Turkish fleet, in the event they sailed into the southern oceans.'

Secretary Miller was lost. What on earth had this to do with anything? Why had the senator wanted the professor dead and why had he specifically asked for the map to be destroyed?

But Byron Silver was warming to his task.

'It maps the land mass of Antarctica and shows it in an ice-free state. Consequently, this map is a curio, a collector's item.'

'You mean it *accurately* maps Antarctica? How is that possible? Correct me if I'm wrong, but is it not entirely buried under ice?'

Byron Silver smiled.

'Well – no one knows. But that is why the map is valuable – beyond and above its historical value, that is. Collectors love items that have a mysterious quality. Whenever we are lucky enough to get such strange artefacts as the Piri Reis map through our doors, we are always inundated with interest.'

Byron Silver reached up to switch off the light and almost absentmindedly added, 'Of course, we also always get a lot of angry complaints from our customers who are, how shall I put it, of the more literal religious bent.'

Secretary Miller froze.

'What? Why?'

Byron Silver turned quickly to look at him – he could sense the tension in his client's voice.

'Well, I just mean that there are some people in the world who don't approve of artefacts that call into question the biblical account of the past.'

Secretary Miller's blood ran cold. He looked down at the map in horror. So the professor had never been a threat to the Corporation. The senator had clearly been using the Corporation's network of agents to achieve his own private ends. This was unprecedented. Was Secretary Miller himself now merely a tool in the senator's plans? Was the entire Corporation in the process of being hijacked in order to further the senator's religious aims?

Secretary Miller could no longer discount the possibility. But he had to take stock. The go-ahead for the Corporation's fait accompli on Monday morning had already been given and he would still have to carry out his part in the plans.

He would challenge the senator face to face before then. But he would choose his moment wisely, or he too would very quickly go the way of Professor Kent.

42

As the car descended the winding and vertiginous road from the Alto Plano to the Bolivian capital, Catherine and Rutherford were lost in their own thoughts. The smiling and energetic Quitte drove with skill and speed.

Catherine gazed at the vast landscapes of valleys and mountain peaks and thought of the professor, wondering what he would have done at this point. She missed him acutely – his gravitas and kindness. Rutherford, who had been silently meditating for some time, admired the spectacular Andean scenery. He frowned to himself and stared out of the window, his eyes roaming over the landscape as if he expected to find answers there. Then quite suddenly, he turned to Catherine.

'Do you know the story of Gilgamesh?'

They looked into each other's eyes. Rutherford raised his eyebrows hopefully. Catherine shook her head. Rutherford changed his position to look at her more easily.

'It's the basis for the Bible story of Noah. The first record wc have of it is from cuneiform inscriptions dating from aound 2000 BC. But it must be even earlier than its origin. Gilgamesh was the king of Uruk in Sumeria, and he tells how he met another king called Utnapishtim who had been alive before the flood. Utnapishtim had been warned by one of the gods that the flood was coming and so he built a boat, brought onboard the different types of animals and all kinds of seeds. There was a huge storm then there was nothing but water as far as the eye could see. Utnapishtim let loose a dove—'

Catherine interjected, 'But this is ridiculous. I mean the Old Testament authors just took the whole tale lock, stock and barrel—'

'And why not? It's a good story. We can assume that Utnapishtim was a symbol, a single figure representing all those who survived the flood. Otherwise the human race could never have regrown to its current size. These myths are graphic first-hand accounts of a cataclysm that nearly destroyed all our ancestors. Humanity was almost wiped out.'

'Wow – that's quite a thought.'

'Yes, it is, but it is the only reason why this frightening story could be at the heart of so many cultures. It is our earliest shared memory . . . and there are lots of other descriptions of destruction that involve earthquakes and fire and cold, and they seem to coincide with the flood stories. The Zoroastrian scriptures, for example.'

Catherine frowned. 'The Zoroastrians. Who are they?'

'They are the followers of the prophet Zoroaster, or Zarathustra as he's also known. They are still in existence today – although there are only a few hundred thousand left living – mainly in Bombay in India. Zoroaster is meant to have received a revelation from God . . .'

Catherine saw a parallel. 'So he's like Mohammed is to the Muslims, or Moses to the Jews?'

'Yes. Only Zarathustra is older, he lived some time before 2000 BC. The Zoroastrians, who believe their people were born in northern Russia, think that one day the devil decided to destroy Airyana Vaejo – the Zoroastrian Eden, somewhere in Siberia. Instead of flooding it he froze it. The scriptures tell how the once beautiful land was covered in snow and ice and plunged into an eternal winter.'

Catherine listened with interest.

'That's a very specific fate – not the sort of thing you would just make up.'

'Yes – and even the Vikings have a similar idea.' Rutherford was on a roll. 'They believe in a time when it looked as though the earth would fall into the abyss of chaos for ever. Crops failed, war broke out, and all around the snow fell. After the cold, the earth was set on fire, turning it into one vast bonfire. Every last speck of life was incinerated. Then finally, as if the earth hadn't suffered enough, the seas suddenly rose up and buried everything under a blanket of water.'

With that, Rutherford clapped his hands together. Catherine pondered the Vikings' terrible vision.

'The problem is that nowhere, in any of the myths you have just recounted, are we told what really caused this global disaster. If we don't know the cause, how can we avoid the same fate?'

Rutherford started to think out loud. 'And yet the professor was convinced that is exactly what the secret message says.'

'Maybe we should be looking at the problem from the other direction.'

'What do you mean?'

'Well, rather than relying solely on our ability to interpret the myths to discover what destroyed the last world, why don't we find other proof of a monumental environmental cataclysm? If we use real geological sources, or fossil evidence, we should be able to locate such a dramatic period in the earth's history. We could match the technical data back to the myths – we could even work out exactly when the last world perished,' said Catherine.

Rutherford nodded encouragingly.

'But will this help us understand why it perished? Will this help us to understand the warning?'

'Absolutely. Think about it. If we know what the real cataclysm was like then it will be easier for us to guess at what the causes might have been.' Catherine's eyes lit up and she slapped the back of the seat in front of her with her hand.

'Von Dechend!'

Rutherford nodded decisively.

'Yes, of course – perfect. And we know we can trust him . . . We've got to get back to Oxford. Now.'

Hernan guided his vehicle along the empty roads of the Alto Plano, back towards Cuzco. He had been in a state of weary shock since the death of his brother; nothing had seemed real. Though they had feared they were in danger, somehow, when the blow came he had not been ready. With the appearance of these strangers he had suddenly felt there was still a slim hope.

Then at least Professor Kent's and Miguel's deaths would not have been in vain. He thought of Catherine and Rutherford making their escape, willing them onwards. *They must get out.* Just then he noticed a car up ahead, parked sideways across the road. On either side of the road the terrain was riven with gullies and boulders: it was impassable.

His car came to a stop five yards from the stationary vehicle. A thickset Caucasian man in black shades
and a dark suit stepped out from behind it. Hernan
watched in horror as the man raised a revolver and
pointed it directly through Hernan's windscreen at his
face.

In a split second Hernan realized what was happening. He pressed hard on the accelerator and shot
forward into the stationary four-wheel drive with an
enormous crash, causing the man to leap out of the way
and momentarily lose his aim. Hernan forced the car
into reverse and rammed his foot to the floor again but
even as he did so, his eye caught sight of a second
man's pistol, pointing at him a yard away from the
driver's door.

Suddenly, there was a terrible bang, and Hernan
found himself in excruciating pain, lying across the
front passenger seat gasping for breath. He couldn't
seem to get any oxygen into his lungs. Everything felt
wet. Grabbing the steering wheel with his right hand,
he tried to lift himself back up to a sitting position but
slid helplessly backwards.

He heard the passenger door open and felt a hand
pushing at his soaked clothing.

A voice said, 'Yeah, it's him – but they're not in
here.'

Then a second voice: 'OK – let's move on. We're

gaining on them. Take his ID and mobile phone. Finish him off.'

Hernan, groaning with pain and shock, tried vainly again to lift himself up. He thought of his brother. He thought of Rutherford and Catherine, and saw them standing together alone in the night. He tried to call out to them, but it was too late . . .

43

On the helipad of the Church of the Revealed Truth, a civilian model of the US air force's Apache attack helicopter squatted like a giant locust, its rotor blades buzzing with a hellish din.

Senator Kurtz and the Reverend Jim White were standing in the doorway of the cathedral. A few last words were exchanged and then the two men embraced for one final time. Their journey was almost over. How far they had come, they were both thinking: they had built the church from almost nothing – it was truly a miracle.

The senator marched purposefully across the lawn, carrying a small suitcase. As he approached the chopper, he instinctively adopted a crouching position and, hurrying across the helipad, bustled his way past two minders and climbed up the retractable steps into the belly of the machine. The door was quickly pushed shut behind him and, with an air of impatience, he straightened his tousled hair. In the porch of the church the Reverend Jim White watched the chopper lurch up into the air and away. All his hopes of bringing salvation to the chosen people went with the senator. He turned his back on the lawn and disappeared into the shadows of the church's sanctuary to return to his prayers.

The interior of the helicopter was a far cry from the usual austerity of its military counterpart. The matt black-and-green colour scheme had been completely replaced. Wood panels and video monitors covered the walls, ammunition boxes and the military specification steel-wrought seating had been exchanged for leather banquettes. An oak office table stood at one end of the sixty-foot-long hull and behind it a comfortable leather chair.

As soon as the soundproof doors were shut, a miraculous silence returned. The senator sat down at the desk and withdrew a slim black phone from his inside breast pocket. He pressed speed dial and held the phone to his ear. As he waited for the line to connect, he studied the view of the headquarters of the Church of the Revealed Truth shrinking before his eyes, until they were nothing more than a tiny collection of white spots on the vast canvas of the landscape.

But his mind was elsewhere. It was now Friday

afternoon. Only two more days and then victory would be assured.

The phone connected. A female voice spoke quickly and brightly. 'Yes, sir, global operations.'

The senator leaned back in his chair, his face contorted with concentration. With a hiss, he said, 'Get me Secretary Miller. This is Senator Kurtz.'

The voice of the receptionist suddenly became nervous: 'Yes, sir. Right away, sir.'

There was a few minutes silence and then the female voice returned to the line – this time it contained a distinct note of fear.

'I'm sorry, sir. Secretary Miller is unavailable at the moment.'

Senator Kurtz's face darkened perceptibly.

'Now listen to me, young lady. I want you to get off your backside and go tell the secretary right this minute that if I haven't heard from him within ten minutes I will hold you personally responsible.'

Secretary Miller was beginning to feel the strain. Sitting in his office he shook his head wearily and studied his telephone. The receptionist continued to pester him. He cursed under his breath and then dialled a number and held his cell phone to his ear. Straight away it was answered. He shifted his position in his seat – he became even more tense. Until he had confronted the senator, he certainly wasn't going to directly disobey orders. It would only arouse suspicion. Two more dead innocents, if indeed they were innocent, were neither here nor there in the great scheme of things. In any case, it was quite possible that the academics had learnt too much about the Corporation. His own safety and the integrity of the Corporation would have to come first.

'Now listen carefully,' said Senator Kurtz. 'Peru has messed up. We are looking for two individuals. One, James Rutherford, UK national, late thirties. Two, Catherine Donovan, US national, late twenties. Have you got that? Liaise immediately with the UK. Get the mobile numbers of these two people, pass them on to the heads of operations in Lima and La Paz and have them traced immediately. I want them shot on sight. This is now global priority number one. Call me as soon as it is done.'

44

Quitte's family home was an apartment in a typical central La Paz tower block of about ten storeys. They parked outside on the narrow pot-holed street. There were a few other cars on either side of the road – all of them looked as if they had seen better days. Quitte led them over to the building's entrance. As he pushed open the rickety double doors, they were greeted by the pungent smell of fried chillies. On the left-hand side of the small foyer was a lift. On the right-hand side was a dilapidated stone stairway that wound its way to the upper floors. Quitte talked away and gesticulated upwards with his fingers. Rutherford craned his neck, following the banister of the stairs as it zigzagged up into the distance, to a grimy skylight ten storeys above. Turning to Catherine he smiled.

'I guess that means the lift is out of order.'

They hefted their rucksacks onto their shoulders and followed the Indian up the winding flights of stairs.

The inside of the apartment was a pleasant surprise after the dirt of the street and the depressing atmosphere of the foyer. The doorway from the landing opened on to a short corridor that led into a decent-sized main room. There was a modest little balcony, barely wide enough for a couple of chairs, but the room was light and airy because the entire wall on either side of the balcony doors was windowed. The view was of the street at the front of the building. A little corridor ran off the main room leading to three bedrooms and a bathroom.

All the furniture was draped in extremely colourful Indian fabrics and a lot of it was made from carved wood. There were children's toys scattered around the place and on the large wooden table that seemed to be the family dining table were bowls and cutlery from the morning's breakfast. The family were clearly not well off, but they had made the most of their meagre resources and the flat had a homely feel. Catherine smiled at Quitte.

He grinned warmly back at her and then led them down the corridor to one of the bedrooms, where they deposited their bags. He showed them the little kitchen with some freshly brewed coffee and then with much gesticulating, he indicated that he would be gone for an hour, before darting out again.

*

As Catherine shut the door behind the departing Quitte, she let out a sigh of relief.

'James, for the first time in a while I almost feel safe!' She opened her phone and began to dial Hernan's mobile.

'I'll just call Hernan quickly and tell him we're OK.'

Rutherford took a swig of coffee and planted his elbows firmly on the table. He was tired. Dog tired.

The phone rang once, then twice and then a third time. Despite herself, Catherine could feel the nausea rising in her stomach.

Suddenly, the ringing stopped. The phone had been picked up. Relieved, Catherine greeted her friend.

'*Holà!* Hernan, it's me.'

There was silence from the other end.

'Hernan? Are you there? Hello?'

There was the noise of someone fumbling with the phone and it went dead, as if it had been suddenly turned off. Catherine and Rutherford looked into each other's eyes; both were thinking the same thing, but neither wanting to admit it.

High up in a brand new office on the sixty-fifth floor of La Paz's newest skyscraper a short, fat man was seated at a desk with a pair of headphones on his head. The office was light, amazingly light, thanks to the floor-to-ceiling windows. All around him was ranged a mass of electrical equipment, TV monitors and computer hardware.

The view out of the great bank of windows was panoramic. Below, a boiling brown smog-cloud blanketed La Paz. The filthy streets seethed with life. Tiny cars clogged the highways and even smaller people scuttled across the pavements.

The short, fat man was dressed in a white shirt and a greasy, dark blue tie. Huge sweat patches were blossoming under his armpits. It wasn't the heat that was causing him to perspire – the offices were air conditioned. Behind him, just by his shoulder stood the professor's killer, dressed all in black and with a frown of almost infinite contempt on his face. The fat man frantically pulled the headphones away from his ears, getting them tangled up behind his neck as he did so, and feverishly scribbled something down on the pad that lay next to his computer keyboard on his desk. He leapt out of his seat, tore the top sheet of paper from the pad and brandishing it, he began to shout, 'Boss! Boss! I've got them—'

The westerner snatched the piece of paper and read the address. With his left hand he pulled a mobile phone out of his pocket and flicked it open. All the time studying the piece of paper, he held the phone to his ear. A second later he spoke. His words were confident. He spoke them with a snarl.

'We have them. Let's go.'

45

In an effort to distract herself, Catherine wandered into the living room. Rutherford slumped on the sofa as she pulled an Atlas down from the bookshelf. She sat down at the table and, opening it, began lazily to flick through its glossy pages. Her eyes settled on a double-page-spread map of the world. As her glance wandered over the page, she read out to herself in a whisper the longitude of various ancient sites.

Catherine shifted uneasily in her seat. A frown appeared on her face as she hunched over the map and scrutinized it with her full attention. Her heart began to race again as the familiar feeling returned to flood over her once more; the feeling that she was looking into the immense black hole of the past and that from out of its depths strange incomprehensible signals were being sent, signals that were as old as time itself.

*

'James, James – wake up!'

Catherine shook Rutherford's shoulder furiously. He moaned, still half asleep.

'What? What is it? I feel exhausted.'

'I almost can't believe it. The implications are just too bizarre but . . . here . . . let me show you.'

Catherine took her pen and began methodically to draw on the map.

Rutherford came over, sat at the table and watched in fascination.

'What are you up to?'

'You'll see. Just look. Now, imagine that the prime meridian is not at London but at Giza, in Egypt – at the Great Pyramid in fact – just like Bezumov said.'

Catherine proceeded to draw the longitudinal positions of all the sites taking Giza as degree zero.

'Look – Kathmandu is exactly fifty-four degrees east of Giza. Fifty-four degrees east of Kathmandu lies the sacred isle of Yap. Angkor Wat is exactly seventy-two degrees east of Giza and Nan Madol is exactly fifty-four degrees east of Angkor. It's almost unbelievable. Yap and Nan Madol are tiny specks in the ocean. Look! Even Raiatea is precisely one hundred and eighty degrees east of Giza.'

Catherine looked up into his eyes to check he had understood.

'Don't you see? They are all whole numbers, which

is pretty remarkable, but what is even stranger is that they are divisible by six or twelve. It is far too unlikely to be an accident.'

Rutherford studied the map and began to grasp the implications of this alarming new discovery.

'You mean all these ancient sites have been deliberately positioned according to an overall global plan?'

Catherine's eyes lit up.

'Yes! And the spaces between the sites are particularly interesting: fifty-four, seventy-two – they are precessional numbers.'

'Precession?' Rutherford asked.

'What do you know about astronomy and the movement of our planet?'

'Not a whole lot. I know the earth rotates on its own axis once every twenty-four hours. I know it completes a full orbit of the sun roughly every three hundred and sixty-five days and I also know it is tilted away from the plane of the ecliptic and that the tilt varies – it wobbles back and forth between twenty-one and twenty-four degrees – a complete wobble takes forty-one thousand years.'

'Good – well, there is one more movement that our planet makes. The axis itself rotates backwards, in the opposite direction to the planet's rotational spin.'

'What do you mean?'

'Imagine the earth as being a spinning top orbiting

the sun. It spins on its axis, it circles the sun, it gracefully changes its tilt and finally its axis also slowly circles around in the opposite direction to the planet's rotational spin. This backward spin is called precession. The great thing is that all these motions are perfectly regular. That is one of the pleasures of being an astronomer. A full rotation of the axis takes 25,776 years.'

Rutherford nodded his head.

'It's all rather elegant. But did the ancients even know about precession? If it happens so slowly it would have taken generations to notice any significant movement.'

'I would never even have contemplated the possibility of the ancients having any understanding of precession before we embarked on this trip, but now I am beginning to wonder. The orthodox view is that Hipparchus, a Greek astronomer, collected data from Alexandria and Babylon. When he compared it he noticed there was a difference in the position of the stars and so he came up with the idea of precession. Maybe he wasn't the first, though; maybe precession had just been forgotten about.'

Rutherford frowned.

'All right – this still doesn't explain why. Why would the ancients be making a reference to precession at all? What is the significance?'

Catherine was silent for a moment. 'Look – when I realized that precessional numbers seemed to play a significant part in the location of these monuments, it suddenly occurred to me that one of the main precessional numbers also keeps popping up in the myths we have been investigating.'

'Really? Which one?'

'Well, you said Osiris was murdered by seventy-two conspirators and that there are seventy-two temples at Angkor Wat – well, seventy-two is arguably the main precessional number. It takes seventy-two years for the earth to precess one degree on its axis. Maybe there are other occurrences.'

Rutherford's eyes widened with excitement.

'My God, you're absolutely right. Seventy-two. That's got to be it. We're close to cracking the code.'

46

Rutherford had never felt more awake. His mind raced through all the ancient myths that he had ever read.

'Are there other precessional numbers? Or are seventy-two and the other base twelve the only ones?'

Catherine thought for a second and then said, 'No, not at all – there are others: 1,080, 2,160, 4,320—'

'Wait! What was that last one?'

'The number of years it takes to move through two houses of the zodiac: 4,320.'

Rutherford looked like he had just seen a vision.

'That's incredible – truly incredible . . .'

Catherine grabbed his arm.

'What?'

His eyes were bright with excitement.

'The most ancient Hindu mystical text, the Rigveda, is made up of 10,800 stanzas and the entire work is precisely 432,000 syllables long. In gematria the key is always the order of numbers – it is not important if there are zeros after them. We know the code has to be global, well here is the central text of the Hindu religion and it enshrines two precessional numbers in its very structure.'

Rutherford turned and looked Catherine in the eyes. She grinned broadly at him.

'That's it: we have struck gold. We are on the scent of the code. Where else do these numbers come up?'

'Everywhere. It is as if all these myths are specifically intended to keep reminding us of the same numbers no matter if the story is different in different places. The ancient mystical book of the Jews is called the Kabbalah. To reach the *ain soph*, or God, one has to pass along the seventy-two paths. And Berossus, the Babylonian historian who described Oannes, says that before the flood there was a line of kings who ruled over Babylon and their reign lasted for 432,000 years. And even more interestingly, Berossus tells us that from creation down to the time of the flood is 2,160,000 years: 2160 is the length of time it takes to move through one house of the zodiac, isn't it?'

'Yes, exactly.'

'And in gematria! Do you remember we calculated the value of the Greek words for Jesus and Mary, 888 and 192. If you add them together you get 1080 – a precessional number.'

'And that number is also the radius of the moon in

miles!' said Catherine, hardly able to believe what she was hearing. 'My goodness – this is becoming positively frightening.'

Rutherford looked over at Catherine, her young face was weighed down by the burden of the knowledge they were discovering.

'Yes. This is starting to make sense,' she said. 'There must be a connection between precession and the destruction of the ancient world.'

Rutherford nodded. 'Yes, it's as if these original myth-makers, these bringers of light are saying that every time the earth completes a 26,000-year wobble, a vast cataclysm is unleashed upon the world.'

Catherine closed her eyes and tried to compose her thoughts.

'James – there's something else in all of this. There's Bezumov. You remember what Hernan said? The electromagnetic currents that he wants to harness are all linked to the orbital motion of the earth. I am willing to bet that the ancients could influence the flows of these energies. I don't know why they did this – maybe to generate power, maybe to alter the motion of the planet. I think Bezumov now believes he can restart their machine. But surely, the consequences of misusing the ancient technology could be fatal.'

Rutherford listened in horror. He cursed under his breath.

'The lunatic Russian! But really, where would he start? It is one thing discovering the ruins of an ancient technology and another thing working out how to use it.'

'Listen, we've got to get Von Dechend to find a true and accurate date for the cataclysm as well as an accurate description of what might actually have happened – then maybe we can figure out why the professor was so sure we were being warned, because it still doesn't all add up: how exactly is precession connected to the cataclysm and why are we being warned? Is whatever happened to the ancients about to happen to us? Professor Kent seemed to think so, but why?'

Rutherford sighed and looked into Catherine's eyes. She smiled and put her hand on his knee.

'James – we can do it. We must just keep trying. We have to finish what we have begun and we must move fast.'

Rutherford took Catherine's hand in his and held it tight. She wanted to hold him in her arms but felt time was ebbing away. She was embarrassed by her nerves. His touch made her want to forget everything – this desperate chase and all the danger they were in.

But just as she opened her mouth to say something, the peaceful security of Quitte's tower block home was shattered by the unmistakable sound of a gun being fired in the street below.

47

Catherine pulled the bolt into place and, turning round to face the living room, pressed her back against the door. A look of ice-cold fear shadowed her face. Her voice was cracked and desperate, 'They're here ... they're coming up the stairs.' She had peered down the stairwell and seen three, or maybe four, men pounding up the stairs, kicking in the doors of the apartments below. The stairwell was filled with the shrieks of terrified families.

Rutherford was on the balcony at the front of the flat. He glanced down and just had time to take in the scene below. He felt himself stiffen with horror as he saw Quitte's body sprawled on the pavement outside the doorway. Around him stood three black-clad figures and, in the middle of the narrow street, two large black four-by-fours were blocking any entry or exit to the apartment block. As Rutherford struggled to absorb what he was seeing, one of the figures pointed up at him and screamed in English, 'There he is! Seventh floor. Let's go!'

Rutherford darted back into the room. In a blind panic Catherine was frantically trying to double-lock the door. Struggling against his fear, Rutherford realized what they must do.

'Grab your passport and money! Quick – do it now! Then follow me . . . and don't forget the maps.'

He ripped open the top of his own bag and pulled out his travel wallet. Stuffing it into his trouser pocket he bounded to the door and unlocked it. Catherine was right behind him clutching her own passport and the precious envelope containing the maps.

'We can't go out there!'

Rutherford wrestled open the door and turned to her, his eyes blazing with adrenalin.

'We don't have any choice.'

Catherine grabbed his arm and followed him onto the landing. The door banged shut behind them. Rutherford peeked over the banister into the stairwell. The gun-wielding men were forcing their way up through the clouds of cordite and wailing crowds of panic-stricken residents milling around on the landings. He turned to Catherine and indicated they should go upwards with his hand. She darted up the stairs without even looking back. Rutherford followed, glancing over his shoulder.

Three flights of stairs up, they reached the tenth-floor landing. An Indian woman was staring at them through the crack of her door. At the end of the landing was another door that clearly led to the roof. They ran over to it. Rutherford grabbed the handle and almost ripped it off its hinges. It wasn't locked. They piled through the doorway, up the short flight of stairs and out onto the roof. The door slammed shut behind them.

The roof was about one hundred yards square. It had a small knee-high wall around its perimeter. TV aerials dotted its surface. Catherine turned to Rutherford with a look of desperation.

'Now what do we do?'

He ran to the back of the roof. Looking over he saw the roof of the adjacent building was only about a yard away and about four feet below the one they were standing on.

Not too far – we can just do it . . .

'Quick, Catherine. We'll have to jump.'

Catherine ran up to the edge and peered over the wall across the gap. Then holding onto Rutherford's arm, she leaned over and stared down at the narrow chasm-like alley that separated the two buildings. A look of desperation and disgust crossed her face.

'I hate heights.'

Rutherford stepped up onto the wall and offered her his hand.

'Come up here. Now just look straight ahead at the horizon.'

Inhaling deeply, Catherine did as she was asked. They were standing side by side on the little wall; Catherine's right hand was locked in Rutherford's left.

'OK – when I say jump, I want you to jump straight out as far as you can and when you hit the ground, you'll have to roll.'

Catherine looked back to the door to the stairs. She was about to scream with fear. Rutherford smiled at her. The beautiful, endless blue sky was all around. She bit her lip and nodded, shutting her eyes.

Rutherford bent his knees, checked his grip on her hand and then saying a silent prayer, focused his mind and body.

'One . . . two . . . three . . . JUMP.'

With a great thud they landed in a heap on the concrete roof of the neighbouring building. In an attempt to break Catherine's fall, Rutherford landed badly on his shoulder. They both got up, Rutherford wincing in pain. In the middle of the roof was a little brick hut with a door to the stairs that would take them out of sight.

The door was open and as they slipped through

Catherine scanned the roof of Quitte's building. Their pursuers hadn't yet appeared. Rutherford was taking the stairs two at a time but leaning heavily against the wall as he did so, clutching his left shoulder. They spiralled down, passing apartment doorways as they went and finally emerging in the foyer on the ground floor. Catherine cautiously opened the front door and peered into the street outside. It was empty. She turned to Rutherford and put her hand very gently on his shoulder.

'OK – I think it's all clear. We've got to run for it now. We can lose ourselves in the alleyways. Are you all right, James?'

He grimaced and nodded.

'Let's get out of here . . .'

Five minutes later, shell-shocked and scared, Catherine and Rutherford emerged from one of La Paz's many side alleys into the bustling street market of San Salvador. Their clothes were dishevelled, their rucksacks were gone – all they had with them now were their passports and their money.

The old street market ran for almost half a mile up the Calle San Salvador: on either side of the road, stall after stall was selling fruit and vegetables, spices, blankets, kitchen utensils and domestic appliances. The road was jam-packed with shoppers and tourists. Catherine was trying to get her breath back. She was standing bent almost double with her hands on her knees. She breathed in a huge gulp of air then stood up straight.

'How did they know where we were?' She looked across at Rutherford in the hope that he might have some answers. 'And who on earth are they?'

Rutherford shook his head, scanning the bustling crowds in the market.

'I've got absolutely no idea. But I can tell you one thing – I have no intention of hanging around to find out. We've got to get to the airport – it's our only hope.'

Pandemonium reigned in Quitte's apartment block. Every room in every apartment had been turned upside down and hordes of screaming, terrified people were milling about on the stairs as the contents of their homes were smashed to smithereens and thrown to the floor. Beds were upended, cupboard doors were kicked in, not a stone was left unturned. Anyone who stood in the way of this outpouring of violence was beaten into submission. Quitte's apartment itself received special treatment. It was as if a maniac had been let loose in it. Not a single piece of furniture or crockery was left in one piece.

Finally, three shaven-headed westerners, wearing black T-shirts, black combat trousers and military boots and carrying an assortment of weaponry, burst onto the roof. Following right behind them was the thin-faced murderer. He mounted the final flight of stairs and pushed his way through the door, now swinging on its hinges after the brutal treatment of the thugs. The sunlight and fresh air seemed to anger him. His quarry had vanished into the nothingness of the blue heavens. He surveyed the rooftop, scattered with TV aerials. His men were stalking around the edge, their guns pointing this way and that. His hands closed into tight fists. Frustration boiled in his veins.

One of his men who was now standing on the little perimeter wall near where Catherine and Rutherford had jumped, gestured to him. Breathing heavily, more out of pent-up fury than exhaustion at running up the stairs, he marched over. The man pointed down to the neighbouring roof.

The westerner took one look and taking out his mobile phone, turned on his heel.

'They are on foot in the barrio. Mobilize all agents. Put people at the bus station, the railway station and the airport. And get the helicopter up immediately.'

With that he disappeared down the stairs at a run.

48

The taxi slowed to walking speed as it drifted along the front of the departures area of the airport building. Other taxis and private vehicles were finding spaces along the curb, pulling up and disgorging their passengers. Bags and suitcases were being hauled from the boots of cars.

Rutherford leant forward to talk to the driver.

'Leave us here – this is good.'

He turned to Catherine. 'I'm mighty glad we're finally leaving South America. I can't help wondering what has happened to that madman Bezumov. Do you think he ran into the men in black? Is he with them or acting alone?'

Catherine wasn't listening. Her attention was focused on the airport crowds. She scanned the faces on the pavement, Indians for the most part, and tourists. Something wasn't right.

'Hold on a minute, James.'

Rutherford was already fishing in his wallet for some money. The driver was nosing the car into a gap behind a minibus. Catherine's view of the pavement was momentarily obscured by a taxi pulling out. Perhaps she was imagining things?

Rutherford took out some dollar bills.

'What is it?'

Suddenly, Catherine's face turned white. There, about thirty feet away from the car, were two dark-suited westerners. They were talking to each other in muted tones, their heads together. There was something about them; they were both very tense and alert – their body language was quite different from everyone else outside the airport. She reached over and grabbed the driver by the shoulder.

'¡Vamos! Go! Now! James, get down.'

Rutherford didn't need to ask what was wrong. He did as he was told. Squashed flat on the seat of the taxi he whispered hoarsely, 'They're here?'

She nodded furiously at him and then addressed the confused driver, 'Quickly, take us along to the arrivals zone.'

Not knowing what else to do, they pressed their bodies to the seat of the taxi, praying that neither of the sinister men would peer inside. Their taxi glided away from the curb and out into the flow of traffic. A hundred yards further on it pulled in for a second time.

Tentatively Catherine raised her head. The pavement was flooded with people who had just arrived. A constant stream of tired-looking travellers spilled out of the arrivals lounge doors. She looked up and down the pavement scanning for any suspicious-looking figures. It seemed to be all clear.

'OK – let's get out of here.'

She opened her door and slipped out onto the pavement, followed by Rutherford, who had palmed a bunch of dollar bills to the driver as he left the taxi. Hand in hand they threaded their way through the crowds, burrowing against the current and on into the arrivals lounge.

Rutherford tugged Catherine's arm, breathlessly he spoke: 'Over there. Do you see it? Back through in the departures hall – it's the American Airlines desk. I am sure they'll have the most flights.'

He pointed down the arrivals hall and on through where it joined, via a gigantic open doorway, the busy departures hall. Catherine checked it out. The American Airlines desk looked so isolated. There was no queue, but it was very exposed. If they went and stood there, they would surely be spotted.

'Do you think they've got people inside as well?'

Rutherford looked over his shoulder.

'I don't know. We have to assume so.'

Catherine was feeling sick to the pit of her stomach.

She looked again at the ticket desk. Just opposite that was passport control and the entrance to the safety of the departure lounge proper. All they had to do was get the tickets.

Suddenly she had an idea. She broke her grip on Rutherford's hand and headed off towards a tourist stall. Rutherford followed her, wondering what she was up to. The stall was selling all sorts of tourist goods: T-shirts, trinkets and items of national dress. Catherine grabbed a black bowler hat and a multicoloured llama-wool poncho, both essential elements of an Aymara's outfit, and quickly paid the smiling Indian assistant. Then she slipped the poncho over her head and tucked her hair under the bowler hat.

I'm too tall, that's for sure, and my skin's too white, but at a glance, I might blend in to the airport crowd – westerners never wear the local costume.

Adjusting the hat so it was pulled down over her eyes, she looked over at the ticket desk.

'Give me your passport,' she said calmly to Rutherford. Hurriedly, he unzipped his travel wallet and handed over the document.

'Are you sure?'

Catherine nodded.

'I'll go up to the desk, buy some tickets and then as soon as I turn around, you walk quickly over to the check-in counter and I'll meet you there.'

With that she was gone. Rutherford waited just out of sight by the entrance to the departures lounge, monitoring her progress but trying his best to blend his big frame into the airport crowds.

Catherine strode as calmly as she could across the floor of the departures hall and up to the American Airlines desk. She could see outside onto the pavement – the two black-clad westerners were pacing up and down, examining the taxis as they arrived to drop people off.

She felt a sharp chill of fear again.

Yes – it's definitely them.

The saleswoman at the American Airlines desk smiled at her costume and then scanned her database for available flights.

'Madam – the best I can do is a flight in one hour. It's not direct though, you have to change in Miami and there is a wait of three hours in the middle of the night. There's nothing else till tomorrow morning.'

'That sounds absolutely fantastic – *muchas gracias.*'

A few minutes later, she tucked the tickets and passports beneath the folds of her poncho and turned on her heel. Rutherford was striding across the hall.

She hurried over to the check-in desk and handed Rutherford his ticket and passport. They snaked their way around the roped-off queuing area until they arrived in front of the passport counter.

Behind the high desk sat two officials. One, clearly the more senior, took the passports and tickets. He had cold, expressionless eyes. He scrutinized their travel documents, his reptilian gaze flicking back and forth from the photos up to their faces. Then after what seemed like an age, he handed the documents back. Trying to stifle a mounting sense of hope Catherine smiled at him. He stared back at her impassively.

'*Gracias*,' she said as she turned to go. He didn't respond. Rutherford had already disappeared past the desk and into the crowds in the departure lounge beyond.

She had barely taken three paces when she heard what she had dreaded to hear – a stentorian bark, 'Madam!'

She stopped in her tracks. What had he found? Had he been tipped off to stop them? Perhaps she should just run for it and throw herself into the crowd.

She saw Rutherford up ahead, searching round for her with an anxious look on his face. With a feeling of complete loss she turned to face the official. Life drained from her eyes, she stared at him with glazed resignation.

And then, suddenly, she saw that he was smiling.

'Madam – we like your outfit!'

Both he and his colleague were grinning at her and pointing at her traditional costume. Catherine almost collapsed with relief. She grinned back at them and then, spinning around, disappeared into the crowd.

49

It was time for the secretary to leave New York. His helicopter landed in a hurricane of noise on the helipad at JFK airport. Like clockwork, a smart new Mercedes Benz raced across the tarmac and swung into position. A burly figure stepped out of the vehicle and scanned around the vicinity. The helicopter door opened mechanically, the steps spilled out and the secretary climbed down and disappeared into the leather-clad interior of the car. Glancing around the barren expanse of tarmac, the minder followed suit and ducked into the vehicle and within seconds the Mercedes was speeding across the dark apron on its way to the private jet compound on the other side of the airfield.

Secretary Miller tried hard to relax, if only for a moment. The meeting in Cairo would be the last opportunity to challenge the senator. With a frown on his face, he leaned forward and addressed the man in the front passenger seat: 'Tell the pilot we are going to

Cairo, but we will be stopping at the base in Switzerland.'

'Yes, sir.'

He closed his eyes and tilted his head back as the car raced across the airstrip. It was time to begin the journey to Egypt – his work in North America was done, at least for the time being. His thoughts turned to the girl and her companion.

Now that she is back in England we will have to be more discreet.

He reached for his phone and dialled a number in Oxford. After several rings, the phone was answered – it was the unmistakable voice of the warden of All Souls.

'I'm phoning about the girl, Donovan. I am expecting her to turn up in Oxford.'

The warden sounded anxious, and extremely tense.

'What do you want me to do now? I've done as much as I can. I've told you all I know. I'm not doing anything more.'

Secretary Miller, sounding derisive, cut him off. 'Don't be ridiculous. I don't rely on old men to do my work. I merely want you to keep close track of her movements and make sure she doesn't go abroad on any more jaunts for the next few days. I don't want her causing us any further problems.'

'Nothing will happen to her, will it?'

'That is not your concern. All I ask is that you keep her in Oxford until Tuesday.'

'She is only twenty-nine, you know – I don't think that she—'

'Warden, you are beginning to try my patience. Do I need to remind you of your obligations? This is your last term before you retire. You don't want your entire career to be blotted by a last-minute revelation, do you?'

There was a long silence.

'Have I made myself understood?'

'Yes, Secretary. You have.'

The line went dead.

50

It was now Saturday morning. After a gruelling flight, including a stopover in Miami, Catherine and Rutherford had finally arrived at Heathrow airport. The flight had, if nothing else, given them an opportunity to succumb to their exhaustion: for the sixteen precious hours they had been suspended in the air, away from the clutches of the enemy who had chased them across the Andes, safe for a brief time, though unable to take any further action.

From Heathrow airport they took the extravagant option and caught a taxi all the way back to Oxford. Living on academic salaries, neither of them had much money, but now was not the time to worry about such things.

They eventually drew up outside All Souls and Rutherford jumped out and paid the driver. Opening the door for Catherine, and grabbing their rucksacks, he stared up at the elegant facade of the building.

'Well, here we are. It hasn't changed a bit.'

Catherine cast a suspicious glance over at the college gate.

'I'm not so sure about that. Anyway, let's just hope that Von Dechend is here. We haven't got a minute to waste.'

As they stepped through the low door into the porter's lodge, Catherine glanced around uneasily.

What is it that is making me feel on edge? It's all so familiar and yet, something no longer feels right . . .

Out of habit she took a quick look in her pigeonhole. As she did so, she thought of the original envelope containing the maps – the maps that had begun their whole dangerous adventure. To her relief, the pigeonhole only contained a couple of notes. She walked over to the porter's desk.

'Fred – are you there?'

A second later, the porter appeared through the doorway.

'Hello, Dr Donovan. Very nice to see you. Lovely day, isn't it?'

Not quite how I would describe it, thought Catherine grimly. But maintaining a positive air, she greeted him in return. 'Hello, Fred – I was just popping in to see Dr Von Dechend. Is he in?'

'Yes – he is. Let me look after your bags for you. Oh – before I forget, the warden is desperate to see you. He keeps calling me up and popping down to ask if you've been into college yet.'

Catherine glanced at Rutherford. But before she could say anything, the dry, sharp voice of the warden assailed the lodge. He was standing behind them in the open doorway. His tall gaunt frame filled the entrance.

'Yes. And I'm here again.' His unsmiling face took in Catherine and Rutherford. 'So you've just returned. How was your trip?'

'Trip where, Warden?'

A flush crossed his face.

'Oh – I thought you must have been away – I've been trying to get hold of you at home as well. I just want to make sure you are aware of the fact that I am calling a meeting of the fellowship on Tuesday morning. It is absolutely essential that *all* fellows attend. I thought I should let you know so there can be no misunderstandings.'

Catherine looked at him with a level gaze.

'Great. Thanks very much – I'll see you there.'

He hovered for a moment longer in the doorway and then, looking a little unsure of himself, spun around and stepped through the lodge gate and into the street.

'James, let's go and find Dr Von Dechend.'

As she walked out into the quad, Rutherford followed behind.

'What was all that about?'

Catherine looked completely bemused.

'I don't know – it's very odd. But I've had a strange feeling about the warden since he called me in and told me about the professor's death.'

51

Dr Von Dechend was overjoyed to see them.

'Catherine! What a delight! And James Rutherford as well – this is really too much. The *jeunesse d'orée* of Oxford. The gilded youth! Again – here in my rooms! What an honour!'

Catherine glanced at Rutherford with a smile, as the old don ushered them in to his cosy book-lined den.

'It's very good to see you again as well, Dr Von Dechend. I hope you are well?'

'Oh yes, my dear,' he replied as he gestured for them to sit down.

Catherine cleared her throat.

'I'm afraid that, once again, we've come seeking your advice.'

'Fire away, young woman, fire away. I am at your service.'

Catherine waited for Von Dechend to settle into his chair and then, drawing a deep breath, she began.

'Well, this may sound cryptic, but we want to ask you a question. I don't have time to explain the background as to why – but we really need your help . . .'

She paused to see if Von Dechend was happy with her strange preamble. He nodded his head slowly, urging her to continue.

'We are trying to locate a catastrophic event that might lie in the depths of the past, that might also have almost wiped out a significant part of humanity. We're looking for any evidence in the fossil record, in geology, in palaeontology, wherever there is anything to indicate a cataclysm of such monumental proportions that it might explain the myths of the end of the last world that can be found in every culture across the globe.'

There was a long pause. Von Dechend stared up at the ceiling as if preparing a speech. Catherine glanced over at Rutherford. They both waited in silence, not even wanting to breathe in case it might disturb that old don's train of thought. After a minute or so of silence Von Dechend spoke. His voice was deeply serious, his bonhomie all gone and his normal jolliness replaced by a tone of absolute scholarly caution. He sounded almost as if he was not at all comfortable discussing such things.

'Before we begin on this topic, let me make one thing clear. I'm not about to endorse any theories that suggest the ancient myths and legends of cataclysm were anything other than myths and legends. There is a world of cranks who will do that for you, cranks and religious maniacs. I am neither of the above, and have no interest in such vainglorious fantasies.'

Rutherford caught Catherine's eye. She hesitated for an instant; he decided to interject for the first time.

'No, of course not, Dr Von Dechend. That's not what we were expecting at all. We simply wanted to have an intellectual discussion in private, off the record, so to speak, and between ourselves. It's just a whim of ours; we'd simply like to speculate as to when might be the most likely time that such a cataclysm might have happened. Obviously, we all know this is merely intellectual speculation.'

Rutherford and Catherine waited with bated breath.

After another interminable pause, Von Dechend spoke again, 'Hmm. I see. Well, now we have made that clear, I can tell you about my own thoughts on this matter.'

Catherine and Rutherford both instinctively drew their breath in. Von Dechend puffed on his pipe and began, first slowly and then gradually with more warmth. 'My immediate instinct has always been that something terrible did happen in the past and that it happened during the end of the last ice age.'

Catherine and Rutherford were on tenterhooks.

With theatrical effect Von Dechend paused again before beginning to speak very slowly: 'Human life before the dawn of recorded history is a series of lucky escapes from total annihilation. In fact, it is no exaggeration to say that the direct ancestors of every one of us must have hung on by the skin of their teeth at some stage. However weak and lazy some of our fellow human beings seem today, you can guarantee they are the descendants of incredibly determined, resourceful and brave men and women who somehow managed to overcome all the disasters the natural world threw at them.

'Our experience as a species over the last few thousand years has allowed us to become far too complacent. We think it is normal for the planet to be a stable and, for the most part, hospitable place. This is a terrible mistake. It would be more accurate to say that for the last few thousand years, we have been passing through the eye of a storm: we have been experiencing the still calm at the dead centre of an endless cyclone of violence and destruction.'

Catherine and Rutherford listened in fascination. Von Dechend, ever the showman, seemed to be preparing to deliver his coup de grâce.

'But to get back to the ice age. Now, like almost everything that happened more than about five hundred years ago, we do not really understand the ice age.

However, we do know that it was massively, terrifyingly destructive and it is fair to guess that humanity was very, very lucky to live through it.

'We are fairly sure that the last ice age began around 110,000 BC with the steady build-up of ice spreading across the globe. Between about 55000 and about 12000 BC it was at its zenith. The whole of the world was affected. From out in space, the earth must have resembled a snowball. The ice sheets would grow and then suddenly melt a bit before growing again, this time a little further than before. The net effect would have been huge environmental instability: floods, earthquakes, storms and so on.

'But it is the final meltdown that I want to draw to your attention. At the zenith of the last ice age – 12000 BC – the ice sheets extended almost over the entire globe. But over the next five thousand years, ice that had taken a hundred thousand years to build up suddenly melted in a truly terrifying thaw. Some scientists even think this great meltdown might have occurred over a much shorter period of time – a few hundred years, or even perhaps as little as ten years. The fossil record shows clearly that massively powerful natural forces were let loose on the inhabitants of the planet as the great ice sheets disappeared. You might have thought that conditions would have improved for the majority of animals, and in the long run they did, but the thaw triggered off natural disasters that in the short term were catastrophic for many species. All over the world the fossil record tells the same story of extinction on a grand scale. You used to get horses and other megafauna in South America – you didn't see the horse again till the Spanish introduced them, and the megafauna are gone for good. And in North America thirty-three of the forty-five genera of large mammals were made extinct. It was a holocaust.'

Von Dechend fixed his guests with an intense gaze.

'Can you imagine living during this period? It would have been truly terrifying. If you and your tribe or family had chosen the wrong part of the world to settle in you would be doomed. The melting ice would have caused massive geological disturbances: earthquakes; volcanic eruptions; tsunamis. It is a miracle that mankind survived at all.

'But what is strangest of all is that the polar regions seem to have been the areas that suffered most. Vast numbers of animal carcasses have been discovered buried under the ice. In fact, even today, perfectly preserved mammoths are still dug up: their tusks are used for ivory carving.'

Catherine was confused.

'But if they are still preserved with the flesh on them

doesn't that mean they must have been frozen incredibly quickly and straight after death – otherwise they would have decomposed?'

'Yes – a very good point. It is odd. Whereas the extinct species of South America and Australia are buried in the earth with their flesh long since decomposed, the animals found around the Arctic Circle – in Alaska and Siberia – seem to have been flash-frozen on an industrial scale. Some of these animals have undigested food in their stomachs, which can only mean they were frozen solid within three hours of their last meal. And what is stranger still is that it is not just mammoths, sabre-toothed tigers and other Arctic animals, but also leopards, elephants, horses, cattle, lions and many other temperate species.'

Rutherford was stunned.

'Leopards and elephants – in the Arctic?'

'It would seem so. Even as far north as the Arctic islands of Svalbard, scientists are still regularly finding fossils of temperate animals and the remains of flora and fauna that can only survive in a tropical climate.'

Rutherford was still having trouble.

'But that's incredible.'

'Yes. It is one of the great mysteries of the end of the last ice age. How did all these temperate species come to end up buried under the ice in what is now the

Arctic Circle? It is clear that, as all over the world the ice age was rushing to its end, these lands were heading in the other direction, they became suddenly colder and less hospitable. Whole herds of animals were flash-frozen.'

'But it just doesn't add up,' James said. 'The end of the ice age should have brought warm weather and, in any case, what were temperate species doing at these frozen latitudes anyway?'

'No. I admit. It all remains a mystery. But what we do know is that by about 7500 BC the great thaw had finished. The ice sheets had retreated. The previous six or seven thousand years would have been the most terrifying time on earth to live through. Volcanoes, earthquakes, violent storms, tsunamis and so on – and then of course, the floods. Millions of tons of melting ice releasing pressure on the earth's crust and causing it to rise, thereby triggered more earthquakes. Sea levels rose. Great swathes of land were swallowed up. The floods and tsunamis were of such scale that the Himalayas could have been temporarily obscured by water.'

'What! That can't be possible!' Rutherford exclaimed.

'Well it is. Whale skeletons have been found in the mountains of North America and even in the middle of the Sahara desert at Wadi Hitan. All over Europe, there are mountainous peaks that must have served as the last refuge for thousands of terrified retreating animals. There are many such mountain-top mass graves all over the world, testament to the terrified migrations of the animals and humans fleeing the rising water. All of western Europe was submerged on several occasions – we don't know for how long, but it definitely went under at least two or three times ... All in all, the period between 15000 and 7000 BC and particularly between 11000 and 8000 BC was characterized by terrible and continuous flooding, sudden freezing and almost universal destruction.'

Catherine, her head shaking in astonishment, had been listening transfixed.

'It would have been absolutely terrifying.'

'Yes. And all the more because these primitive peoples would have had no understanding of why it was happening. It would have been only natural to think that the gods were angry and they were being punished.' He sighed. 'Was this what you were looking for?'

Rutherford and Catherine exchanged glances.

'Yes. Thank you very much for taking the time to tell us about all this – I had no idea that humanity had been through such a terrible storm, particularly in the comparatively recent past,' Rutherford said.

Catherine chimed in: 'Yes – many thanks, Dr Von Dechend. There are not many people who have the range of knowledge you do and your knowledge of the period has been very useful. But we must go. We've taken up enough of your time.'

'Not at all, Catherine, it's always a pleasure. I am glad I have been of use. It is important to remind people that we are living in an unusually quiet and calm time. It will not last though!'

Catherine and Rutherford rose to go. The old don looked at her with a sly expression on his face.

'Maybe one day you'll tell me what all the questions are about.'

Catherine smiled ruefully.

'I will, Dr Von Dechend. One day, I promise I will.'

52

Once again, Catherine and Rutherford left Von Dechend's company buoyed with hope. As they descended the stairs, they talked excitedly.

'James! That was all we could have hoped for and more! That explains everything, including the fact that the flood really did happen. And precession must be linked to the end of the ice age – to the meltdown! It makes perfect sense. As the earth's orbit changes over the 26,000-year cycle, the north and south poles are exposed to different amounts of sunlight. At some point in that cycle, when they are closest to the sun, the poles will start to melt . . . the end of the ice age is the answer!'

Thoughts flashed through Catherine's mind. Everything seemed to be falling into place. Rutherford was equally excited.

'I know. It does all start to make sense . . . the flood

myths are true accounts of the disasters that almost wiped us out.'

Catherine, speaking almost at the same time, said, 'Yes – and the end of the ice age also brought the sudden, paradoxical freeze in certain areas that the Vikings and Zoroastrians talk of . . .' Suddenly, she slapped her forehead with the palm of her right hand. 'James – I've got it! I can't believe I've been so dim: we've known the answer all along . . .'

Catherine threw open the door to Professor Kent's study and strode over to his desk. On it was a large globe and at the touch of a button she had illuminated it. Turning back to James she began: 'Hapgood's theory of earth-crust displacement!'

Rutherford looked blank for a moment.

'You remember. Dr Von Dechend told us about it when we were talking about the maps. He said that Hapgood had used the Piri Reis map to help prove his earth-crust displacement theory. According to him, Antarctica used to be further north, but the earth's crust slipped and Antarctica sank to the bottom of the planet.'

She slowly turned the globe round to illustrate her point.

'The whole crust moved, remember, not just one or

two tectonic plates but the whole lithosphere. Formerly temperate land must have suddenly moved up beyond the Arctic Circle. No wonder all these lions and camels and other such temperate animals are found frozen under the Siberian ice.'

Rutherford suddenly understood. His face lit up.

'And that also means that before this crustal displacement happened people could have lived on what is now the Antarctic landmass. Suddenly, when it shifted south, they would have found themselves frozen out – not to mention destroyed by tsunamis.'

'Exactly! And that means Antarctica could have been where the bringers of light were from. This explains the Piri Reis map, this explains everything. The Zoroastrians fleeing their homeland on the plains of Russia, when it was suddenly transported northwards and froze, and the bringers of light suddenly having their civilization destroyed when it moved south.'

Rutherford's forehead was furrowed in concentration.

'And it even explains one of the main problems I have been having with everything we have discovered so far: it explains why there is no record of the original civilization of the bringers of light.'

'Exactly, all evidence has been buried under two miles of Antarctic ice, and that is why no one has ever found it. The survivors were scattered to the four winds.

They arrived on the shores of South America and the Middle East and tried to rebuild their legacy: Viracocha and Osiris and Oannes were all refugees from an ancient Antarctic civilization that was destroyed when the earth's crust moved.'

'I really think this is right.'

'And it also explains the speed of the great thaw. The more the ice melts, the more the earth's surface weight is redistributed. This caused the crust to slip; it suddenly moved the poles down into warmer latitudes and caused even more melting. No wonder the sea levels rose so quickly.'

Rutherford was lost in thought again.

'Yes – but there is one piece missing in our jigsaw. Why was Professor Kent convinced that the same fate is about to befall us? We are nowhere near the same point on the precessional cycle . . . we are not even close to coming to the end of the ice age like the ancients were, so why did he think we are in danger of suffering another similar cataclysm?'

'I think we should go to Giza – we now know that Giza was the centre of the old world. Bezumov will go to Giza, I am sure of that. And when he gets there, he will try to work it out for himself. We can beat him to it; stop his crazy schemes and then we can finally work out why the professor thought we were in danger.'

Rutherford smiled and shook his head.

'OK, Catherine. Our last throw of the dice. I guess if it doesn't work, we're all doomed anyway. So why not go away on one last jaunt, before the end of civilization?'

PART FOUR

PART FOUR

53

The receptionist at the five-star Nile Hilton in Cairo stared in confusion at the tall, smartly dressed Caucasian man who stood on the other side of the desk, carrying nothing but a briefcase. He was dressed in what appeared to be a pristine white suit, brown Oxford brogue shoes, a white shirt with an elegantly patterned blue tie, and he seemed to have not a single piece of luggage. He had just strolled into the hotel and demanded the best room available.

'I am very sorry, sir, but how do you spell that?'

'C-H-E-K-H-O-V, Andrey Chekhov.'

Ivan Bezumov slid a brand-new Russian passport across the top of the marble reception desk and into the waiting hand of the receptionist.

'Now get a move on – I'm in a hurry.'

The sun streamed in through the huge windows that looked out onto the majestic river below. In stark contrast to the noise and sweat outside, diligent waiters hurried silently across the vast and airy marble atrium, ferrying drinks to the well-heeled tourists who were scattered in comfortable seats across the enormous floor.

The receptionist cleared his throat nervously. 'Yes, I'm sorry, sir. How many nights will it be for, Mr Chekhov?'

'Oh – let's say three for now. That should be plenty.'

'Would you like a room with a view of the Nile?'

'Yes. Can we hurry this up, please?'

'Of course, sir. Here is your key.'

'And I want a car with a driver – a four-wheel-drive vehicle – and the driver must be a fluent Russian speaker. And he has to be available twenty-four hours a day. And before you ask, money is no object. Here's my credit card. I'm going up to my room for a few hours. Please make sure that when I come down the driver is waiting for me in the lobby.'

Bezumov spun round and strode across the marble floor towards the lifts.

High above the Mediterranean, Catherine and Rutherford once again found themselves speeding headlong into the unknown. Feeling slightly claustrophobic, trapped again in a crowded aeroplane so soon after their last flight, Catherine closed her eyes. In a bid to offset the dehydrating consequences of prolonged air travel, she began to drink her way through a bottle of spring water. After taking half a dozen hearty swigs she looked over at Rutherford. His face was a study in concentration; he was speed-reading a book on hieroglyphs. Catherine put her head back and, letting out a long sigh, rubbed her tired eyes.

'Ahh . . . I feel shattered. But we've simply got to keep going. I am more determined than ever to end this.'

Rutherford, his eyes bloodshot, answered grimly, 'Me too. I'm exhausted. But I get the feeling that if nothing else, Egypt is the end of our trail.'

Catherine agreed.

I just wish I knew more about ancient Egypt – in fact I wish I knew more about everything. This has been an intellectual roller coaster.

So much seemed to hinge on whether their combined knowledge and intelligence could help them understand why the professor thought the world was in danger of another cataclysm.

And even when we've understood why we are in danger of suffering the fate of the ancients, we still have to find a way to avert the disaster and we still have to stop Bezumov . . . I just wish the professor was still with us; if only he was here for me to talk to.

She opened her eyes again and gingerly stretched her neck from side to side.

'James?'

Rutherford, deeply immersed, murmured without looking up, 'Hmm?'

'I'm hoping you know a lot more about where we're going than I do.'

Rutherford slowly shut the book and stuffed it into the pocket in the back of the seat in front of him. He looked round at her and forced a weary smile.

'Well, I can't say I'm a world authority. But, I've been here several times before. I'm definitely on firmer ground than I was in South America – I know the orthodox thinking about ancient Egypt, at least. The thing is, that after what we've learned I'm beginning to wonder if the orthodox thinking is worth the paper it's written on.'

Catherine sighed. 'I agree. And I'm willing to bet we will uncover some disturbing anomalies here as well. I'm also willing to bet that the precessional numbers will be behind it all again. But I am a complete beginner. All I know is what you've told me about Osiris and what little I can remember from school. I've spent too many years reading about the stars.'

'You can't know everything. And without your knowledge of the stars, we wouldn't have got where we are now. Anyway, you could have spent years learning about stuff we might shortly discover is all wrong.'

'Well – we've got to start somewhere. Maybe, if

you've got the energy, you could fill me in on some basics?'

Rutherford sat up straighter and shook his shoulders to wake himself up.

'Before we get on to the history,' he began, 'there are a couple of interesting geographical things to note here. Firstly, Giza, where the pyramids are built and where the great River Nile splits on its way to the Mediterranean, is at exactly thirty degrees latitude. This means the pyramids are located exactly one-third of the way between the equator and the North Pole. I had never really thought this was important before, but because of Bezumov's theory and, more importantly, because of what you discovered about the precessional link in the placement of all these global monuments, it suddenly seems to be a bit more significant.'

'That *is* interesting – I mean it can hardly be an accident. What is the other thing?'

'Ahh – well, again, I had never really thought about it before, but the site of the pyramids is also at the centre of the world's dry land.'

Catherine frowned.

'What do you mean? Surely somewhere in the middle of Russia or North America is the centre of the earth's dry land?'

Rutherford shook his head.

'No, not in the sense that I mean. I mean that if you

drew a line from pole to pole running down the line of longitude that passes directly through the base of the Great Pyramid, it would also run through more dry land than any other north–south line of longitude on the globe. Furthermore, if you drew a line east–west, along the line of latitude passing directly through the pyramids, it too would go through more dry land than any other line of latitude. Here, look.'

He found a world map in the airline magazine and then took out a pen and drew a line up and down the map, crossing the site of Giza. He then drew a second line, east–west crossing the first line. Catherine stared at the drawing. Suddenly her expression changed – her eyes flashed with inspiration.

'Doesn't it make you think of the flood?'

Rutherford tilted his head in surprise.

'Now you mention it, yes. I suppose the seas would have to cross more dry land to touch the pyramids than at any other site on earth.'

'Yes – and also, it might have been one of the first parts of the world to dry out once the waters started to recede!'

Rutherford laughed.

'Of course – yes! I hadn't thought of that.' He paused, considering. Then he continued: 'It is assumed that ancient Egypt as we know it began with a pharaoh called Menes in 3000 BC. The pyramids and also many of the other important sites are thought to have been crafted during the first five hundred years – to 2500 BC. It's also during this time that they say the religious texts that have come down to us were carved and painted onto the various buildings.'

Catherine thought through what Rutherford was telling her.

'And what about before then, before Menes?'

'Well, supposedly there were just a whole load of little kingdoms and principalities. These tiny states never achieved anything of significance; they were for the most part very primitive societies – Neolithic farmers hugging the banks of the river Nile. Everything we regard today as the great achievements of the ancient Egyptians came during the pharaonic times that began with Menes.'

'This all sounds too familiar. It reminds me too much of the way the Viracochas have been totally airbrushed from history.'

Rutherford pulled another book from his bag.

'I agree. Here, read this. I'm going to try to get some sleep.'

He slid his blindfold over his eyes and leant his head wearily back on the headrest.

Catherine was anxious but also relieved because she felt the journey was coming to an end, that perhaps they might find a conclusion somewhere in the ancient desert sands.

She recalled the expressions of the men who had come for them, their air of menace, the real threat of gruesome violence lingering around them. She was frightened by these memories; they made her want to run away, find somewhere safe, if anywhere was safe any more. But she knew she had to finish this, to understand the truth. She looked across at Rutherford, and thought how glad she was that he had come, that she hadn't had to do all this alone.

54

Two hours after landing they had finally cleared customs and were making their way at a snail's pace in a hired car through the gridlocked traffic of Cairo. Suddenly Rutherford spotted what he had been looking for. There, stuck out on the outskirts of the Egyptian capital city were the dominating forms of the three largest Giza pyramids: the Great Pyramid, also called by modern Egyptologists the Pyramid of Khufu, the second, the Pyramid of Khafre, and finally the third, much smaller, Pyramid of Menkaure. Although they are situated in the desert beyond the fringes of the city, they are so massive that when viewed from suburbs of Cairo they seem to rise up from within the city itself, looming over everything else.

Rutherford pulled the car up onto the side of the road. The sea of traffic continued to rumble past.

'Look!'

Catherine leaned forward and stared out into the

heat. What she saw took her breath away. Rutherford was ecstatic as he pointed to the largest of the three.

'The Great Pyramid. The biggest man-made structure ever built.'

'Surely not! What about all the skyscrapers of the twentieth century?'

Rutherford laughed. 'Child's play by comparison! The Great Pyramid is in a league of its own. You'll see when we get closer and you will really feel its enormity when we get inside.'

'No one ever warned me quite how awesome they look.'

Rutherford continued, 'Yes – and it's all the more amazing if you remember that the Great Pyramid was also one of the first buildings ever constructed. It appears out of nowhere at the very beginning of history – archaeologists reckon on it having been built around 2600 BC – using astonishing levels of technical accuracy. Given that the builders of the pyramids didn't have cranes and diggers and all the other paraphernalia at the disposal of the modern builder, it is nothing short of a miracle.'

Catherine stared across at him. His eyes were glued to the gigantic structure.

He looks like he's under their spell . . . the spell of the pyramids.

'Doesn't it strike you as a little odd?'

Rutherford was still staring up at the pyramids. He answered without looking over at her, 'What?'

'Well – it's a bit like deciding to design the first-ever car and building a Ferrari, and from then on being content to build go-karts for thousands of years before even approaching being able to build Ferraris again.'

Rutherford was listening to her intently.

She continued, 'I mean, one could hardly describe this as the normal model of development. I don't know much about the history of architecture, but before they built Warwick Castle in England or the great crusader castles, they built lots of far more primitive types of castle. There was a learning curve, a gradual progression – they didn't suddenly one day in the depths of history decide to build the biggest most perfect castle ever conceived. The pyramid defies that pattern, it is just there at the beginning, looking down inscrutably on everything that comes after it.'

Rutherford had a very serious look on his face. 'You're right. I guess we are beginning to see just how flimsy the official history really is.' He frowned to himself and then turned his furrowed brow to Catherine. 'Come on – I want to show you something.'

He put the car into gear and they swung out into the busy road. They continued along the highway for another mile before turning off and then taking a series of side roads that brought them up to the edge of the desert. They had left the tall ugly concrete buildings of central Cairo far behind, and even the shabby office blocks that hugged the highway had disappeared. The buildings here were almost rural in character; it was as if the suburbs had petered out to become a village, or had simply run out of steam on the edge of the desert. The roads were not tarmacked and the dust the tyres threw up hung in the air. Rutherford drew the car to a halt. The pyramids seemed to tower above them, even though they were still far away over the sand dunes.

'Here we are. From now on we're on foot.'

The sun was harsh, it was one in the afternoon. They winced as they climbed out into the fierce sunlight. The heat seemed to be reflected up at them from the burning sand. A stench of horse manure hung in the air, flies buzzed around their ears. The Giza plateau was almost empty. One or two beleaguered-looking guards walked around the base of the Great Pyramid, but the tourists were back at their hotels, safely out of the sun. After an exhausting trudge through the sand, they finally reached the enormous flanks of the Great Pyramid itself.

Rutherford walked up to the first step of masonry. He was looking far less sure of himself. He patted one of the massive blocks. It came up to his chest and was at least ten tons in weight. He craned his neck and stared upwards toward the summit of the huge pile of stone. Catherine shielded her eyes with her hand and looked around the vast Giza plateau.

'Do you think we are safe here? Do you think they are still following us?'

Rutherford scanned the horizon anxiously. The whole panorama of the plateau was drenched in an oppressive heat.

'I don't know. We have to assume they are. By now they have probably found what flight we took. We must work fast.'

Catherine's mouth was dry. She looked up at the unassailable heights of the ancient pyramid.

'And we've got to find Bezumov. He must be somewhere in Cairo.'

Rutherford shook his head and looked over at her.

'Well, he will be here by sunrise tomorrow for the spring equinox, that much we can be sure of. Quite what we can do about him I'm not so certain.' He squinted back up at the Great Pyramid. 'But for now, let's concentrate on solving the mystery.'

He turned and rested his right hand on the flank of the lowest course of stone.

'It is a miraculous structure, isn't it? It is made of more than two and a half millon blocks of masonry, each block weighing anything from two to fifteen tons, which is an enormous amount. If each block was not positioned exactly in the right place, then phenomenal pressure would build up very quickly and the whole structure would collapse.' He stroked the ancient stones. 'Originally, the whole pyramid was encased in a shell of cladding stones similar to white marble. So the entire structure, and the two neighbouring pyramids, gleamed like mirrors in the bright sunlight. The effect would have been absolutely incredible.'

Catherine walked up to the base. She ran her fingers over the stones.

'How do we know it was covered like that? What happened to the casing?'

Rutherford confidently answered her question.

'Firstly, we have descriptions from the time of the ancient Greeks, but also, in some places pieces of the casing still remain. Each of these pieces of casing stone weighed over ten tons, but the joints between slabs are so perfect you couldn't slip a piece of paper between them. Much like the stonework in Peru,' he added.

Catherine leaned back and tried to look all the way up towards the top. Like a great mountain, it was impossible to see the summit, just the never-ending staircase of stone. Rutherford stepped back a few paces to get a better view of the structure.

'But this is not all. As you can see, the base of the pyramid forms a square.'

Catherine stepped back to join him.

He continued, 'The four sides of this square are lined up with the utmost precision to the four points of the compass. What I mean by that is that the north face, which we are now looking at, is lined perfectly to true north. And the east face to true east and so on.'

Catherine looked right and left down the length of the north face.

'Surely they can't be *perfectly* aligned?'

Rutherford answered, 'Well – as near to perfect as is humanly possible when building a structure of this size. They have all been measured by experts using the most advanced high-tech tools and it was calculated that they are only out by less than 0.1 per cent.'

'How amazing!'

Rutherford watched Catherine's reaction with satisfaction.

'Quite. It also doesn't really make sense.'

'Too right it doesn't make sense – it's totally insane.'

'No – I mean it is completely unnecessary. As far as the human eye is concerned, we wouldn't notice a margin of error of one per cent. A modern builder, for example, wouldn't be too fussed about even 1.5 per cent either way. What makes the whole thing even more incomprehensible is that to reduce the margin of error from one to 0.1 per cent is very, very difficult.'

Catherine was astounded once again.

'Then why did they bother? What was the point?'

Rutherford stroked his chin with the fingers of his right hand.

'That's just what I'm getting at. No one really has an explanation for it. Anyway, the mania for precision doesn't stop there. The lengths of the sides are also almost exactly uniform. And all the corners are, as near as humanly possible, precise ninety-degree angles. It's inexplicable.'

Catherine marvelled at the skill that had gone into this ancient construction.

'But how did they achieve such technical brilliance?'

Rutherford took his hand from his chin and raised his index finger as if to emphasize the point he was making.

'Ahh – there's another problem. This level of skill isn't reached again until the twentieth century. No one can work out how such accuracy can be achieved without the most modern surveying tools. Even *with* the tools it's nigh on impossible. Another mystery for us to solve.'

Over at the Nile Hilton, the Nubian doorman, dressed in red turban, smart red uniform and white gloves, swung open one of the hotel's glass front doors as Ivan Bezumov marched purposefully through.

As he stepped out into the shimmering heat of the Cairo afternoon a nervous-looking chauffeur, who had been lounging around in the shade of one of the palm trees that decorated the hotel grounds, jumped to attention, stubbed out his cigarette and leapt into his waiting vehicle. It was a white Toyota Land Cruiser four-wheel drive, just as Bezumov had requested.

The engine roared as the driver turned the key in the ignition. Bezumov waited impatiently as the Land Cruiser came to a halt outside the front entrance of the hotel. Before the chauffeur had time to get out of the car and run around and open the passenger door, as he had been trained to do, Bezumov jumped in.

'The pyramids – and make it fast.'

55

Catherine followed Rutherford up to the corner of the Great Pyramid. When she reached it she positioned herself so she could clearly see the whole of both the north and west faces, albeit at an oblique slant. Her eyes were drawn remorselessly up to the summit. She noticed that the last few courses of masonry seemed to be missing.

'What happened to the apex?'

Rutherford stood back and admired the view to the west, off into the rolling sand dunes.

'No one knows exactly. At some point in the last few millennia it was taken down. At least two and a half thousand years ago, travellers were already reporting that the last few courses below the summit were not in place.'

'What would have been on top?'

'The thinking is that the very tip would have been the Benben stone.'

'The what?'

'A Benben is the name for the final pyramidon that sits on top of the main body of the pyramid. The myth goes that at the beginning of time Atum, the Egyptian god of creation, stirred in the void and caused the other gods to be born. A few mounds of dry land were revealed by the receding waters of chaos. Onto one of these mounds of dry land fell the Benben stone.'

'Wow – yet another flood myth.'

'Yes – exactly.'

'But if it's a myth then isn't the Benben stone more likely to be just a symbol, or a metaphor?'

'I wouldn't be so sure. Perhaps it was part of a meteorite – there are other cases of ancient people worshipping such objects. Or perhaps it was simply a sacred rock or a man-made object – but there is no reason to believe it didn't exist. Apparently the Benben stone sat on top of the gleaming marble casing, shining brightly, casting a divine light that could be seen from miles and miles around. Even at night, the starlight would illuminate it.'

'But what was it made of?'

'Diamond, polished granite, gold, who knows? Some say it had the eye of Horus in it – you know, that rather disturbing eye you still see in the pyramid shown on the dollar bill. Tradition has it that the Benben was taken down by the high priests when they realized the days of the old religion were drawing to an end. Christianity was in the ascendant – they knew they would have to remove the Benben, or sooner or later someone would just steal it. So, they took it down and hid it. It's just one more mystery of the pyramids.'

Catherine turned to look into the desert.

Sand, sand and more sand, all the way to the Atlantic coast. Not many sources of rock around here . . .

'Come to think of it, James, how on earth did they build the pyramids at all? How did they get all these gigantic blocks of stones over the desert and then erect them in such perfect order?'

Rutherford had been waiting for her to ask this and found himself smiling.

'You're not going to like this answer, but, again, no one knows.'

Catherine stared at him, a look of surprise on her face.

'There are two and a half million blocks involved and not one of them weighs any less than a car. How would *you* set about moving them all without even the use of a crane to help?'

Catherine looked at him sternly. 'I'm not the Egyptologist or an engineer – I've got no idea. What are the theories?'

'I suppose the most popular theory – the one they

seem to teach most in school – is that the blocks were pushed, dragged and lifted into place using brute force. It took a hundred thousand men twenty years to complete it.'

Catherine thought for a second.

'That's a hell of a lot of people. A lot of mouths to feed. Were they war prisoners?'

'No – they were supposedly agricultural workers. They only worked on the pyramid during the three-month period the Nile flooded its banks – when they would have been on forced holiday from farm work.'

Catherine started to think out loud. 'Some holiday! OK – so three months a year for twenty years, that's sixty months. Let's imagine that they were working twelve hours a day. Thirty days in a month at twelve hours a day is roughly twenty thousand hours in total. So, if there were two and a half million blocks all weighing at least a couple of tons, they would have to shift about a hundred and twenty blocks an hour, I reckon. Or basically two blocks per minute.'

Rutherford made an exaggerated expression of disbelief.

'I have to say, two blocks per minute does sound totally incredible.'

'But what makes it more unbelievable was that they weren't just moving the blocks and dumping them anywhere, they were lifting them up hundreds of feet into the air and then placing them with the exactitude of a neurosurgeon.'

Rutherford laughed and shrugged his shoulders.

Catherine had another question on her mind. 'You haven't yet told me what the pyramids were for in the first place.'

Rutherford suddenly looked almost depressed.

'I really don't know what to think any more. I am beginning to believe that Bezumov is far closer to the truth than the conventional wisdom.'

Catherine's forehead was knotted in mystification.

'What do you mean?'

'Egyptologists say the pyramids are tombs. They are the final resting place of the pharaohs . . . I used to agree with them. But I really don't any more.' He stared up at the mass of the Great Pyramid. 'It just seems too simplistic. Why go to all the trouble? There simply must be more to the pyramids than being burial chambers of dead kings. Sorry – I'm probably not making much sense. It's just my gut feeling . . .'

'What evidence do the archaeologists have for saying they are tombs anyway?'

Rutherford paused to collect his thoughts and then began again, 'It was Herodotus, the Greek historian of the fifth century BC, who first reported the theory that the Great Pyramid was built by Khufu, that his brother

Khafre built the second pyramid and that Khafre's son built the third. Ever since then Egyptologists have tended to agree with his suggestion, and whenever they find circumstantial evidence they take it as final proof. For example, they have found various inscriptions around the Giza site that attribute the Great Pyramid to Khufu. But this isn't proof – it would be only natural for a later pharaoh to appropriate the sites from his forefathers. When the pyramids were opened, they were found to be completely empty – no treasure, and only in the third, smallest, pyramid were there any bones. But even those have been dated to around the time of Jesus Christ, long after the pyramids were built. They say that in the case of the Great Pyramid, it must have been emptied by tomb raiders. But we really don't know.'

Catherine pondered what he was saying.

'OK. What all this means is that we really don't know anything at all?'

Rutherford smiled sheepishly.

'Yes.'

Rutherford looked up again at the great blank side of the pyramid.

'It's another mystery in a land of mysteries. We don't know what they were for, we can't understand how anyone could have built them, we don't know *who* built them, and, in all honesty, we don't even know *when* they were built. They're just here from the beginning of human history and quite possibly from long before that.' He stepped back and smiled at her. 'Come on, let's go and have a look inside.'

56

Over on the other side of Cairo, Dr Ahmed Aziz was returning to his office after a long lunch. In addition to his role as director of Egyptian antiquities, Dr Aziz was also keeper of the Great Pyramid and deputy governor of the Egyptian museum. He was a youngish man – he looked to be in his late thirties or early forties, with a full black moustache, and today he was dressed in an elegant dark blue suit. He was a little on the portly side, probably as a result of the many dinners and lunches he was obliged to attend, either before or after showing foreign delegations around the fabulous sites of Egypt – but he glowed with pampered good health.

How he had risen so quickly to the pre-eminent position in one of the most important antiquities departments in the world remained a mystery – even to many in the Egyptian government itself. It was not that he was unqualified – he was an undisputed expert on certain areas of ancient Egyptian pottery and had done post-doctoral work in the US – but to be promoted to the exalted heights of the directorship at such a tender age was unprecedented. Life had been kind to him.

He looked at the clock on the wall of his comfortable office. It was 3.30 p.m. The lunch had been longer than he had planned, but that was so often the way when entertaining important foreign dignitaries.

He sat down in his chair, and at once his direct line started to ring. Picking up the receiver in a plump hand adorned with two heavy gold rings, he answered, '*Salaam aleikum.*'

'Aziz – it is I.' Senator Kurtz's distinctive voice echoed down the line.

Aziz's expression instantly changed. Gone was the look of mild annoyance and frustration that had been playing on his face. He was now visibly alarmed.

He glanced over at the door to his office. It was open. He could see into the outer room where his secretary sat along with his aide, Mr Poimandres, a short, frail, sixty-year-old Coptic Christian Egyptian. Both of them appeared to be busy – the secretary was typing and Mr Poimandres was on the phone.

But he wasn't going to take any risks – particularly with Poimandres. Aziz never felt entirely comfortable around his aide. Perhaps it was the fact that Poimandres was a member of one of the oldest Christian Churches in the world that caused Aziz, a devout Muslim, no small amount of unease. The Copts had been a powerful force in Egyptian society for two thousand years – disproportionately powerful, some said. Were it not for the fact that Poimandres was so very reliable and so very good at his job, Aziz would have had him discreetly moved on years ago.

Aziz could hear the senator's impatient breathing.

'Please – one moment, sir.'

He put the receiver down on top of the leather writing pad on his desk, walked over to the door and, after peering into the outer office to check there was no one else in it, shut and then locked it.

'Sir – please. I am back.'

'Listen very carefully, Aziz. If anyone pays you a visit today, asking questions or offering theories about the pyramids, I want you to respond as follows . . . Are you listening?'

'Yes. Yes, sir!'

There was a pause.

'Tell them their theories are quite wrong. Tell them their ideas are not new, they have all been discussed in the public domain and that, interesting as they may be, they have no foundation in reality. They will try to get you to discuss their points in a rational manner. You must not engage with them. Do you understand? Do not engage. Do not argue. Just tell them that what they are saying is wrong.'

'Yes, sir. Maybe you would just like me to go on leave – or not agree to see them at all?'

'No – don't do that – it's too suspicious. They are not cranks, we are talking here about highly regarded academics from Oxford University. Meet them, do not get into a debate with them and refute all they say. Is that clear?'

'Yes, sir – absolutely, sir.'

'And Aziz – no mistakes, if you value your prestigious position. I will shortly be in Egypt and will personally take care of them.'

Aziz gulped nervously and dabbed his sweating forehead with his handkerchief.

'Sir – you are coming to Egypt?'

The line went dead. Aziz's pulse was racing as if he had just completed a hundred-metre sprint.

57

Catherine and Rutherford walked halfway down the west side of the pyramid to where modern scaffolding carried a staircase up to the entrance. As they got nearer, Catherine looked at the sand, the tourists and day-trippers and wondered if someone was coming for them. She saw a man on his own, away from a group, wearing Arab dress, but he seemed not to be looking at her. She watched a family moving slowly across the sand. It seemed OK, she thought, but everything could change so quickly, and she didn't like the idea of being trapped underground. Sooner or later Bezumov would appear and she was quite sure he wouldn't be pleased about their reunion.

Rutherford looked at her. 'Come on then, let's get this over with. This is why we came.'

He was worried, too, and they moved quickly inside, clambering up the stairs with their heads bowed. Then they entered the cave-like mouth. Catherine looked over her shoulder, back out across the sands to the car park. Cars were coming and going. She hadn't even set foot in the massive tunnel, but already claustrophobia was gripping her by the throat.

Rutherford stepped forward and reached his hand out and ran it along the uneven sides of the walls.

'Don't pay attention to this tunnel – it is an aberration. It was made by the Arab labourers, not the original pyramid builders, that's why it is a bit of a mess. It's called Mamun's hole after the Egyptian caliph who ordered the break-in.'

In silence they made their way through the poorly lit passageway until they stumbled into the main tunnel.

The descending corridor plunged downwards into the dark. Despite the fact that lights had been attached at intervals to the ceiling, it was impossible to see the bottom. The corridor itself looked like the inside of a gigantic piece of steel machinery. The stone walls were as smooth as glass. The sight took her breath away.

This is just extraordinary. It can't be a tomb. It must be a machine of some sort. It radiates functional purpose.

Rutherford smiled at her.

'I thought you would be impressed. It goes straight down for three hundred and forty-nine feet at an angle of exactly twenty-six degrees, half the fifty-two degrees of the slope of the pyramid's sides. But what is most incredible is that it doesn't deviate by more than a fraction of an inch the whole way down. Even today, such accuracy would be pretty much impossible to achieve.'

Rutherford led the way along the passage.

'We're going up to the gallery.'

As they went, Catherine looked around, checking the semi-darkness. Their shadows made shifting shapes on the walls. She heard every step, magnified by the surrounding silence. Then she thought she heard echoing footsteps, someone behind her. There was nothing to do, she thought, but keep going. She noticed her breathing was shallow, nervous, and she tried to calm herself. She negotiated some modern steps and came out in an ascending passage. It was a mirror image of the descending tunnel. The same machine-like perfection and impossible angle of climb, but this time heading upwards. Her sense of claustrophobia increased. The ceiling was less than four feet high and the air was stiflingly close. Bent double, they continued their ascent.

After struggling along for several minutes, the narrow passageway suddenly opened out into a far more substantial chamber, one hundred and fifty feet in length and about thirty feet high, with a sloping, vaulted ceiling. Rutherford drew himself up to his natural height and stretched with relief.

'Phew – I was beginning to get a little panicked there.'

Catherine wiped her brow, not saying anything. She didn't want to confess the extent of her fears. She had a mounting sense that someone had followed them into the pyramid to exact some sort of terrible revenge. Trying to shrug off the crushing sense of foreboding, she stared at the floor that sloped up and ahead of them.

'What is *that*?' She pointed to a trench running the entire length of the floor of the chamber. 'It looks like a kind of groove for a piece of machinery or something. Please don't tell me we don't know what it is.'

Rutherford made an apologetic face. Catherine shook her head, as they started to climb up through the grand gallery.

After going through another passageway, they entered a final large room. Rutherford stood up, rubbing his lower back, and readjusted his bag.

'So here we are in the king's chamber.'

Catherine arrived at his side and was struck by the oppressive nature of the room. She was conscious of the tons of masonry pushing down from above. It felt almost as if the great dark slabs of stone that formed the walls were closing in.

If someone came now to kill us, no one would hear anything. No one would ever know . . .

Rutherford's face was covered in a sheen of perspiration.

'What is that?' Catherine pointed to the man-sized stone box that lay on the floor at the far end of the room.

'That's a granite coffer. It's empty – come on, let's have a look.'

They walked over to the box and peered in. Rutherford, consulting his guidebook, muttered its dimensions out loud. Then suddenly he exclaimed, 'My God! The imperial measures we still use today in England and America, the inches and feet, are related to the measuring system used in the construction of the pyramid and the coffer.'

'What! So somehow this was used as a basis for our measuring system?'

'It appears so. I hadn't contemplated the pyramid in these terms before, but now I feel as if it is the source of everything. The box must have been in here from the beginning because it's much too big to get out along the tunnel we just came through. What is also interesting is that the *inside* corners are absolutely, perfectly square. It is inexplicable how this could have been achieved using anything other than modern technology. Tons of pressure and diamond drill bits are needed to hollow out granite in this fashion.'

Just then something struck Catherine. With a distinct

note of fear in her voice she said, 'Wait a minute, what were those measurements you were just reading?'

Puzzled by her request, Rutherford studied her face before looking back down at the guidebook. 'The inside is six feet six point six inches long—'

'Yes,' interrupted Catherine. 'That's what I thought you said. It can't be accidental, given all we know about their mania for precision. The internal length of this ancient coffer at the heart of the world's oldest and strangest building is six six six – the number of the devil.'

Just then the lights flickered off and for a second the chamber was plunged into absolute darkness. Catherine's pulse leapt. Rutherford could feel a wave of pure panic spreading from his stomach and into his chest.

Then the lights flickered back on again, and the room emerged from the darkness. Rutherford looked like he had aged ten years.

'Right, we're not staying here a minute longer than we have to.'

Catherine breathed again.

'I couldn't agree more.'

The light held. Rutherford wiped his brow on his sleeve and then began again. He sounded very nervous.

'Six six six isn't really the number of the beast.'

Catherine, staring around at the oppressive tomblike room, didn't understand.

'How do you mean?'

'Well – it's far older than Christianity. It's the pagan number of the sun, or of earthly power. The alchemists associated it with sulphur. In gematria, the biblical phrase *theos eini epi gaia* – "I am god on earth" – has a value of six six six. Later Christians, who had lost touch with the old knowledge, became afraid of the number and its symbolic power.'

Rutherford rubbed his feverish brow with his fore-arm and glanced nervously around.

'But there's one more important thing. Quick, over here.'

He walked over to the southern wall of the king's chamber. Catherine followed, all the time worried that the lights might fail again, and wishing she had brought a torch. Rutherford pointed to a small hole.

'Here – this shaft leads directly out through the blocks of the pyramid. Like everything in here it's perfectly straight. It slices its way right up through the core masonry, at an angle of exactly forty-five degrees. Thousands upon thousands of blocks would have had to be individually carved so as to allow the shaft to run through them. But that is only the half of it. If you extend the shaft into outer space, at times it crosses perfectly through the meridian path of Orion's belt, a sacred area of the sky in the Egyptian religion. Similarly, in the queen's chamber, the southern shaft is lined up perfectly with the path of the star Sirius, which was also extremely significant. The hieroglyph for Sirius is made up of a star, a pyramid and a Benben stone.'

At the mention of Sirius, Catherine felt a pang, as she was instantly transported back to the sunny All Souls lecture hall and her lecture on the mystery of the Dogon tribes. *How far we've come that these matters are no longer amusing academic games but matters of life and death.*

Rutherford continued. 'And each chamber also has another shaft which lines up with a specific star. Usually, when one is aligned, the others are just pointing into the cosmic wastes. But apparently, all four shafts align correctly when you turn the star clock back to 2450 BC.'

'I wonder what the significance was to the builders. Perhaps it was the date they finally managed to re-establish themselves after the chaos of the flood? But there is something about the Sirius connection . . .' Catherine couldn't help but think of the Dogon again. 'Maybe the bringers of light were also visited . . .'

Rutherford didn't quite catch what she said.

'What?'

Catherine stopped herself.

'Oh, nothing. It is strange. In any case, it can't be an accident that the shafts line up on the stars.'

Rutherford eyed the lights nervously, as if expecting them to go out again.

'Let's talk about this outside, I don't think I can take any more of this pressure. It's really getting to me, this enclosed space.'

Catherine made to go.

'I couldn't agree more – let's get out of here.'

58

The door to the secretary's plane swung open and the North African heat hit him like a wall. Cairo international airport sweltered in the burning sun. The aircraft's engines were still running – white noise prevented any communication. There was an overriding stench of aviation fuel.

With a look of distaste on his face, he marched down the giant steps and set foot on the runway, followed by his two most trustworthy bodyguards. As they did so a four-ton truck with a canvas roof trundled to a stop a few yards from the plane. A fit-looking Caucasian man in desert-camouflage fatigues leapt down from the driver's cab and walked briskly over to it. The engines were still slowly whining to a halt; he had to shout above the noise.

'Sir – I have six men here. All armed and ready to go, and we have agents at the ready all across Cairo. I can report that the targets came through customs three hours ago and are now at Giza.'

'And the man in white? Have you found him?'

'No, sir, we haven't been able to pick up his trail again. Global ops say he is a former Russian army officer, a renegade scientist and spy – which probably explains why we've lost him. He worked with Professor Kent a couple of years ago; he has a history of interest in the ice caps.'

The secretary looked up at his minion and, speaking decisively, laid out the plan.

'We need to get the targets on their own, then we will take them. I don't want a repeat of what happened in La Paz. This has to be done discreetly – but I want armed men standing by at Giza. As for the Russian, it's time we shut him up as well. We can't take any risks at this stage. Get a photo of him out to all the agents immediately and have him shot on sight.'

He fell quiet and looked across the runway out over towards the airport buildings, where distant human figures moved in the rippling heat. The spring equinox was now only a matter of hours away. He looked tired, old even. For the first time his eyes betrayed a certain vulnerability – he seemed almost to wince.

He glanced at his two bodyguards, both of whom he had briefed on the plane. They were highly experienced and he knew he could count on their loyalty in dealing with the senator, who would be focused on the coming days' plans. The last thing he would be expecting was an interrogation session from one of his own.

59

Emerging from the bowels of the Great Pyramid, Catherine and Rutherford were almost blinded by the blazing sunshine. The cloudless blue sky stretched away in all directions and even the desolate sight of the empty desert brought a sense of relief after the intense fear and claustrophobia generated inside the subterranean passages of the Great Pyramid.

Catherine shielded her eyes with her left hand while brushing the dust off her clothes with her right.

'Ah! Air! Fresh air and sunshine. Thank goodness we're outside. I wouldn't like to have to spend the night in there.'

Rutherford dug his sunglasses out of his bag and breathed expansively. 'I agree!'

She turned around and looked back up at the ponderous mass of the Great Pyramid.

'Well, one thing is for sure: this wasn't built by a primitive people. And it certainly wasn't simply a burial chamber. If only Professor Kent were here to talk to. He would have known what to do.'

Rutherford shook his head and with dogged determination in his voice, said, 'We must keep moving forward. Eventually we will work it out.'

Catherine walked over to him, put her arms around his shoulders and hugged him in silence. They remained locked in the embrace for half a minute, then she stepped away and swung her rucksack over her shoulders.

They rounded the north-east corner of the Great Pyramid and the Giza Necropolis came into view.

'There it is.'

Rutherford pointed in a south-easterly direction, out over the gradually descending rock plateau leading down to where the sphinx lay, nestled in its man-made trench. With the body of a lion and the head of a man, it lay with its forepaws stretched out in front of it, the bulk of its body merging into the solid rock behind. For incalculable millennia it had waited there patiently – on many occasions it had been buried entirely by the constantly encroaching sand, but an emperor or king or governor would come along eventually and dig it out.

'It's facing east, I think,' said Catherine.

'Yes – due east, straight at the rising sun. This time

the builders are marking the astrological age of Leo, which begins in 10970 and ends at 8810.'

'That's amazing, it fits perfectly with Von Dechend's dates for the end of the last ice age. Do you think that they were marking when their civilization was destroyed?'

Rutherford didn't even answer. They were approaching the flanks of the gigantic sphinx. It was about sixty feet high and two hundred and forty feet long – the biggest sculpture ever made. He craned his head up.

'And you see how it has weathered?'

Catherine studied the great hollows and crevices in the ancient stone from which the beast had been created. It looked in parts like a giant melting waxwork model. Great gouges ran down the stonework from top to bottom.

'It takes literally thousands upon thousands of years to cause erosion like that.'

'And how is such erosion caused?'

'Rain, rain and more rain. The Sahara is a young desert. It wasn't always like this here. It was once green, fertile and pleasant. And clearly it rained a lot and for a very, very long time.'

'So when do people think that it was carved?'

'Ahh, well, that depends on who you ask.'

They walked down to the front of the sphinx and looked up into its ancient face.

'Experts on the weathering of limestone have concluded that it must have been carved at the very least nine thousand years ago – and that's conservative. It is enormously, almost incomprehensibly old. And of course, as we know, orthodox history says that around that time we were all running around in loincloths, using stone-age implements.'

Staring up at the inscrutable face of the sphinx, Catherine thought of the great people who must have created it all those millennia ago.

'OK,' she said, 'so we have a pyramid built to specifications that NASA would be hard pushed to achieve. The pyramid itself seems to hint at knowledge of astronomy and higher mathematics if you so much as look at it and also has star shafts that line up at 2450 BC. We have a sphinx that is at least nine thousand years old – probably much older – and it indicates a clear affinity with the age of Leo. On top of all this, we have total denial of these incontrovertible pieces of evidence by the entire historical community.'

Catherine walked slowly around the front paws of the strange beast. 'What's more, the makers of the very maps that prompted us to begin this quest considered this to be the centre of the world. And further, we have myths throughout the world describing a band of civilizers coming after the great flood to reinstall their shattered civilization. These myths also contain, as

Professor Kent suggested, a lot of technical information which may be related to a cataclysm caused by the shifting of the earth's crust. And finally, thanks to Von Dechend, we can date this cataclysm to sometime at the end of the ice age, around 11000 BC. This gives the refugees time to make their way from Antarctica to Egypt, to begin to re-establish themselves, and sculpt the sphinx.'

Rutherford looked over at Catherine. He had a sheepish smile on his face.

'And there's one more thing.'

Catherine frowned in anxious expectation.

'What?'

Rutherford looked at his feet.

'I forgot to tell you about the boats.'

60

Catherine felt as if her head was about to start spinning.

'What boats?' she asked, warily.

Rutherford looked up – he was almost embarrassed at having to reveal yet another mystery.

'Archaeologists have dug up several boats from the sand next to the pyramids. They are huge, ocean-going vessels that marine archaeologists say can only have been the result of a long tradition of experiment in boat design.'

Catherine threw back her head and laughed. There was one last avenue of enquiry that she wanted to follow.

'Do we know what the ancient Egyptians had to say about their own origins?'

'Yes. And in a way the Egyptians' own version of the past tallies better with the evidence than conventional history. That is, if we are willing to read the myths with sympathetic eyes.'

'What do you mean?'

'Well, for example, Osiris is one of the Egyptian gods. The neteru, as they were called, arrived from their own mystery homeland just like Quetzalcoatl and his followers, or the Viracochas. But if the neteru were from a more advanced civilization, with huge amounts of technical and religious knowledge, it is hardly surprising that the original inhabitants of Egypt found them godlike.'

Catherine was a picture of concentration.

'So the neteru – whom the Egyptologists dismiss as mythological deities – must have been the bringers of light.'

'It certainly looks like it. There are hieroglyphic inscriptions on the inside of the Pyramid of Unas at Saqqara that date from around 2400 BC. They are interesting because, like the pyramids here at Giza, they suddenly appear out of nowhere.'

'In what sense?'

'Well, prior to their sudden appearance, there is no primitive writing. There are no early simple hieroglyphs used for counting supplies or marking the passing of days, as is the case with the early cuneiform scripts from Babylon; instead we move straight to the most sophisticated hieroglyphs that Egypt will ever see. And what's more, the subjects under discussion are highly developed abstract theological and metaphysical ideas, complete with a huge cast of highly symbolic gods and goddesses. Wallis Budge, who was the greatest British scholar of Egyptology, once said that it was simply inexplicable that such a sophisticated civilization should suddenly appear overnight. It would be like the Bushmen of the Kalahari giving birth to the entire culture and religion of the Jews in the space of a hundred years – while also building the world's greatest building in the African desert.'

Catherine was working her way towards an idea of what to do next.

'Who is responsible for all these ancient sites? I mean, who is it who ultimately grants permission to study these buildings and to test new theories? Who has the power to overturn this erroneous orthodox opinion?'

Rutherford studied her face.

'Dr Ahmed Aziz, the director of Egyptian antiquities. He can end any Egyptologist's career with a stroke of his pen by refusing them permission to visit the sites or even refusing them entry to Egypt. His power is absolute.'

Catherine nodded definitively.

'Good – so at least we know where the buck stops. If he were to initiate an effort to re-date everything then it might actually happen. If he thought the version of Egyptian history people have today was hopelessly bankrupt, then he might try to change things.'

Rutherford looked back at the awesome sight of the pyramids.

'We've got to ask ourselves why he hasn't already done just that. We have to assume he is at least aware of some of this evidence. Maybe he won't review the evidence because of religious pressure on the government.'

Catherine couldn't follow the logic.

'Why might that be a factor?'

Rutherford pulled his glasses off and ran his hand through his hair.

'Well, the fundamentalist Muslims – who do have significant influence on the Egyptian government – aren't much different from fundamentalist Christians in America, or the Jews for that matter. They too have their own view of the history of the world, a sort of Muslim version of the Christian creationist view. I doubt they want to have to explain suddenly a whole new world that precedes this one . . . but I don't know – I'm just speculating.'

Catherine sensed some truth in this.

'I think we should go and have a sniff around. Perhaps we can even meet this guy Aziz. What do you know about him?'

'Very little. I met him once, years ago, though I'm not sure – he gave a lecture at Oxford. This was long before he was appointed director. His predecessor died in a car accident, I think. I remember Aziz's appointment created a bit of a stir – he's very young and he studied in the US.' Rutherford paused. 'It's worth a try, I suppose. There's no sign of Bezumov so far, but the equinox is still twelve hours away. Quite what he is planning I don't know – what can you do with millions of tons of stone?' Rutherford shrugged his shoulders.

'OK – let's try Aziz and see what he has to say about all these inconsistencies.' He took one last lingering look at the motionless face of the sphinx and then swung his bag over his shoulder.

'Let's get back to the car.'

Catherine stared up at the immortal face of the ancient sculpture and muttered, almost to herself, 'We'll find out your riddle yet, great sphinx.'

Turning on her heel she followed Rutherford up the gentle incline of the Giza plateau to the car.

'*Stop!*'

At the barked command, Bezumov's chauffeur drew the Land Cruiser to an abrupt halt on the edge of the Giza car park. A cloud of dust lifted into the air behind the vehicle.

Bezumov couldn't believe his eyes. He squinted at the two westerners he could see walking over the sand towards the car park, away from the sphinx. His face was a contorted mask of anger and surprise. As the two figures gradually drew closer, his suspicions were proved correct. He followed their progress to their car. First Donovan and then the irritating Englishman got in. Bezumov slammed the palm of his hand on the dashboard.

Instinctively he reached under his jacket and felt in his shoulder holster. The gun was there.

But this is not the right place . . .

The car pulled away from the car park.

'Driver, follow that car. Don't lose sight of it – not even for a second.'

61

Cairo is not an easy city to drive in. A lot of the roads look exactly the same, the street signs are few and far between, the traffic is appalling, and the Cairo drivers treat the highway code at best as a set of vague guidelines, and at worst as a total irrelevance.

After many wrong turns, and much honking of horns, Rutherford and Catherine finally pulled into a car park behind the department of antiquities. Rutherford was looking extremely stressed.

'That was a nightmare. I thought we were never going to find this place and I thought we were being followed, until I realized even the most determined criminal in the world couldn't possibly deal with this traffic.'

He jumped out of the car and stared across at the building housing the department of antiquities – somehow he felt it had a forbidding look about it.

'Do you really think it's worth trying to get a

meeting with Aziz? I mean what's he going to say even if he does agree to meet us?'

Catherine slammed the passenger door shut.

'James – our approach has worked so far. If nothing comes of it, we can go and find a hotel and try to think of another plan. I just want to see his reaction.'

A guard dressed in an ill-fitting brown uniform and peaked cap wandered out of a sentry box and waved them towards the back entrance of the building. Catherine and Rutherford walked over to him.

'*Salaam aleikum.* Passport please.'

They produced their passports and after a token gesture of scrutiny, the guard motioned for them to go through the door.

Inside, a shabby linoleum corridor ran straight ahead, leading – according to the overhead sign – to the reception desk. On either side of the corridor were closed doors and, occasionally, further corridors heading off to who knew where. Peering down the gloomy, badly lit main corridor Catherine looked at Rutherford.

'What do you reckon?'

He hesitated and then answered, 'I don't know, I suppose we ought to go to the reception desk.'

After a few paces Rutherford noticed a sign in English and Arabic pointing down a corridor that led off to the right. It read 'To the Director's Office and Conference Room'.

'On second thoughts why don't we just skip the receptionist and cut out one layer of bureaucracy. She'll only keep us waiting for ages. If our friend the director wants to see us, he will see us straight away and if he doesn't, then he can tell us so face to face – assuming he isn't at lunch, that is.'

'Or out of the country,' added Catherine.

Halfway down the corridor was the door to the director's office. Rutherford raised his hand to knock and then paused for a second. He glanced at Catherine.

'OK – here goes!'

He knocked loudly.

They waited in nervous anticipation. After about thirty seconds the door was opened by a young woman dressed in the customary Muslim head shawl. She looked surprised to see Catherine and Rutherford standing in the hall.

'Hello, can I help you?' She spoke good English with a strong Egyptian accent.

Rutherford glanced at Catherine and then began, 'Er, yes – we've come to see Dr Aziz. Is he in?'

The secretary looked at them both suspiciously.

'Do you have an appointment?'

Rutherford wasn't sure how to respond but before he could think of what to say next Catherine seized the initiative. In a tone of righteous indignation she addressed the woman.

'Excuse me . . .'

She stepped in front of Rutherford.

'Yes, we do have an appointment. Please can you tell Dr Aziz that Catherine Donovan and James Rutherford from Oxford University are here to see him? And will you please let us in – I do not appreciate being made to wait in the corridor, particularly after a long flight.'

This did the trick. The secretary immediately swung the door open, revealing Ahmed Aziz's spacious outer office. She beckoned for them to come in. The office had large windows looking onto a well-kept Egyptian garden, and a second door that Catherine supposed must lead to Ahmed Aziz's private office. There were two big green leather sofas, with accompanying ornamental hookah pipes, and as Catherine's gaze scanned the room she saw that there was one other person seated in the office – a short, thin-framed Egyptian who occupied the second desk. He smiled at her, his dark eyes twinkling. The secretary, looking very anxious, led them towards one of the sofas.

'Please, have a seat. Mr Rutherford and Miss Donovan – yes?'

Catherine replied haughtily, 'Dr Rutherford and Dr Donovan, actually. Thank you.'

With one more anxious glance at them, the secretary

walked back round her desk and sat down. She picked up her phone and dialled a number. Rutherford followed her every movement.

After muttering in guttural Arabic for a moment she hung up the phone.

'Dr Aziz will see you shortly.'

Catherine smiled conspiratorially at Rutherford and they both sat down on one of the large leather sofas. A minute later the door to Dr Aziz's office swung open and the man himself stepped out.

'Hello. Welcome to Cairo. Please – come in, come in.'

Catherine and Rutherford were both slightly startled by the friendliness of the reception as they followed him in. It wasn't meant to be this easy; it was meant to be damn hard to see such important people at such short notice, anywhere in the world. *This is very strange*, Rutherford thought. He had come here expecting a struggle, at best to be told to come back the next day, or the day after. And now they were being shown in, immediately, no further questions asked.

Aziz's office was lavishly furnished with Turkish carpets and leather-clad chairs. The walls were adorned with Egyptian Ministry of Tourism posters of the great sites of the country and on his desk was a paperweight: a miniature, five-inch-high, bronze reproduction of the Benben stone.

Aziz gestured for them to sit, settled himself behind his desk and began to speak; he had a definite Egyptian accent, but his English was fluent. His tone was indulgent and, Catherine thought, slightly sleazy.

'So – my apologies. My secretary must have mislaid your appointment.'

He lolled back in his chair, one arm hooked over the armrest, and smiled at them. He didn't seem to be in any hurry.

'Coffee? Mint tea?'

Rutherford couldn't understand why he was being so friendly. Catherine leant forward.

'The reason we are here is because we wanted to ask you some questions ... some questions about the dating of the pyramids and the sphinx.'

Aziz rocked forward and leaned his elbows and forearms on his desk, his hands clasped together.

'Of course. I know a little bit about that subject!'

Aziz started to chuckle at his own joke. Rutherford decided to get to the point.

'We wanted to know what you thought about the evidence that geologists have that proves – conclusively, in my opinion – that the sphinx is thousands of years older than has been previously thought.'

Aziz's expression changed in an instant. Suddenly he

was serious. The charm melted away from his face. His voice had an edge of aggression.

'Of course, I have heard this wild theory. Our geologists have examined the sphinx and dismissed these claims. I can hardly believe that two academics from as prestigious an institution as Oxford University would be prepared to entertain such ludicrous ideas. Hundreds of years of scholarship have gone into working out the correct chronology of our Egyptian past. Hundreds of years. Many notable experts from all around the world have contributed to this great work, including many men from your countries.' He looked over at them, his eyes burning. 'Your insinuations are preposterous and insulting, not just to me but to the entire Egyptological orthodoxy. I am stunned.'

Catherine could hardly take in the sudden ferocity of his response. Aziz sat back in his chair and regarded them coldly.

'I suggest you go to a library somewhere – maybe back in Oxford – and do some proper, thorough research, before bothering someone in my position again. And' – he dropped his voice – 'I would suggest that for your own professional reputations, you don't tout this sort of foolishness around too much. It takes many years to build up an academic reputation, and yet it is so very easy to destroy it.'

Catherine looked over at Rutherford, who raised his

eyebrows in a gesture of incomprehension and surprise and shook his head at her – they were getting nowhere. She stood up.

'Thank you very much, Dr Aziz, it has been a pleasure talking to you. We are just amateurs in this field – please forgive us if we have offended you.'

Aziz rose to his feet, walked over to the door and opened it wide. He stood in forbidding silence, making any further questions or conversation very awkward. Catherine and Rutherford left the private office and re-entered the main room. Aziz called over their shoulders.

'Poimandres – please show our guests the way out.'

Addressing the two westerners for one last time Aziz bid them farewell in a cursory manner, his face devoid of warmth.

'Good day, Dr Donovan, Dr Rutherford – it was a pleasure meeting you both.'

The dark Copt got up from behind his desk and smiled at them both.

62

Catherine stared incredulously at the door to Aziz's office. Its blank face summed up the finality of his goodbye.

'Good afternoon, my name is Mr Poimandres, I am Dr Aziz's aide.'

The diminutive Copt held out his hand to Catherine. Slightly taken aback she shook it.

'Pleasure to meet you, Mr Poimandres. I am Catherine Donovan, and this is James Rutherford.'

Rutherford reached out and shook Poimandres's hand.

'Hi, nice to meet you. So you're going to make sure we leave the premises?'

Poimandres smiled at Rutherford. He had the bony, honest face of an ascetic monk. 'Yes – you could say that. Would you please like to follow me?'

Rutherford smiled. There was something other-worldly, almost ethereal, about the small dark man.

After the hostility and condescension of Aziz, Poimandres seemed to exude warmth and calm. He walked past the secretary, who sat in silence at her desk, and back out into the hall. As they entered the gloomy, silent corridor, Poimandres shut the door behind them. Then he looked quickly up and down the corridor, as if to check that it was empty.

'You came to ask Dr Aziz about the origins of Egyptian civilization?'

Catherine glanced quickly at Rutherford – he was looking as nonplussed as she was.

'We have various theories we just wanted to run by him. He didn't have much time for them, though.'

Poimandres continued to probe.

'Dr Aziz finds himself in a difficult position. He is not at liberty to speculate.'

Rutherford was intrigued. Why was this strange little man telling them this? Sensing an opportunity, he asked, 'Mr Poimandres, do you think our line of questioning is reasonable?'

Very slowly, the dark eyes of the Copt shifted over to focus on Rutherford's face.

'Dr Rutherford, that depends very much on *why* you are asking.'

Catherine said, 'What do you mean "why" we are asking these questions?'

'I mean, what is your motive? Are you hoping for

academic glory or . . .' He paused for a second. His glistening dark eyes flickered across her face, as if scanning her mind for another reaction. 'Or are you seeking something else?'

Catherine could sense from his penetrating gaze that this was a critical moment in their quest. She did not understand what was going on, but she knew instinctively her answer to his question might make all the difference. *He understands. He is on our side.*

She could feel Poimandres waiting. In a sudden flash, she saw in her mind's eye one of the often-reproduced images from the hieroglyphic pyramid texts. It was the hall of judgement of Osiris. Osiris, sitting resplendent on his throne, is presented with the soul of the recently deceased. Before him, in his hands he holds a set of scales. He is weighing the human heart against a feather – the essence of lightness and truth. Is the heart pure? Looking Poimandres in the eye, she made her decision.

'We believe the world is in danger. We think there has been a deliberate attempt to pervert the historical record and cover up the truth about the past. Knowledge of the civilization of the ancients is being deliberately kept from us and it is only this knowledge that might save us. If we do not discover what the ancients knew, we will perish as they did in a terrible environmental cataclysm. The pyramids were not built by pharaohs in 2500 BC, they are the monuments of the people who survived the great flood.'

Poimandres lowered his gaze. In a whisper he responded, 'Please – you must come with me to Giza. But first . . .'

He led them through a door off the corridor. It opened into a workmen's storeroom. Among the tools, cans of paint and other materials were some Egyptian work clothes.

'Here – put on these jellabas.' Poimandres handed each of them an ankle-length Egyptian gown. Catherine and Rutherford looked at each other and then slipped the cloak-like outfits over their heads. With the hoods up they were now completely unrecognizable. Poimandres opened the door to the corridor again and gave the all clear.

'Follow me.'

63

On the other side of the street from the antiquities department, a white Toyota Land Cruiser waited. Dusk had fallen over Cairo, but Bezumov remained as alert as ever, patiently watching for any sign of activity. Suddenly, after what seemed like hours, there was movement.

'Now what's happening?'

The wait had been getting to Bezumov. His patience was wearing thin: he was basically a man of action. He looked on as a small emaciated man dressed in a white jellaba cautiously came out of the building. He was clearly of some authority judging by the way the guard came to attention. The old man shuffled forward, followed by two other people, both wearing dirty, hooded cloaks. Bezumov looked over at his driver – he was half asleep. Bezumov whacked him on the arm.

Then in the half light of the open doorway, Bezumov spotted the smart western shoes that Catherine was wearing, just visible under the cloak as she walked.

It's them!

64

In the darkness, Poimandres's jeep pulled up at the base of the Great Pyramid. He had spoken to the night guards on the way in and had been waved on through. They had gone past the car park and had driven right onto the site itself.

Rutherford and Catherine looked at each other in silence and then got out of their car. The stars were spectacular under the clear North African sky. Catherine shut her door, looked up at the great mass of the pyramid and then over at the Copt who was waiting patiently for them on the edge of the causeway.

Under her breath she muttered, 'OK, let's see what he's got to say for himself. Keep your eyes skinned for the Russian.'

Poimandres looked at them solemnly. The driver waited just out of earshot by the Land-Rover. Poimandres bowed his head and then began: 'The construction of the Great Pyramid was the last attempt of a dying civilization to preserve its ancient wisdom.' He scrutinized their faces. 'If I am not much mistaken, you already know this. It is why you are here – why you came to see Aziz.'

Catherine and Rutherford nodded cautiously.

He continued, 'And you are also right to think that the world is in danger. I don't know how you know these things and I do not need to know. You have been brought to me because you are pure in heart. There are no accidents in the universe. It is my obligation to help anyone who seeks the truth. I will reveal the secrets of the Great Pyramid to you to help you on your quest. We have been waiting for you to come – a long, long time.'

Poimandres turned to face the pyramid. It was glowing a dull yellow thanks to a spotlight positioned somewhere near the guard post. The last few tourists were long gone and an eerie calm engulfed the site. The sand dunes rolled on for ever, for thousands upon thousands of miles, until they hit the Atlantic coast. It was an apocalyptic landscape, fantastically beautiful and at the same time strangely depressing: a landscape devoid of life and love. Poimandres's face was thin, his cheeks were hollow and even his bony eye sockets seemed unusually sunken. He spoke in a soft voice, which nonetheless had a trace of urgency to it.

'The Great Pyramid was built to preserve the old

knowledge for ever so that, even if the civilization that built it should one day perish, future generations would still be able to learn the truth. The ratios of its dimensions contain all the mathematical formulae that govern the universe. It is a scientific "glyph" which, when meditated on by an initiate, reveals the secrets of life itself. The layout of the heavens is indicated by the positioning of its blocks. It is a message designed to be read by us in the future and at the same time it is a fully functioning energy accumulator, capable of attracting and harnessing prodigious power. But first, before I explain these secrets, I want to be absolutely clear that you understand there have been worlds and civilizations before our own. I think that you realize this?'

Catherine nodded her head.

'Yes – we have seen too much evidence to possibly think otherwise.'

Rutherford added his assent. 'There is no doubt in our minds.'

Poimandres thought for a second and then began cautiously to explain.

'The earth was mapped during the last world by the previous great civilization. Its dimensions were accurately calculated . . .'

Catherine nodded again.

'Yes – we have seen their maps linking their buildings throughout the world.'

The Copt glanced up at them to check they were still with him.

'The global network of the system of energy lines, which you in England called ley lines, is one manifestation of their work. The disaster that destroyed the former civilization was one of such ferocity that it caused the alignment of the continents to shift beyond recognition, changing for ever the patterns of solar and terrestrial energies, and thereby altering the arrangement of the ley lines. The handful of men and women who did survive the disaster found themselves homeless and powerless. Their entire civilization had rested on a knowledge and understanding of these energies. In a desperate bid to save their world, they found the position of the new energy centre, here on the Giza plateua, and began to rebuild their civilization, starting with their sacred technology: the Great Pyramid.'

Poimandres turned to look at the pyramid – its tip glowing in the artificial light.

'Imagine a ball, covered in fur, or the hairs on a human head. Somewhere on the ball's surface or on the head, one single fibre will stand straight up and all the other fibres on the ball will align themselves with it. It's the same with the planet's magnetic field.'

Rutherford thought of Ivan Bezumov. *The Russian was right – just as Professor Kent suspected.*

Poimandres walked away and addressed the driver in Arabic, then turned back to them.

'But we are not safe out here. We must go down into the *bir* – that is Arabic for well. Only there can I reveal the secrets of the pyramid and explain why the world is in danger. Please follow me.'

Through the dark, Poimandres led them over to the causeway that ran in an easterly direction from the second pyramid, the Pyramid of Khafre, downhill to the sphinx. The last tourists were leaving and the guards were about to begin their nightly checks, to ensure no one was trying to climb the pyramids.

They followed the path of the causeway towards the flanks of the sphinx. About halfway down, Poimandres stopped. He said a few words to the driver and then beckoned to Catherine and Rutherford to follow as he jumped down from the causeway onto the sand. The driver stayed where he was. *Probably posted as a lookout*, thought Rutherford.

They followed Poimandres down onto the sand and to their surprise they saw the mouth of a tunnel sloping back under the great limestone blocks that were the foundation of the causeway. About six feet into the tunnel was a heavy barred iron gate. Poimandres fished in the pockets of his jellaba and pulled out a set of large keys. He motioned for them to come into the tunnel mouth to keep out of view of the tourists and any passing guards.

He unlocked the gate and ushered them through into what was in effect a little cave. He bent down and turned on a feeble electric lamp. In the corner of the cave was a well with a steel ladder descending down the shaft. Poimandres shut the gate behind them.

'I will go first – come after me. And be careful: it gets very slippery.'

Catherine and Rutherford looked at each other in amazement. He wanted them to follow him into the bowels of the earth. As Poimandres vanished into the blackness, Rutherford drew in his breath.

'There are only five hours left before dawn – there's no turning back now. Do you want to go first?'

Catherine steeled her nerves and then grabbed hold of the top of the ladder.

'OK – see you down at the bottom.'

If there is a bottom, thought Rutherford as Catherine slipped out of sight.

65

Secretary Miller and his two bodyguards climbed out of the truck at the heliport hangar. The secretary brushed himself down. Three muscular Caucasian men, wearing wrap-around shades, black T-shirts and carrying assault rifles, guarded the entrance. The secretary felt out of place and vulnerable in his dusty business suit.

He felt a sudden rush of resolve. It was now or never. His right arm moved up to touch the bulge of the pistol that he kept in his shoulder holster and then, with a quick nod to his two bodyguards, he stepped through the narrow gap between the enormous corrugated doors of the heliport hangar.

But as his eyes adjusted to the gloom of the interior, he realized he was doomed. Before he could take two steps forward, he felt the cold steel of a gun barrel pressed against his temple. Then, in the next second, the hangar lights flickered on, revealing the terrifying extent of the secretary's mistake. Before him stood a dozen well-armed men, all with their weapons raised.

Secretary Miller and his two bodyguards didn't even have time to think. A voice barked at them, 'OK – you two, at the back. Lie face down on the floor, immediately.'

The secretary's two bodyguards looked at each other with fear on their faces and then did as they were ordered, spread-eagling themselves on the cold concrete floor.

The man pointing the weapon at the secretary's temple silently slipped his hand into the secretary's shoulder holster and removed his pistol. Then, poking him in the ribs with his own gun, the assailant indicated for him to walk up the hangar towards the lonely door at the far end.

With a feeling of terrible anguish and dread, Secretary Miller began the long walk. A dozen silent helicopters were scattered around the cavern-like space, casting bizarre shadows, like dinosaurs in a museum.

He walked uncertainly forward, the clicking noise of his heels echoing around the massive hangar. There was no other motion, no other sound. He felt his heart beat quickening with each step – his senses were in overdrive. What was he to do now? What was he to say?

In the darkness at the far end of the hangar, a chink of light appeared in the back wall and then increased to the size of a perfect door-sized white rectangle. He quickened his pace, but then slowed as he approached the doorway. The light from outside was so bright he couldn't see anything – it was like looking into a parallel universe. He knew he had to go through. He glanced over his shoulder at the vast, airy room and felt a strange wave of grief flood over him. And then he stepped through into the light beyond.

He saw tarmac and the pale dunes beyond and there, in front of him, some kind of strange aircraft. It was black, and about the same size as a stealth bomber – but it was rounder, flatter – like a massive circular deepwater fish, evolved specifically to withstand the millions of tons of pressure of the ocean floor. Its black velvet colour seemed to absorb all the light into its surface – it was beautiful, truly beautiful. And yet it radiated terrible power. From its underbelly, a retractable staircase descended to the ground and at its base stood Senator Kurtz with two other men. The secretary's blood froze. Senator Kurtz, his face as impassive as a cliff face, raised a pistol in his right hand and pointed it at the secretary's forehead.

In a blind panic Secretary Miller stammered, 'No! Please, there's no need for this.'

Without even blinking, Senator Kurtz pulled the trigger. The secretary's head was blown to smithereens and his body collapsed like a rag doll to the ground.

Calmly Senator Kurtz walked over to inspect the damage. He looked down at the disfigured corpse and shook his head.

'Rest in peace, sinner. May God spare you at the coming judgement day.'

He turned on his heel, replaced the gun in his shoulder holster and walked slowly back to the strange aircraft.

66

Thirty feet down, the ladder stopped at a platform. Poimandres pulled three little torches out of his robes.

'Here – take these. Further down there is no light at all.'

Catherine and Rutherford put them in their pockets. A second ladder plummeted downwards from the other side of the platform. There was still just enough light to see that the well shafts were man made and not merely fissures in the rock

Rutherford ran his finger over the wall. It was wet. *How old is this well?* he wondered.

Poimandres had disappeared over the edge of the platform into the blackness. Catherine grasped the top of the ladder in her hands. She offered up a desperate prayer.

Don't let us get stuck down here, please!

Thirty feet further down, the ladder ended in the corner of a damp subterranean man-made cave.

Poimandres quickly switched on his torch. Its feeble glow was just enough to reveal the room's dimensions. It was about forty feet by twenty feet and about ten feet high.

As Catherine's eyes adjusted to the gloom she suddenly noticed that there were two granite coffers – one on either side of the dark cave.

'What are those doing here?'

Rutherford dropped down beside her.

'My God. Sarcophagi.'

Poimandres pointed to the corner of the claustrophobic room. There was an even darker hole – another *bir* going even further down.

'We haven't finished yet. Follow me.'

In silence, they went over to the black mouth of the well. Poimandres turned his torch off and slipped it into the pocket of his robes and then, gripping the ladder, swung himself into the inky blackness. Shaking her head, Catherine followed. Rutherford, hardly able to believe what they were doing, took one last look around the cave before following them into the unknown.

Forty feet lower down, Rutherford dropped into a spacious room. Catherine was already looking around in awe, pointing her torch this way and that. The room, though it was hard to get a real sense in the dark, appeared to be about sixty feet square. The ceiling was low and water was streaming down the walls. Rutherford pointed his feeble torch towards the centre. There was what appeared to be a small island surrounded by a moat, about ten feet wide. On the island he could make out chunks of stone strewn about, as if they had once been part of a structure that had long since been dismantled or vandalized.

Poimandres waited for them to get their bearings and then said, 'This is the bottom. Or more precisely "a bottom". The Giza plateau is riddled with tunnels and rooms.'

Catherine couldn't believe her ears.

'You mean there are other caves like this?'

'Catherine – this room is nothing. There are vast vaults down here. Giant chambers containing whole libraries of ancient knowledge. The main chamber, the most important chamber, is the hall of records – the repository of all knowledge from before the great flood.'

Rutherford was dumbfounded. His whole life had been spent in studying ancient myths and religions and trying to reconstruct the past and here they were, deep beneath the surface of the world, being told that the secrets of history were right down there with them.

'But, Poimandres – why don't people open up the hall of records? Have you seen it? Has Aziz seen it?'

Poimandres shook his head solemnly.

'No. I could count on the fingers of my hands the

number of people who have been allowed to see this chamber.'

Catherine couldn't understand.

'But why don't you tell the world? Why doesn't Aziz tell the world?'

Poimandres's face was grim.

'Aziz only knows about this room. He doesn't know about the hall of records, which is just as well otherwise I am sure he would try to get into it and then seal it up or destroy it . . . Aziz doesn't want to find anything more. Or more precisely, his masters don't want anyone to find anything more. They are afraid of the pyramid and the secrets it holds. In fact they are terrified. They don't want anyone to know what's down here, they don't want anyone to ask about it, and they certainly don't want people conducting research down here.'

Rutherford was gobsmacked.

'But why? And who are Aziz's masters?'

'There is an organization called the Corporation. Those who think they control the Corporation are themselves the slaves of power. They think that by controlling other people and the world around them they will be able to do good. In order to achieve this end they will bring the whole world under their dominion. It is very much in their interests to maintain our belief in the orthodox version of history.' Poimandres paused and looked seriously at them. 'If the truth came out, the whole world-view of modern mankind would have to change. Most importantly, the beliefs that underpin the modern growth-obsessed world would be shown for what they are: dangerous, short-term plundering of the world's resources that will lead us inevitably to another cataclysm. If the truth came out, the general public would no longer be able to stomach the "growth at all costs" mentality and the enormous avarice and greed that lies behind it, leading us inexorably to our doom.'

Catherine was completely stunned. She turned to Rutherford.

'This Corporation must have been responsible for the murders of Professor Kent and Miguel Flores.' She shook her head. That was too much to deal with at this moment. Rutherford put his hand on her shoulder and turned back to Poimandres.

'It is still incredible that the existence of the underground rooms and the hall of records has never come to light.'

The Copt's steady gaze was in stark contrast to the shocked expressions on the faces of the two academics.

'All I know is that Aziz and these terrible people he works for don't want anyone to discover the truth about the ancients.'

Rutherford was completely baffled.

'Why don't you want people to know?'

'Knowledge in the hands of the unwise is lethal, as we can see all around the world. People today are in no way prepared for such knowledge; they are not wise enough, they would only end up doing harm. We have to wait until such a time as people can be trusted not to abuse the power that knowledge brings. The men behind the Corporation, mad as they are, are normal for this dark age we live in. Imagine what they would try to do if they got hold of the power of the ancients. So you see, it is in all our interests, both ours and Aziz's, to keep all this quiet.'

Rutherford could hardly believe what he was hearing. A great treasure trove of knowledge, the actual records of the bringers of light, was there almost within reach, and yet the only people who knew about it were bent on making sure it was never found.

'But what if there *is* another cataclysm? What if the world is destroyed before people are ready?'

'That is a risk we have to take. Eventually, another world will grow up, just as our present world grew up after the cataclysm of the great flood. We can only hope that the next world develops more harmoniously and that these future peoples will be more fitting inheritors of the ancient wisdom.'

Poimandres started to walk towards the water's edge.

'Come. To the island.'

In the darkness, it was impossible to judge the depths

of the oily black water but Poimandres didn't hesitate. He stepped out onto the surface of the water and instead of sinking he continued to walk across. In five paces he had reached the dry land.

'Step where I stepped. There is a causeway half an inch beneath the surface of the water, just where I crossed.'

Catherine looked at Rutherford and then walked to the water's edge at the point where Poimandres had stepped out. Holding her breath she reached out with her right foot.

As her boot broke the surface tension of the water, she felt the comforting presence of hard stone – just as Poimandres had said. Nervously she walked out to the island. Rutherford clenched his teeth and followed. On the island Poimandres had started to light candles. Among the large stone blocks that lay scattered about was a stone dais. He placed six candles on it and then moved among the other blocks, balancing candles where he could, until the island's megaliths were dotted with bright pinpoints of candlelight. The flickering flames illuminated his taut face. His cheekbones were high and hard. His forehead was bony and strong. His face looked tired. He looked almost desiccated in the twilight, like a mummy.

'I am a member of the oldest Christian Church: the Egyptian Coptic Church. The gospel writer St Mark arrived in Alexandria on the Egyptian coast in AD 45 and started to preach the word of Jesus. We trace our Christianity straight back to him. But as well as being a Coptic Christian, I am also a Gnostic, a seeker of gnosis. Gnosis is ancient Greek for "knowledge".' Poimandres paused for a moment. 'We Gnostics are the inheritors of the last remnants of a spiritual tradition that stretches back to before the flood. The forefathers of the designers of the pyramids, who came to Giza long ago, knew that souls were immortal and they knew we are all fragments of the universal consciousness.

'We are all one: all people, all plants, all matter, everything contained in the space–time continuum. We inherited this knowledge from the ancients who lived before the flood and we hid it within the gospels of Jesus Christ. True Christianity is simply a continuation of the ancient knowledge. St Mark was of course a Gnostic, as were all the early Christians.

'Today though, people do not realize this. Instead, they take the story of the gospels literally and they read other books claiming to be Christian, like the writings of St Paul. But St Paul and the other writers who came after the gospels were not Gnostics and so their books do not have the old knowledge hidden within them. Christianity was hijacked by the Church. A priesthood was constructed, the truth became obscured and knowledge of the original message was lost. Instead of being a vehicle of truth, the Church became a vehicle for power and repression. And finally, in the modern age, western society discarded the Church. All that remains is the lust for power and control – the desire to enslave each other and nature.'

Poimandres shook his head and then continued, 'In the past few years, another danger has appeared in the world. A radical Church has been born that preaches the literal truth of the Bible. This Church attempts to destroy any evidence that contravenes the biblical account of creation, including evidence of the last world. But worse still, it is intent on bringing the terrifying visions of the Book of Revelations to reality. Even as we stand here now, they are working to bring about the final Armageddon. Our fear is that if they can infiltrate the Corporation, we are all doomed, for they will have access to the Corporation's unlimited wealth and earthly power. This new Church is the final embodiment of the rejection of the old knowledge – rather than embracing the cosmos and regarding all nature as one, it seeks to destroy the material universe in order to reunite its followers with God. It does not realize that we are all God.'

The old man sighed. 'We Gnostics are peaceful. We cannot take up arms against our enemies for to do so is against the way of the old knowledge and against the way of Christ. Violence only leads to further violence and power corrupts anyone who attempts to ally with it or use it. So we will simply never reveal the secrets of the old knowledge to these people, nor will we tell them what lies beneath the pyramids.'

Rutherford couldn't believe what he was hearing. He knew about the Gnostics and their ancient tradition but they were supposed to have died out long ago.

Poimandres pressed his point home. 'After the last flood, the surviving humans were scattered in isolated bands all over the world. Mankind had been greatly reduced in numbers but not altogether destroyed. The ancients came to Giza, and to a few other places round the globe to try to rebuild their world among the remnants of the human population. When they arrived in these lands, the earth was green and fertile and the people were receptive. The ancients brought agriculture and technological know-how and most importantly of all, they brought the old knowledge of the universal nature of God. This knowledge survived for thousands of years until Pythagoras, the father of western science, came to Egypt. When he returned to Greece, he brought back this knowledge and it became the basis of Greek philosophy and science. Soon afterwards, our forefathers, the first Gnostic Christians, sought to bring this knowledge of the truth to the Jews and so the gospels were written. The son of a carpenter from Nazareth, the product of a virgin birth, was presented as the symbol of Osiris and Dionysus to the Jews.'

Rutherford couldn't contain himself any longer.

'What! You mean Jesus is just a symbol of Osiris and Dionysus? You mean he definitely didn't exist?'

'Yes and no. He was a real person but he was also a representation. They are all representations of the same idea. Osiris died and was resurrected, so too did Dionysus and Jesus. All were born of virgin mothers. All have twelve followers. All are born under a star. All are god-men who willingly let themselves be persecuted . . . All die for our sins and are reborn, so that we may be reborn as they are . . . All preach the same creed: if someone does wrong by you, then turn the other cheek, there is but one God. The Gnostics wanted to bring the ancient truth to the Jews, who laboured in error under a tribal god. The story of Christ was their attempt to do this. We wanted to pass on the ancient knowledge before we were destroyed.'

Suddenly Poimandres stopped.

'But enough. We have little time. I must show you the secrets of the pyramid.

'Only through understanding the harmony of numbers can the harmony of the universe be comprehended. Where modern western science sees numbers as nothing more than tools for expressing quantity, the previous civilization saw them as interlocking components in a cosmological puzzle.' He held his hands together as if in prayer.

'A proper understanding of numbers and ratios can unlock the essential laws of the universe itself. The divine numbers are those that resurface again and again in different areas of life – in the musical scale, in the electromagnetic spectrum, in the movements of the stars. Every effort of the former civilization was based upon and referred to these governing numbers and formulae and it was of course precisely these numbers and formulae that were buried in the sacred texts of the world, using gematric codes.'

Catherine felt the familiar tingle of excitement as she listened in amazement to Poimandres's explanation.

'Equally, every last sacred building of antiquity was also laid out in such a way that its dimensions should be significant in terms of gematria. Even in its design it could communicate the divine ratios. The art of gematria was not a Greek invention – the Egyptians knew of it, for it had been preserved by them after the collapse of the old universal order.'

Poimandres looked up – he seemed to radiate patience and wisdom.

'There are many doors into the past. They lie concealed, just out of reach, unless you know what you are looking for. The Great Pyramid is one such door – it is one of the physical monuments that link us directly with the civilization that existed before the flood. To understand the secrets let us begin with the physical object itself. Do you know the dimensions of the Great Pyramid of Giza?'

Catherine answered quickly, 'Yes – I think we do.' She turned to Rutherford. 'James?'

'Yes. The length of each of the sides at the base is 755 feet, which means that the perimeter of the whole pyramid is 3,020 feet. And the height is 480.5 feet or 275 Egyptian cubits.'

'Yes – that is correct. And do you know anything of gematria?'

Again, Catherine looked at Rutherford.

'Yes, we do, a little.'

Poimandres paused for a minute as if working out how to begin.

'Well, 755 – the length of the sides at the base – is equal in value to *o petros* – the rock.'

He stepped around the dais towards them and continued cautiously, as if he was worried that his explanation might confuse them if he went too fast.

'Now, Jesus said that his disciple Peter was the rock on which he would build his Church – Petros, as well as meaning rock, is also the Greek name Peter. Remember, as I said, we Gnostics do not take the new testaments as literally as most Christians, because we have not forgotten that it is written in gematric code: it is a way of passing on the old knowledge via a story. The story is the life, death and resurrection of Christ. Peter, the rock, is the old knowledge of the ancients as embodied in the Great Pyramid at Giza. Jesus was building his new Church on the ancient knowledge and it's right there, for all who know how to see.'

Rutherford listened in fascination. He was a world authority on myths and religions, but he could feel that Poimandres was leading him into entirely uncharted waters and that this was no academic game. Poimandres was about to reveal secrets that had been carefully guarded for millennia.

67

Poimandres gathered his thoughts.

'As you will have seen the Great Pyramid is missing its tip. The top five Egyptian cubits of the structure were removed long ago, before the power of the old knowledge finally waned. With the tip removed the pyramid shrank to its present height of 275 Egyptian cubits. This is the same as five great cubits because one great cubit is equal to fifty-five Egyptian cubits. This is no accident, of course – five is the number of creation and regeneration. Pentagonal symmetry is the key to life. It is the quintessence – the five parts that make the whole: earth, air, fire, water plus the fifth element, the divine spark that makes life out of the other four. Fifty-five is also itself a pyramid number: the entrance to the Great Pyramid is, naturally, on the fifty-fifth course of masonry.'

Catherine and James waited, both of them transfixed by what Poimandres was saying.

'The tip that was removed is itself another pyramid. Its height, you won't be surprised to hear, is five Egyptian cubits. The central tenet of the ancients, or the bringers of light as you call them, was "as above, so below". The same rules that govern the growth of a single human cell also govern the motions of the galaxies.'

He began to move backwards towards the granite dais.

'This second, small pyramid that was removed from the Great Pyramid itself had a tip. That tip was the Benben stone. It had a volume of exactly five cubic inches – It would sit comfortably in the palm of your hand ... For thousands upon thousands of years, people have speculated about what became of the Benben stone: who removed it; where was it hidden; what was it exactly and so on.'

Poimandres had his back to them now, leaning over the dais.

'And this – this is the Benben stone.'

He turned around. In the palm of his outstretched right hand rested a beautiful, shining golden pyramid, a few inches in height. At its tip was a crystal, glinting in the candlelight and showering the walls and ceiling of the cave with a million flickering lights.

Catherine and Rutherford both gasped in awe. Catherine couldn't quite see what it was made of.

'What is that at its tip?'

'It is a diamond. It is "the grain of the mustard seed" – *kikkos sinapeos* in Greek. Which has a value of 1,746 in gematria. A circle with the circumference of 1,746 has a diameter of 555. Once again we are back to fives.'

Rutherford's jaw had dropped. He was speechless. The whole structure was beginning to make perfect, divine sense, the numbers seemed to flow upwards and downwards in waterfalls of cosmic perfection.

Poimandres continued. 'It is also the sum of the sun, 666, and the moon, 1080. As you probably know, the alchemists thought that life was created from the fusion of sulphur and mercury – sulphur being the sun and mercury the moon. Everything on the earth is fed by the sun: all life, even the earth's rotational motion, derives from the pull of the sun's gravitational field. Mercury, the divine spark, combines with sulphur to create life.'

Poimandres looked at them with utmost gravity.

'The power of the pyramids can be used as a force for good but in the wrong hands, it is a force that can cause immense evil. No one who has not been properly trained and whose soul is not completely pure should be allowed to use this power. That is why the top of the pyramid was dismantled as the old knowledge declined. The ancients knew that a dark age was coming and it was decided to remove the Benben stone and the top five cubits of masonry so no one could restart the machine.'

Rutherford immediately thought of Bezumov.

'So it is a machine!'

The Copt looked up at Rutherford – his face was a mask of seriousness.

'Oh, yes – the pyramid is the greatest machine ever built. Its bulk is specifically designed to accumulate the energy of the universe. The pyramid's position meant that terrestrial energy could be funnelled and stored, and then channelled to the many other sites around the world. As soon as the Benben stone is returned to the top of the pyramid, the machine will restart. The energy that drives it is today called the magnetic field and is still a little-understood force.'

Poimandres turned and carefully placed the Benben stone on the dais. It seemed to generate its own internal light – though this, of course, was impossible. Its immense simplicity and power drew Catherine to it.

'Inside the earth – right at its very centre – is a solid spherical lump of iron about the same size as the moon. It is suspended in a boiling fluid of molten iron that itself is surrounded by a layer of lava, thousands of miles thick all encased in the lithosphere. This massive iron ball in the middle of our planet is spinning slightly faster than the outside of the globe. Perhaps this helps to create these magnetic forces, no one is really sure; the knowledge is now lost. The ancients knew how to store and manipulate these forces. As you have seen, they could create vast structures, they could quarry and carve materials that are harder than iron, and they could control and adjust the orbital motion of the planet.'

Catherine was thinking of the secret message.

'Poimandres – I must ask you a question.'

'Of course.'

'Our quest is to discover what caused the last cataclysm and also to discover how we might avoid it happening again. We know now that the cataclysm was caused by the entire lithosphere slipping at once and we know this was related to precession and the earth's orbital motion. But we don't really understand why this will happen again.'

Poimandres nodded slowly. His wise face overflowed with understanding, as he smiled at her.

'You have come a long way. I can help you with the last steps. You are right; the modern world is being warned. We are heading towards another apocalypse. Every year that goes by, the old knowledge diminishes, those who understand it are fewer in number while its enemies increase in strength. The masters of the Corporation are ever more powerful. Their obsession with the material world, with the subjugation of nature and the enslavement of their fellow man is rushing us headlong over the abyss. Their machines and systems devour the world and every day more of nature is added to the great bonfire. They are literally setting the world aflame.'

His face was incredibly sad, almost as if he saw no hope.

'As the wicked men stoke their fires, so the ice caps melt. The more they fuel the fiery furnace of their greed, the quicker the ambient temperature of the world grows, the faster the great ice sheets liquefy.'

Catherine nodded encouragingly. She sensed that she was about to learn the fate of humanity from the lips of the frail Copt.

'The position of the lithosphere of our beautiful planet is determined by the distribution of weight across the planet's surface. Although the earth is a sphere, weight is not evenly distributed over the surface of the crust. In some regions there is mountainous dry land, and here the lithosphere is thick and heavy. On top of Antarctica lies a blanket of ice a mile thick weighing billions of tons. It creates a huge weight at the bottom of the planet which helps to keep the lithosphere stationary. The centrifugal forces are balanced by this and also by the weight of the millions of tons of ice at the North Pole.

'It took millennia for this ice to build up and, if nature was allowed to run her course, it would remain in place until the precession of the globe moved Antarctica closer to the sun and then, finally, after countless further millennia, it would begin to melt. It is as regular as clockwork.

'That is the secret message. That is what those ancient geniuses are trying to tell us and it is one of the reasons they built the global grid – so as to influence precession and save us from the inevitable fate. But they were too few in number. Not enough of them survived their own cataclysm. Within a few generations they had all gone, leaving us with only the ruin of their technology and their secret warning in the myths.'

Catherine was appalled.

'But I still don't see why we are in danger today. Surely it will take millennia for precession to cause another flood? It might be regular but it is a very slow process.'

The old Copt looked at her solemnly.

'Today the earth is balanced, the crust is in a position that is correct for the distribution of weight at the present time and there is little movement. If, however, the ice melts, and drains away, as it did at the end of the last ice age, all this colossal weight will be redistributed into the oceans. Eventually, as at the end of the last ice age, the lithosphere will be forced to rearrange itself so that the earth can continue to spin.

At this point, it will slip again and bring to an end life as we know it.

'What we are witnessing today is a man-made start to this inevitable development. We don't need to wait for the slow process of precession; we are melting the ice ourselves. The ancients never foresaw this. They would never have dreamed that we would consciously bring about our own destruction.'

Catherine's eyes widened in terror. It made perfect sense.

'Poimandres, is it too late? Can we still stop this happening?'

But before he could answer, there was a sudden noise, emanating from the well shaft. It was the sound of footsteps moving as silently as possible down the rungs of the ladder.

68

Out of the blackness of the well shaft stepped Ivan Bezumov. In tones rich with sarcasm he spoke.

'I'm sorry – am I disturbing you?'

His white suit made him a ghostly presence in the dark shadows of the subterranean chamber.

Bezumov slipped his hand inside his jacket and as he removed it Catherine saw he was holding something. Her heart thumped with terror.

'Bezumov – what is that?'

'This, Catherine, is a gun. A Heckler and Koch to be precise.'

The Russian cocked the hammer with practised ease. Catherine, Rutherford and the Copt froze where they stood.

'What are you doing? Have you gone mad? Put that thing away.'

'No, Catherine, I'm not mad. And I'm afraid the gun is staying. I want you all to move back away from the rock – over there. Please don't try anything rash, as they say in the movies. You won't be the first people I've ever shot, and I doubt you will be the last.'

Rutherford, very alarmed, joined in. 'Why are you doing this, Bezumov?'

Holding the revolver almost casually in his right hand, Bezumov threw back his head and laughed scornfully.

'An intelligent question at last, Dr Rutherford. I was tiring of your painfully slow grasp of astronomy. Let me tell you why I am pointing this gun at you. It is time the great educators of Oxford were taught a lesson.'

Gesturing with the barrel of the gun, he shepherded them to the back of the island.

'I am doing this because a fabulous scientific instrument lies waiting to be restarted.'

Keeping his gun trained on them, Bezumov crouched down and picked up some pebbles. With these in his hand he advanced to the water's edge. He then scattered the pebbles over the surface of the water. The ones that landed on the causeway remained partially visible. He began to advance across the moat.

'This machine is the greatest piece of technology mankind has ever created. So subtle and sophisticated is its design that it harnesses the earth's own motion around the sun and puts it to the use of protecting the planet. Our modern ideas of energy production are unbelievably primitive by comparison. You are right, Catherine, this machine is a monument to precession, but it was also designed to control the grinding of the mill. The energies of the earth's rotation can be mastered and used.'

He was now only a few feet away from them. Catherine could clearly see his eyes. They seemed almost vacant, as if he was operating on autopilot. He was consumed by his thoughts, deeply engrossed in them. And yet he was grinning.

'Now, finally, I have the Benben stone, I will return it to its place on top of the Great Pyramid and the invisible currents that play endlessly around the world will once again be under mankind's control.'

Catherine could restrain herself no longer – gun or no gun.

'No! Bezumov, you are making a terrible mistake. The ancients removed the Benben stone for a reason. You don't know what you are doing.'

Bezumov ignored her and stepped forward towards the Copt.

'Mr Poimandres, thanks very much for the lecture; I found it very interesting but it merely confirmed all my work. Now, if you don't mind, please hand over the stone.' With a sickly smile on his face the Russian took another step forward. 'And to think I was beginning to worry if I would ever find it in time.'

Poimandres clutched the stone to his chest.

'Never! Over my dead body . . .'

Raising his right hand and carefully aiming the gun at the Copt's chest, the Russian answered dryly, 'I thought you might say that. If you insist.'

When the gun went off in the confined space of the room, the noise was so loud that Catherine thought her eardrums must have exploded. Instinctively, she fell into a crouch and covered her head. When she regained her senses and opened her eyes a second later, she saw Rutherford had adopted a similar pose – half crouched, half ready to pounce. In the corner, Poimandres's body had fallen awkwardly, and she couldn't see if he was still breathing. He had been shot at close range, and she was afraid he was dead. She felt a spasm of rage grip her body. As with the professor, all his wisdom had been annihilated with a single act of insane violence.

The stench of cordite raked her nostrils. There were tears running down her cheeks, and she gritted her teeth, trying to stop herself from howling at the vicious Russian.

When Bezumov spoke again, his voice was firm, 'You two stay right where you are. It is not my wish to harm anyone unnecessarily.'

Catherine's ears were ringing, and she gazed at the crumpled shape of Poimandres. There was blood dripping onto the stone floor. For the sake of Poimandres and the professor and all these holders of ancient knowledge, the last bulwarks against the craziness Bezumov represented and the still more sinister Corporation, she had to do something.

'Bezumov – what you are doing is madness,' she said, her voice weak with emotion.

'Rubbish! I am the only person prepared to put his hand on the tiller of the globe and steer it to safety. Only I understand the great machine. If I am not allowed to fulfil my ambition, then the earth will be destroyed.'

Bezumov weighed the stone in his hand. His eyes were bright and his face radiated a manic energy. His voice was very grave and he spoke in what was almost a whisper, 'For five thousand years we have lived in an environmentally peaceful period on the planet. But this is an aberration. Very soon now, the world will return to the violent place it normally is and we will be swept away. Can you imagine what will happen when a supervolcano erupts, as any day now one surely will? It has been common over the life of our planet and only one thing is for sure: it will happen again. And when it does, the lights will go out. The ash and refuse will, as has happened before, fill the sky with dust that will obscure the sun. Crops will fail, industrial civilization will collapse instantly, chaos will reign. Do you doubt this future scenario? Do you really question me? The history of the past is also the history of the future. Even Mr Poimandres would have agreed with me on that. Both the past events and the future events exist. Neither can be altered or avoided unless I restart the machine and steer us to safety.'

Catherine looked at him in horror – his awful predictions might be true but he was still completely crazy. He had to be stopped.

'This isn't right. You will destroy everything.'

Bezumov's teeth flashed as he smiled at her, his self-confidence was almost tangible in the gloom. 'I am not going to stand here arguing like a petty academic, I have too much to do.'

With that, he turned and re-crossed the moat. Like a phantom he glided over to the well shaft before addressing them one last time.

'Do not attempt to follow me. If you do try to climb up behind me I will not hesitate to shoot you. I shall lock the trap door at the top. Don't worry – you won't suffocate, and perhaps you will even be freed later, before you die of thirst or hunger! Goodbye.'

With a flick of his torch he was gone.

69

Catherine rushed over to Poimandres's side. He was lying on his back next to the dais. His right hand was clutching the blood-soaked front of his white jellaba while his left arm lay uselessly by his side. Catherine squatted down and touched his cheek and then tried to find a pulse.

'James – he's still alive!'

Rutherford was standing over them both.

'We have to get him to a doctor immediately. I'm going to try and get out up at the top.'

Catherine turned her head to look up at him.

'There's no point. You heard what Bezumov said.'

Rutherford was looking desperate.

'What else can we do? We can't just sit here while Poimandres dies and Bezumov restarts the machine.'

Catherine looked at her watch.

'There's only one more hour until dawn.'

She stood up, her hands hanging by her sides in uncertainty. Shaking her head from side to side she spoke quickly, 'OK – go and check – but, James, please be careful. I can't believe we have come so far, only to have handed the Benben stone to Bezumov.'

Rutherford turned, splashed through the water and made his way quickly to the well shaft and the ladder. Meanwhile Catherine turned to Poimandres. She knelt down next to him and carefully moved his head onto her knees. Quietly she addressed the unconscious Copt, 'Please don't give up hope, Poimandres – just hang on . . .'

Ivan Bezumov stepped off the top of the ladder and out into the grotto under the causeway. After the intense blackness of the underground caves, the starlight that filtered into the grotto was a blessed relief. Even without his torch, Bezumov could make out the outline of the driver's body lying prone on the floor. Bezumov dusted himself down and then shut the steel trapdoor over the well shaft. He then threaded the heavy padlock into place and clicked it shut. He stepped over the driver, slipped out of the gate and locked it behind him. The wind was up – a storm was brewing. Sand clouds were beginning to chase across the Giza plateau and in the far distance the black sky boiled and thunder rolled across the ancient desert planes.

Within seconds, Bezumov was striding up the causeway towards the Great Pyramid – the hyena whine of the cold desert wind his only companion.

70

Rutherford reappeared at the bottom of the ladder and splashed back across the water, sweat dripping from his brow. Breathlessly he panted, 'It's locked – I don't know what we can do.'

Catherine was stroking Poimandres's forehead with a handkerchief dipped in the cool subterranean water. Poimandres's eyes seemed to open a fraction. Immediately Catherine spoke, 'Poimandres! Be strong. We *will* get you out of here.'

She looked helplessly up at Rutherford, who was staring down in horror at the dying Copt. Continuing to stroke his forehead, Catherine addressed her patient in a very calm voice – trying with all her might to hide the waves of emotion that threatened to engulf her. 'Poimandres – is there another way out of here? Is there a hidden exit?'

His mouth opened and shut and then with a supreme effort he said, 'In the water . . .'

Rutherford dropped onto his right knee.

'Where?'

Poimandres let out a quiet moan and then spoke again in an almost inaudible voice. Catherine leant forward to better hear him.

'There is a secret tunnel in the water, behind the dais. Take it – swim – you will emerge in the sacred chambers. Take the right-hand fork, it leads out by another way. Don't, whatever you do, go on into the hall of records. And if you live today, don't ever tell anyone of what you have seen. Please – you must promise, you must . . .'

With that his eyes closed. Rutherford was on his feet. He looked at his torch, it was fading fast. He strode round the dais and stopped at the edge of the black moat. It was ten feet wide and on the far side was the rock of the cave wall, rising in a broken fashion to the roof. The underground water might as well have been oil – it was impossible to see how deep it was or to see what was down in its depths.

Catherine carefully laid the wounded man's head on one of the rolled-up jellabas and extricated herself from underneath him. As she did so she whispered a solemn oath to him, 'Poimandres – I promise . . . Hold on . . .'

Rutherford paced up and down shining his torch, trying desperately to get an angle on the surface of the water that would reveal what lay beneath. Catherine arrived at his side.

'Can you see anything?'

'Not a thing. It's hopeless.'

Catherine looked back at Poimandres and then down at the water.

'We have no choice – we've got to try it – or we'll be stuck here – Bezumov will succeed and Poimandres will die.'

Holding James's arm, she kicked off her shoes and stepped into the water. It shelved steeply. She sat down on the edge of the moat and carefully lowered herself into the water. It was ice cold and absolutely black. Every atom in her body felt as if it was having an electric current passed through it as the freezing water enveloped her. Gasping she paddled to keep her head above water. She grabbed onto the side, looked up at James and caught her breath.

'Are you coming?'

In silence he slipped his shoes off and slid into the icy water – his eyes widened with the shock.

'OK – now let's see what's down there . . .'

He took a deep breath and then disappeared beneath the surface. All was black. All was silent and cold. He kicked downwards and a moment later he touched the rock wall of the far side. He felt around with his hands. The wall was rough and it undulated in and out. His breath was beginning to run out and he was having difficulty staying down. He groped about like a blind man and then suddenly, there it was. Below him on the right, the wall disappeared and there was the tunnel. He searched around. It was wide, a yard across probably. That was enough. Exhaling as he rose, he exploded to the surface of the cave.

'I found it – he's right – it's there.'

He swam over to the shivering Catherine.

'I'll go first. Follow me through. If you run out of breath turn back.'

They both inhaled deeply and then plunged their heads beneath the icy water and into the silent subaqueous realm.

Rutherford made straight for the tunnel. Ascertaining its location again, he hesitated for a second before propelling himself into the unknown. Three strong strokes later he was still swimming. His lungs were beginning to feel the strain. Catherine, an excellent swimmer, was right behind. She could feel the swirling vortices caused by his kicking feet. She tried to remain calm. Another stroke and then another. Panic was beginning to set in and then suddenly, Rutherford could see his hands in front of him in the water – there was light.

He burst upwards in relief, closely followed by Catherine. In confusion they floundered together, gasping for breath, unable to understand where they were.

'What is this place?' blurted Rutherford.

They were in a narrow pool of water, two yards square. The sides of the pool were made of neatly turned granite. Around them was a small room – about twice the size of the pool and a yard and a half high. Two perfectly carved steps led up out of the pool to a doorway opening into a dark tunnel. The room itself had smooth walls – perfectly smooth – like the inside of the king's chamber. They were decorated with hieroglyphs, painted in some kind of gold substance that made them glow gently in the dark. The ceiling of the small room also glowed. It was covered in thousands of tiny dots of light. Catherine gasped at the beauty of it all.

'That's incredible! They're stars! Look, it's the constellation of Orion overhead.'

Rutherford hauled himself onto the steps and then helped her out. They stood for a minute transfixed by the amazing light effects.

Awestruck, Rutherford spoke: 'These hieroglyphs – I've never seen any of them – not one . . . they're all unknown symbols. Imagine what the world would think – imagine what it all means . . .'

Catherine was looking through the doorway down the dark passage.

'What do you think is down there?' They both stepped over to the doorway and peered into the gloom of the passage.

'I've got no idea – this is totally incredible . . .' He could hardly take his eyes off the dazzlingly beautiful walls.

Catherine stepped into the passage. It wasn't as dark as it had seemed – it too had a sprinkling of stars on the ceiling lighting the way. With her heart pounding she began to explore along the passage. Rutherford, taking one last look at the extraordinary array of symbols, turned and followed her.

As Bezumov reached the bottom course of masonry on the south side of the Great Pyramid the first shot rang out across the Giza plateau. He could hear voices on the wind shouting – not in Arabic but in English. Someone had seen him. He grasped the Benben stone to his chest and with his free hand helped himself up onto the first step. He felt like a Lilliputian in a land of giants. The huge ten-ton granite blocks came up almost to his neck. He turned to face the desert, his back pressing against the dead weight of the massive stone-work of the second course. There was no one around – who were they shooting at? Where were they?

Suddenly, high above in the night sky, near the top

of the pyramid, a flare exploded like a firework in a brilliant white phosphorescent light.

So they haven't seen me yet . . .

Carefully, he turned on the narrow step, reached up again and hauled himself up onto the next level. The flare, which had momentarily lit up the south face as it hung in the heavens, was picked up by the wind and carried off at tremendous speed into the desert. He was immersed once again in darkness.

Frantically, he scrambled up, each level an enormous effort in itself. Minutes ticked by; another flare went up. He cowered against the stone, trying as hard as he could to make himself invisible. He was now halfway up. The view downwards was dizzying. He could see figures running towards the base of the pyramid. The second flare was also swept off into the desert by the wind, which was lifting the sand off the dunes and carrying it upwards in huge swirling clouds. Did they know he was up there? He turned back to the cold rock and continued his climb. There was nowhere to hide – he had to carry on. The granite blocks were smaller now he was higher up, which was a blessed relief. His pace accelerated. Suddenly to his horror, a torch beam passed over his outstretched right arm. It shot onwards across the vast face of the pyramid and like a yellow ghost flickered this way and that, a dancing circle of light. He froze again. He was not far from the top.

Looking down, he could just make out four men standing at the base of the south face, one of them holding the torch. Desperately, he looked right and left along the course he was on. He wasn't far from the top and the corner of the southern and western faces was now only about ten yards to his left. Pressing himself harder still against the stone, he began to shuffle sideways along the stone ledge. The torchlight weaved across the stonework around him. He was only a couple of yards away. And then the beam stopped right on him – picking him out in the darkness, lighting up his chest and head like an angel in the night.

Immediately he heard gunfire, and bullets flew into the stone on either side of him. As they struck the granite they made a vicious cracking noise. He scampered desperately to the corner almost losing his grip and then, in a last desperate lunge, pulled himself round onto the western face. His pursuers began to run around the side of the pyramid. He had seconds to act. He looked up – there wasn't much further to go. Carefully he placed the Benben stone on the step above him, and then pulled out his revolver and, using all his years of Soviet military training, he began methodically to shoot.

71

Hand in hand, Catherine and Rutherford tiptoed onwards down the passageway into the mysterious gloom. How long it had been there undiscovered was impossible to know or tell. Nor was there any indication of when it had been built, other than the fact that its superlative craftsmanship was on a technical par with that of the inner chambers of the Great Pyramid itself. With wonder in his eyes – he could barely contain his amazement – Rutherford whispered breathlessly, 'Catherine – this is it! This is the secret of our origins – the human race *was* great before. The former world *did* exist. This is its last monument.'

Catherine, her jaw hanging open in awe, peered onwards into the gloom.

'Look! It joins another tunnel.'

Sure enough, fifteen yards further on, the passageway hit a T-junction. The second passage was built from the same perfectly joined slabs of granite. The gaps between the great blocks were as fine as a human hair and the surfaces of the walls – even the star-studded ceilings – had been polished to an icy smoothness.

To the right, the tunnel descended and appeared to narrow and then disappeared into darkness. To the left it rose imperceptibly and then thirty or forty yards further along was submerged in a golden glow of warm and comforting light. Rutherford let go of Catherine's hand, transfixed by the beauty of the strange light that seemed to draw him towards it.

'My God – I've never seen anything like it . . .'

Catherine stepped up beside him, her face lit by the lambent glow.

'What is it? What could lie through there?'

They looked into each other's eyes and then Catherine grabbed Rutherford's hand and squeezed it.

'Remember what Poimandres said – he told us to take the right-hand path.'

Rutherford looked at her, his unblinking eyes hardly registering her words.

'We must see – we must go and look. We can't miss this opportunity.'

Catherine was torn – the golden light drew her towards it, but her conscience was battling to remind her of Poimandres's words and her promise to do as he had asked. They began to advance down the passage, powerless to look away from the light and seemingly powerless to turn back.

As they approached the source of light, the corridor opened abruptly onto an unimaginably strange view. Before, beneath and above them was a vast chamber the size of a cathedral – hundreds of yards long. Never in their wildest imaginings had they expected to see such a vision, so far below the ground. The corridor had disgorged them onto a granite ledge halfway up one of the 80-yard-high sides of the chamber and they stood on this precipice, aghast at what they saw. Beneath them, more than thirty pyramids rose up from the floor, their tops reaching halfway to the ceiling – each one was cased in beautiful white stone, their tips made of some kind of white metal. A wonderful diaphanous blue electric light played rhythmically between them, licking its way from one to the next like the tongue of an otherworldly flame. The entire structure emitted a low humming noise and as the twenty-yard-long tongue of blue light slowly coiled its way around the room, jumping from tip to tip, it made a crackling noise, like the sound of dry wood in an oven. Catherine looked on in horror and fascination.

'What on earth is this place?'

Rutherford, equally appalled and entranced by the eerie vision that lay before them, answered, 'I have absolutely no idea. But I think we are in the presence of some form of natural technology, far beyond what we understand.'

It was true: as Catherine marvelled at the extra-ordinary sight that lay before them she could not help thinking this must be the heart of the machine. The ledge upon which they stood circled the entire vast room. At intervals, stone staircases went down to the floor below and at spaces of fifteen yards or so around the ledge, other corridors like the one they had come in through disappeared off into the rock. Rutherford's eyes were on stalks. He spun round to Catherine.

'We must go on – look!'

With his arm outstretched he pointed down the length of the great room to the far end, directly opposite where they stood. A huge doorway was bathed in light. Light radiated from the opening, and above the door-way in strange, giant beautiful glowing hieroglyphs was an incomprehensible ancient message.

'The hall of records!' He could hardly contain his excitement. 'It must be. I know it. Just through there . . . we can go round the ledge – come on!'

Catherine stared at him in horror.

'No, James, we're going back. I promised Poimandres, and he is dying, even as we speak. And we must stop Bezumov – this is what he was talking about – this is the machine he wants to restart. And yet he can't possibly know what he is doing, just what he is tampering with. We have to stop him *now*!'

Rutherford looked at her with an expression of desperation. He gestured with his open hand at the extraordinary room.

'But – we can't just leave . . .'

Catherine took both his hands in hers and looked into his eyes as if trying to steal him back from the spell of the machine. Quietly she said, 'We can come back. It will still be here. We have work to do in the present world; we will deal with the last world when we can. Come. We have to go – before it is too late . . .'

Rutherford looked back across the massive chamber, his eyes lingering on the great doorway. He shook his head and looked down at his feet.

'But we have seen it, haven't we? We're not dreaming?'

Catherine looked at him and then across the wondrous site that lay before them, deep beneath the Giza plateau.

'No, we are not dreaming. Now we know – another civilization existed with its own extraordinary technology – and it perished just as ours will.' She looked up at him again. 'James – we have no time to waste. We don't need the hall of records. We have all the knowledge we need – don't you see? There are no more secrets. We have to stop Bezumov and the Corporation and we have to change the way people live. It's everything Professor Kent always said. But I don't want Poimandres to suffer a lonely death like the professor did. I want him to be rescued, whatever it takes. There are too few such people remaining in the world, and we need them.'

Rutherford listened in silence and then, turning to her, nodded his head slowly. 'You are right, Catherine.'

She reached up and kissed him on the cheek and then, turning, pulled him after her as she dived back into the tunnel from which they had come. At a run they retraced their steps, back past the turn to the room with the pool and on down the right-hand passage Poimandres had told them to take. With every step the passageway darkened. It began to bend to the right and soon it had curved so far that looking back, they could no longer see the opening to the enormous chamber. Finally, after another fifty or sixty yards, the stonework changed. The incredibly well-cut and polished granite gave way to rough, unworked rock and the ceiling dropped several feet, forcing them to crouch. After another hundred yards, the corridor gave out altogether and came to an abrupt end in a pile of rubble and sand spilling out of a large two-foot-wide horizontal fissure in the rock. Rutherford looked at it in dismay.

'It's collapsed. How are we going to get out now?'

Catherine scrambled over the rubble up to the fissure.

'We will crawl.'

She hoisted herself up and slid into the gap in the rock. It felt like putting her head in-between a lion's jaws – it might collapse at any moment. Trying not to think of this she began to slide forwards on her belly, pulling herself along with her hands. She could hear Rutherford scrambling up behind her.

After ten yards of this gruelling work, sweat pouring from her face, her path was blocked by sand. Frantically, she scrabbled at it, furious it was impeding their escape.

This can't be the end. Not here, not now, please . . .

She fought and dug her way through and suddenly she felt it: the cool night air of the open plateau. A spray of fine sand dusted her face – but she could feel the breath of fresh air on her skin. She dug feverishly like a mole, using her hands as trowels. At last, she pushed her face out into the air – and the howl of the storm around her was a blissful sound.

'We've made it!'

Scrambling desperately, like a creature emerging from an egg, she hauled herself through the debris of sand and rubble and into the outside world. Exhausted, she collapsed on her side. A moment later Rutherford's head emerged into the wind and then he squirmed out and joined her in a heap, spread-eagled on the empty sand, exposed under the storm clouds and the stars . . . The sky was brightening towards the dawn. They lay together for several seconds, gasping for breath until Rutherford rolled over and looked around. There, about two hundred yards away, was the west face of the Great Pyramid and there at the base, around the side, Rutherford could clearly make out several figures moving. Before he could really take them in, or even take on board everything that had just happened to them, the shooting began. Instinctively, they both flattened themselves to the ground.

'Who is it? Are they shooting at us?'

There was a round of answering fire from automatic weapons.

'No – it's coming from over by the Great Pyramid.'

Then suddenly a flare burst high in the sky, its phosphorescent light illuminating the sand below. Rutherford crawled up to the edge of the dune they were lying on. He could hardly believe his eyes.

'My God – look! It's Bezumov, he's almost at the top.'

Catherine scrambled up next to him and swept her hair from her face. There, high up on the side of the pyramid, only a few levels from the summit, was Bezumov. First the flare and then a torch beam picked out his strange figure against the vast stone edifice. He looked like a man about to commit suicide, wavering on the top of a building – except that he was remorselessly moving up, like a crab, towards the summit. Bullets were flying into the granite around him, but patiently, like a seasoned climber, he was mounting the granite blocks, one at a time, levering himself higher and higher.

Almost without thinking Catherine and Rutherford stood up. Before their very eyes Bezumov was slipping out of reach. Dawn was almost breaking. There seemed no way now they could possibly stop him. Had their whole journey been in vain?

72

With one last mammoth exertion Bezumov pulled himself onto the summit of the Great Pyramid. It was about seven yards by seven yards across. The wind tore at his clothes and threatened to push him off the edge. As he crawled and rolled out of sight of the marksmen below, protected by the millions of tons of stone, he let out a maniacal laugh.

'I have made it! I am here! Now we will see – now the world will know that I am right.'

He stood up and held the Benben stone before him in his hands as if it were a precious jewel. His wild eyes searched the horizon for the burning orb of the rising sun, but the stormy sky was so cloudy it was impossible to see it. As he gazed, he heard a terrible noise drowning out even the sound of the howling wind. It was as if a thousand jet engines were starting up in unison. In confusion, he looked around, clutching the stone to his chest. Panic flooded his face. He spun around; the biting wind and the impenetrable darkness adding to his feeling of disorientation. And then he saw it: barely ten yards away, a monstrous black aircraft rose into view. It hovered before him, like some kind of strange dark insect. Its huge, round, flattened body had a diameter of about twenty yards across. At its front, two spear-like antennae stuck out aggressively towards him. In-between the antennae was a black windscreen, level with him. He took one look at it and then turned to face the east. There in the midst of the gloom was the unmistakable first glow of the dawn sun. Spinning round, Bezumov cried into the dying night, 'Never! You will never stop me! You are too late!'

He planted his feet firmly on the centre of the summit. Beneath him rested the entire phenomenal mass of the pyramid. He raised his hands above his head and thrust the Benben stone up towards the dying stars. At that very moment, the electrical storm seemed to break. Flashes of blue lightning burnt through the clouds all around, racing in from all directions like a celestial forest fire.

Catherine and Rutherford, although standing hundreds of yards away in the desert, couldn't help but flinch as all the lightning in the sky seemed to rush across the heavens, before crashing down in an enormous blinding flash onto the top of the Great Pyramid. There was a monumental thunderclap and an enormous explosion – hundreds of times brighter than the phosphorescent flares that had been fired into the sky moments earlier. They tried to turn away but were knocked to the ground by the force of the blast. Then there was a second blast – even louder than the first. It was the strange aircraft: it seemed to have been struck by a great wave of lightning, and had combusted instantly. A shower of metal debris was scattered in all directions. Catherine curled up into a ball and Rutherford wrapped himself protectively over her, praying that none of the red-hot shrapnel falling from the sky would touch them.

The last shards of debris crashed to earth, and then all was silence. Even the wind seemed to have died down, blown away by the massive blast. Catherine peeked out from behind her hands. The pyramid stood firm. Night was melting away behind its vast frame; the sun was rising. It was the morning of the spring equinox, and the scene looked once again as it had looked for ten thousand years: the grandeur of the pyramids bearing mute witness to the folly of mankind. She crawled up the dune. Scattered across the desert were burning pieces of fuselage. Nearer to the pyramid, she could make out in the light of dawn the bodies of several people, lying on the ground. Rutherford crawled up to join her. They stared at the oddly silent scene in a state of absolute shock, not knowing what to say.

They could see Egyptian police cars arriving and startled policemen cautiously getting out of their cars, poking at the debris smouldering at the base of the pyramid. Suddenly, Rutherford spotted something glowing in the sand about twenty yards in front of them.

'Hey, look – what's that?'

Catherine started up:

'My goodness – it can't be . . .'

She began to half crawl, half run towards it. She turned round and shouted to James, 'It is! It's the Benben stone!'

Rutherford joined her and on all fours they cautiously approached it. There it was, seemingly unscarred in any way – its perfect golden surface glowing warmly in the night, its diamond sparkling like a star. Catherine leant forward to pick it up.

'That's incredible. How on earth did it survive? Ow!' She dropped it as soon as she touched it. 'It's scorching.'

Rutherford tore the sleeve off his still damp shirt and threw it on top of the shimmering prize. Gingerly, he picked it up and rolled the cloth around the metal to completely cover it.

'Got it.' He glanced across the plateau towards the causeway and the entrance to the *bir*. Policemen were running and shouting.

'Look down there,' he said. 'They must have found the driver's body. Good. They're going down the well and now they'll find Poimandres.' He scanned the plateau, looking for an escape route.

Police sirens filled the air with their awful shrieking and a series of searchlights, normally used for son et lumière productions for the tourists, joined with the rising sun in lighting up all four faces of the pyramid, bathing the sands in reflected light. Rutherford grabbed Catherine's hand.

'Right – that's definitely our cue to leave.'

With that, they turned and, quickly getting their bearings, headed off into the dunes and the peace of the desert.

73

Later that day, Rutherford awoke lying on top of crisp cotton bed sheets in a clean, sparsely decorated hotel room. Sunlight streamed in through the windows and a warm breeze rustled the diaphanous white curtains. Outside was the cloudless blue sky.

Instantly, the night's adventures came flooding back to him. He turned his weary head to see Catherine lying next to him fast asleep. So he hadn't just imagined it all.

His eyes scanned the hotel room and alighted on his torn piece of shirt, which was on a chair opposite. Glancing quickly at her and trying to be as quiet as possible he slipped off the bed and grabbed the shirt and its contents. Gingerly, he laid the bundle on the bed and carefully unravelled it. There before him in all its mysterious glory, was the Benben stone. At that moment Catherine rolled over and opened her eyes.

'James! Where are we?'

He smiled warmly at her, leant over and kissed her gently on the lips.

'We're in the hotel we found last night, somewhere on the outskirts of Cairo. And I don't know what time it is.'

Catherine gazed at the Benben stone.

'So we *did* get it back; it wasn't just a crazy dream. And Bezumov—'

Rutherford finished her sentence: 'Bezumov is gone. So too are the masters of the Corporation, I think. The strange aircraft that was blown into a million pieces must have been theirs. It's over – we're safe for now. Look!' He turned to the window with a smile. 'It's a beautiful day.'

Catherine sat up on her elbow and looked out into the peaceful blue sky.

'What about Poimandres, though? We must check to see if he's all right.'

Rutherford stood up.

'I'll go down to reception right away and get them to ring Giza hospital to see if he is there. I think we should pay him a visit.'

Catherine studied the beautiful designs on the stone. She patted it gently.

'Yes – and we have to find some way of returning this extraordinary object.'

Rutherford did up his shirt, pulled on his boots and tied the laces.

'Why don't you have a shower and wake up – I'll be back in ten minutes and then we can set off.'

Catherine smiled at him. The breeze blew through the window, wafting the curtain to one side and causing the sunlight to shine on her face.

'James!'

He turned round – his hand was already on the door.

'Yes?'

She beamed at him.

'Thanks for everything.'

Poimandres lay motionless on the hospital bed. The crisp sheet was drawn up under his chin. Warm, life-giving sunlight poured in through the blinds. His face looked more than ever like the stern death mask of a long dead pharaoh. The nurse walked round the side of the bed and gently touched his shoulder. Then she leant over and whispered something in his ear. Instantly, Poimandres opened his eyes. For a moment he looked lost and his pupils darted around the room, but as soon as he saw his two visitors, he smiled.

Somehow, the act of smiling seemed to bring colour and life to his face. Catherine walked round the bed and sat down on the chair next to the bedside table. Rutherford remained standing at the foot of the bed. The nurse nodded at Catherine and then left. Catherine leaned towards him. She didn't really know where to begin. She hardly understood what had happened herself.

'Mr Poimandres, everything is OK. We have the Benben stone – we rescued it after the explosion last night.' Catherine picked up her bag and put it on her lap. 'How can we give it back?'

She looked around the ward. Poimandres's bed was cut off from the surrounding patients by a curtain. It didn't seem the right place for such an important artefact. Poimandres opened and closed his mouth. A feeble but determined smile broke his lips. Then summoning his remaining resources of energy, he spoke.

'It doesn't matter. The Benben stone isn't important.'

He could see the look of shock and surprise on their faces. Coughing weakly he began again. He was desperate for them to understand.

'It is nothing. It is a symbol.'

Catherine could hardly believe her ears.

'You mean it doesn't work? But we saw – last night, it—'

Poimandres coughed again.

'No – it works. It just doesn't have to be that

particular stone. The Benben is a component of the machine. Those who know how can simply build another. Fortunately, this knowledge is not very widespread.'

Rutherford chuckled to himself. *Well, that was worth almost dying for.*

Poimandres looked over at him.

'Please, just dispose of it. That would be the safest thing to do.'

Rutherford nodded his assent. Poimandres licked his dry lips and began to speak again, 'Miracles have been worked. We came close to certain death. The man in white has been stopped. The Corporation has been prevented from understanding the power of the pyramids. Some of its number, at least, have been killed, and for the time being their evil plans have been delayed.'

Catherine frowned.

'But they are still destroying the world. We have only stopped them for a day. Now we understand that the melting of the ice will cause the lithosphere to slip, what can we do?'

Rutherford looked to check that the nurse was nowhere to be seen.

'Maybe we can work out how to use the machine ourselves? We could harness its power and pull humanity back from the brink. Perhaps Bezumov had the right idea, just the wrong technique,' he said.

With an urgent, dry cough, Poimandres stopped him.

'No, James. No one is ready yet to master its power. The temptation to use the machine or to open the hall of records must be resisted. You already understand enough. If you try to fight the Corporation with power, you will either be destroyed by it, or power itself will corrupt you just as it has corrupted those who believe they are the Corporation's masters. There is only one way in which you can defeat the Corporation.'

'How?' asked Catherine.

'It is simple. You have to explain to people the truth. And you cannot coerce people into changing their minds – you would eventually turn yourself into a new Corporation. Remember, the truth is more powerful than any physical force in the universe.' Poimandres smiled. 'We are entering a new age. The Corporation seems ever more powerful but that is a mistake – we are also closer than ever to defeating them. If people can just be made to see the truth, they will realize that the modern cures of "development" and economic growth are in fact diseases themselves; that they lead only to enslavement. We just need the next generation to believe and to spread their belief to their children.

Then we will be free, finally, from the grip of the Corporation and we will avert the coming cataclysm. I believe we can. We must. And if we don't, then our species isn't worth saving anyway. It is all very simple, you see, in the end.'

Poimandres stopped to catch his breath.

'You see now why the hall of records is not important, nor is any other secret knowledge. We must voluntarily give up all desire for power and wealth, for it is through such desires alone that the Corporation can control us. If we can turn our backs on such materialism, then the Corporation – and its corrupt offshoots – will be exposed for what they truly are – a shortcut to doom. But it will take a great effort. Go now. Return to your countries and spread the word. The present still belongs to them but the future – the future belongs to us . . .'

With his last words, Poimandres broke into a fit of dry coughing. The nurse returned. She looked sternly at Rutherford and Catherine. The Copt made one final attempt to speak: 'You are safe now.'

Rutherford was worried.

'But what about the explosion – won't it attract attention from the Egyptian police and media? What about the debris of that strange aircraft?'

Summoning his last reserves of strength Poimandres

said, 'The Egyptian government will cover it up. A lot of strange things happen at Giza. You have nothing to fear. Concentrate on the future.'

The nurse stepped over to Poimandres's bedside and turned to the two academics.

'You must go now – Mr Poimandres is not well enough yet for long conversations.'

Catherine stood up.

'Yes – of course, we're sorry . . .'

She leant forward so that Poimandres could hear her without effort.

'We will do as you ask. We will warn people and persuade them to change their ways. We will spread the truth. We promise.'

74

As they walked out of the hospital into the sunshine Catherine suddenly realized it was the first time in what seemed like a long while that she had stepped into a public place without instinctively looking over her shoulder. It was the first time she had felt relaxed since the day she had learned of the professor's death. She let out a long contented sigh.

'So – we definitely have our work cut out for us now. But first, I think we deserve a rest. Shall we go to the airport and see if we can get a flight back to London?'

Rutherford smiled at her.

'Yes – I think we have seen and learnt enough for one trip. It's time to go home.'

She shut her eyes and enjoyed the feeling of the sunlight warming her skin. By the time she had opened them again James was gone. She looked around anxiously and then saw he was standing in the doorway of a decrepit-looking tourist shop just along the pavement.

'I'll just be one minute, there's something I promised myself I would do before we left Egypt.'

He had a grin on his face. Catherine looked at him, mystified.

'James! What are you doing?'

'Hold on – I won't be a moment.'

Rutherford darted between the passers-by on the pavement and disappeared into the ramshackle gift shop. The interior was an Aladdin's cave of trinkets and tourist knick-knacks: leather bags, souvenir stuffed leather camels, Persian rugs, nargil pipes and great trays of jewellery – rings and necklaces and earrings, all made from different materials, some with Egyptian symbols carved on them. Rutherford scanned the boxes and trays of jewellery. On one small table there was a sheet of sponge into which were stuck a few dozen rings. The rings were all simple silver hoops with clasps that held colourful but non-precious stones in place. Scanning the tray, Rutherford picked out one ring in particular. An old man, clearly the shop owner, shuffled over to him from out of the shadows at the back of the shop – slightly surprised to see a customer at all. Rutherford turned to him and grinned.

'I would like to buy this ring.'

The shop owner grunted, 'A hundred Egyptian pounds.'

Rutherford didn't mind paying over the odds.

'Done. But I want you to remove the stone.'

The old man looked at him in incomprehension. Rutherford made hand gestures to show what he meant. The old man was confused.

'Remove stone? But still a hundred pounds. Not cheaper with no stone.'

Rutherford nodded.

'Yes, I understand. I'll pay the same, don't worry. Here – here's the money.'

The old man shook his head and smiled – *Crazy tourists!* He shuffled to the back of the shop and rummaged around among various boxes. Rutherford glanced through the glass of the shop door. Catherine was standing on the pavement in the sunshine, watching the passers-by. His heart glowed as he looked at her. The old man touched his elbow.

'Give.'

Rutherford handed him the ring.

The old man had a pair of pliers in his hand. Skilfully he unbent the metal clasp that held the stone in place on top of the ring. He then tipped the ring upside down and the stone dropped into the palm of his hand. He offered it to Rutherford, who smiled and shook his head.

'You keep it! Now this is what I want you to do next . . .'

From his pocket Rutherford pulled out the Benben

stone. The old man's eyes widened in delight as he saw the diamond that was attached to the top of the little pyramid. Rutherford made a gesture with his hand to indicate that he wanted the diamond removed and then stuck into the clasp of the ring.

'Ahhh!'

Now the old man understood. He smiled happily at Rutherford and, taking the Benben from his hand, he bustled off to the back of the shop and again rummaged through his boxes of tools. After a little muttering and various attempts on the stone with different metal instruments he let out a little cheer.

The old man held up the diamond for Rutherford's inspection and then busily began to fit it into the ring's clasp. A minute later, after much fine tuning, he presented the finished item back to Rutherford.

'Present!' said the old Egyptian with pride.

Rutherford grinned.

'Exactly!'

Rutherford paid him and then turned around and pushed his way through the glass door and out onto the street. The old man, fascinated, walked up to the door to watch his strange customer go.

Rutherford took a deep breath and then, crossing the pavement, walked straight over to the bemused Catherine.

'What did you do with the Benben stone?'

With a twinkle in his eye, Rutherford answered.

'Oh, I thought I'd make an engagement ring out of it.'

A blush flooded her pretty face, turning her cheeks into beautiful roses. She smiled as she had never smiled before and, taking the ring without hesitation, she slipped it onto her finger and fell into a passionate embrace, wrapped in the strong arms of her star-crossed lover.

Visit **www.panmacmillan.com** to read more about all our books and to buy them. You will also find features, author interviews and news of any author events, and you can sign up for e-newsletters so that you're always first to hear about our new releases.